Memories

Tr

HOLLOW VOICES

Michelle Corbier

M. CORBIER

Michelle Corbier

415 Pisgah Church PMB 342

Greensboro, NC 27455

For more information:

www.MichelleCorbier.com

Cover and interior design by Karen Phillips at PhillipCovers.com

Hollow Voices

979-8-9870408-2-9   Hollow Voices, eBook

979-8-9870408-3-6   Hollow Voices, paperback

979-8-9870408-4-3   Hollow Voices, hardback

979-8-9870408-5-0   Hollow Voices, audiobook

Publisher MJM Creations LLC

For Jean-Michel, all my love.

Books by M. Corbier

Write Club Mysteries
Murder Is Revealing
Murder In Gemini

Mwindaji series
Dark Blood Awakens

Acknowledgements

Special thanks to my family and friends
for their encouragement.

This book discusses issues of sexual assault and suicide. Read with caution.

FindTreatment.gov is a confidential and anonymous resource for people needing treatment for mental and substance use disorders in the United States.

Suicide and Crisis Lifeline 988 provides 24/7 confidential and anonymous support for people in distress.

Epigraph
Pain consumes so much energy.

CHAPTER 1

The clinic resembled a three-ring circus. Medical assistants recorded vital signs near the weight scales. Nurses cajoled children into receiving vaccinations as physicians navigated exam rooms with the practice of high-flying acrobats. Chatter bounced off the clinic walls like popcorn as I hurried from the exam room.

"Javier, room two needs their vaccines," I said, speaking over my shoulder while hurrying inside my office.

"No problem," he said.

"Where did I put that book?" For half a minute, I searched inside drawers and on shelves for a comic book. My next patient, a pre-teen with an addiction to superheroes, received all As on her report card. The comic was a promised reward for her academic success.

"There it is." I scooped up the comic and rushed out of the office.

Down the hall, Camile approached. While I appreciated my best friend stopping by, this was not the time. Because she was chief of staff at the medical center, I feared she brought news about another mandatory meeting. Her grim countenance made me wary.

I had promised Evens a dinner at his favorite restaurant and had no interest in another boring administration meeting. My son's college break was shorter than my patience. With

Noughton's recent expansion into the Central Valley, the medical center held weekly meetings discussing patient statistics and insurance reimbursements.

Raising my hand in protest, I said, "Not now. A patient is waiting in room three."

Camile gently squeezed my arm. "Julia, come in here."

"Give me a minute," I said, pulling away.

Tears pooled in her eyes. "Now," she said, choking back a sob.

My body stiffened. "Is it Momma?"

The neurologist suspected Momma had dementia. She hadn't completed testing yet, at least not the last time I spoke with her. When was the last time we spoke? I'd been busy—

"It's Evens."

My eyes widened as I clutched her hand. "What happened?"

A painful scowl zigzagged across Camile's forehead. I hyperventilated. The comic slipped from my hand as I slumped against the wall. Camile leaped forward and eased me onto the floor. Javier rushed over, cuddling my head on his lap.

"No," I said, my voice small against the conversations of parents and children echoing against the clinic walls.

"I'm so sorry." Camile's tears splashed onto my face.

Gazing up at her, my head shook. "It can't be. He… I saw him this morning." My eyelids fluttered, and the room began spinning. A caped superhero grinned up at me from a bright blue sky as everything went black.

CHAPTER 2

This tacky, wallpapered office had become my tomb. If I looked closely, etchings of departed souls hid in the creases. How many people like me lay on this recliner, wondering how they ended up in a psychiatrist's office? Sticky faux-leather cushions resembled the plastic seat coverings on my grandmother's sofa. Maybe Dr. Griffith chose this material because it was easier to wash away the blood of her victims. My laughter reverberated off the walls.

Dr. Griffith scowled.

Did I laugh out loud? I hadn't realized it was audible. She really would think I was mentally ill.

Careful, Julia, or you'll be committed.

It's the drugs. They make me…strange. Each movement of the wall clock hammered in my ears.

Tick, tick, tick.

I gripped the sides of the recliner.

Dr. Griffith's bony hand supported her knobby chin. A pen dangled between her fingers. "Try to relax, Julia."

No matter what position I assumed, the recliner remained uncomfortable. I closed and reopened my eyes, straining to bring the doctor's face into focus. She brought the chair closer to my side.

"You have to trust me. We can't progress if you don't confide in me."

"I trusted Jean." My voice trailed off. "Then he died."

"Your husband didn't want to die."

"I know," I snapped, squirming along the recliner. Time passed as I sipped from a water bottle.

Paneling and cheap flooring dated the room's décor to sometime in the 60s. It smelled of disinfectant and desperation. Deep inside my core, a scream ripened. I wanted to unleash it. Hurl it in Dr. Griffith's face. But I couldn't.

It wouldn't make any difference. She'd simply jot down what occurred. Add it to the other items she'd collected about my aberrant behavior.

Hold it together, Julia. Prove her wrong, and you'll regain your freedom.

The single item of individuality in the room was a floral rug. But it lay askew, not squarely positioned underneath Dr. Griffith's desk. I grimaced, disturbed by its asymmetry. My head lolled right as I stared at the floor.

Dr. Griffith reclined into her chair. "You suffered a severe depression after your son's death—became disconnected from reality."

Why tell me what I already know?

Tapping the pen against the chair, she said, "Tell me about your last dream."

My eyes refused to focus. "I can't see."

"It's a side effect of the medication. It'll go away."

"Two months. You said in two months. It's been four."

"Obfuscation. We've discussed your avoidance tactics before."

Her office appeared wrong, fake. It tried too hard to look like a psychiatrist's office should. I glanced at the plastic human brain on her desk. Artificial, like the wig improperly positioned on her head.

Dr. Griffith's lips hung irregularly on her face. They grew

4

larger, puckered, and came closer. They were red—blood-red, like the puddled blood gathered around my son's head after the car slammed him against—

Snap. Snap.

"Julia, you're drifting away," Dr. Griffith said, snapping her fingers. "Focus on me—on my words."

My gaze drifted over her expensively tailored suit, which clashed with cheap, off-the-rack shoes. Dr. Griffith's clean, austere respectability conflicted with those long, bejeweled fingernails. Contradictions.

"These medications make me drowsy." I pushed myself up along the recliner. "I can't...can't make sense of my thoughts—of facts."

"You'll acclimate. It takes time."

"I don't want to take them. I have a job, responsibilities. How do you expect me to work like this?"

She leaned forward, hovering over me. "We've discussed this before. You can't go back to work until you improve. Now, control your thoughts." A tiny grin formed along her lips. "I want to hear more about your *urges*. We barely touched on them last week."

Words and faces lumbered across my mind. I glanced up, peering into her eyes. So clear. They held little color other than the pupil. Similar to the woman...

What woman? Can't remember. Too many things I can no longer remember. Drool pooled in the corner of my lips. Wiping my mouth, I sat up straighter.

Despite the outward adornment, Dr. Griffith seemed artificial, a simple shell—not human.

Don't confide in her, Julia.

"I don't want to talk about dreams."

"Trust me." She wiggled her fingers, dropping the pen. "See. I'm not taking notes. No one will know what we discuss."

Peripherally, I spied the white noise machine on the ground beside the door. Would it prevent our conversation from being recorded? Inhaling deeply—like she taught me—I thought about the people I trusted, like Jean. But Jean was dead.

She crossed her legs. "Tell me about your urges."

"What urges? I don't remember any."

"Well, compulsions—if you prefer. You mentioned them on the tapes. An urge to kill. Have you suppressed them, Julia? Hidden the desire to kill in the recesses of your mind?"

Had I? I couldn't recall suppressing anything—but then, I didn't remember having them.

"Impulses can remain dormant for years. Perhaps the death of your son brought them to the surface."

Was she correct? How long had I hidden my impulses? I *had* killed before or had that been a dream? An aberration. My head throbbed, trying to recall what happened.

Would I be able to suppress homicidal impulses? I couldn't care for children if I was a murderer.

Something touched my arm. As if disconnected from my body, my head rolled to the side. I viewed her hand—bony with spidery, inhuman fingers. With effort, I made my arm move away from her touch.

"I'm your psychiatrist. What we discuss stays between these four walls." Her honeyed voice sounded sickly sweet. I recognized it. The same one nurses used when lying to children about shots not hurting. *Liars! Be honest.* I told the truth to Jean. We shared everything.

My stomach churned, burning my throat with refluxed acid. I swallowed and sipped more water.

"You'll feel better if you share. I'll understand."

So hard to resist. I wanted to tell someone. Release my thoughts. My mouth opened, ready to explain those desires and needs. "Sometimes—"

A ringtone blared in the dense air.

Dr. Griffith raced to her desk. "Wait a minute. Let me turn my phone off."

Like dawn cresting over a dark horizon, an awareness grew in my mind. In a brief moment of clarity, I recognized an incongruity. "Why is your phone on? You said phones weren't allowed in the office."

"I'm a physician. I have to be available for my patients."

"Do you see patients in the hospital?"

"No."

"Do you make house calls?"

"Julia—"

"Why was your phone on?" I stood up.

"You're exaggerating the significance of a call."

"No, I'm not."

"Remember when we discussed your paranoia? You believed people were following you. I'm not recording our conversations."

"Let me see your phone. Do you have a recording app on it?"

"No, I don't."

"Let me see."

"You have to learn trust. This is a test. Believe me."

"Believe you?" In slow motion, I scanned the entire room. "Give me back my tapes." I stepped forward.

She interposed herself between me and the desk.

"Julia, you're regressing. If this continues, I'll have to notify your office *and* the state medical board. Your behavior is becoming threatening—a risk for working with children."

I threw my head back to better view her.

Her narrowed eyes returned my gaze. Her lips pressed together and disappeared like a lizard.

Seconds later, my shoulders slumped, and I retreated toward the recliner.

A smile teased at the edge of her mouth. "Much better."

Herding me toward the door, she said, "This was fine for today, but next time, I want to move forward. We have to work on trust. Record your thoughts on the audio tapes, and we'll listen to them together. And remember to take your medications. If you deviate from the treatment plan, you're not ready to return to work."

Her skeletal hand rested on my shoulder—a lifeless fragment of humanity. I didn't bother moving it away. Those hands wouldn't touch me again.

The threat in her voice strengthened my resolve. For a moment, I had visualized a hint of truth. Without responding, I entered the lobby where Camile waited.

Dr. Griffith had lied. She was hiding something.

Did it concern my urges, those impulses? I didn't know—yet. But I would uncover the truth. Rediscover my secrets. I had to. My sanity depended upon it.

CHAPTER 3

Sunlight streaked through the bedroom window and across my face. Squinting, I crawled out of bed. My head felt heavy as I struggled to shake off drowsiness. Medication slackened my movements.

Despite Dr. Griffith's reassurance, the side effects hadn't resolved. I decided not to take the morning pill, preferring to be conscious enough to understand the court proceedings.

An acrid smell clung to the air. I hated coffee. Because my parents drank it each morning, I tolerated it—had tolerated it—for the past two weeks. They had arrived after I received news from the district attorney regarding our court date. Could this nightmare finally be over?

In the bathroom, my head drooped over the sink. The reflection in the mirror was distorted and foreign, but it would have to do. After splashing cold water on my face, I prepared for the day ahead.

"Morning, Julia. You hungry?" Camile squeezed by me and into the closet at the rear of the bathroom. "Do you need help picking something out to wear?"

"I can dress myself."

Although Camile was my best friend, I bridled at her intrusion.

She returned to my side. "I thought you might need—"

"I know you're trying to help, but I'm fine." Was I?

While I brushed my teeth, she filled a cup with water and removed a pill from my prescription medicine bottle. Toothpaste dribbled down my chin.

"What're you doing?"

"Helping." In one hand, she held a pill and in the other a cup. "Here."

I accepted the pill and cup, placing them on the counter while I finished dressing.

"Aren't you going to take them?"

"Later."

"Julia, you're supposed to take one pill twice a day."

"I'm a physician, too, Camile. I know how to take medication."

"Fine." She frowned, resting her hands on her slim hips. "You should follow up with Dr. Griffith. She's a highly recommended forensic psychiatrist."

"My internist said he would prescribe my medication—and I'm also seeing a therapist."

"Humph. It's not the same."

"You still think I need a psychiatrist?"

"Dr. Griffith thought you needed more intensive treatment. She was worried about your dreams."

Without answering, I rubbed moisturizer across my face. But from the corner of my eye, I watched her.

"Have you had any more of those dreams?"

"What dreams?" From the mirror, I observed her response.

She gazed distantly, twirling a hairbrush in her hand. "Well, I guess they weren't actually dreams, more like thoughts—or urges. At least, that's what Dr. Griffith called them."

"Have you been talking to her about what I told you?"

"No, of course not," she said, averting her gaze.

Had she been speaking to Dr. Griffith? In the future, I'd keep my own counsel. It hurt not to have someone I could trust—not even my doctor. But I wouldn't let anyone deceive me—not again.

"Dr. Griffith called me a psychopath."

"No, she didn't. She said you experienced delusions from a psychotic break brought on by severe depression."

"She wanted to institutionalize me."

"Remember how bad you'd become? You wouldn't eat—couldn't sleep. She wanted you to heal."

Why eat? Food held no pleasure, serving simply as fuel to keep my body functioning. My whole reason for existing ended with the murder of my son. After Jean died, I had Evens. Caring for him gave me purpose. Now, with Evens dead... nothing mattered.

"Don't you believe I'm doing better?"

"I wonder sometimes." Camile slid the cup and pill across the counter in my direction.

With a sigh, I picked up the pill and swallowed it, chasing it down with water.

"Good. Need help with your hair?"

"No, I got it."

After Camile left, I spit the pill into the sink and watched it dissolve and float down the drain—like my life. My hands trembled. With concerted effort, I twisted my hair into two vines on the sides of my scalp. Presently, simple tasks confounded me.

Antipsychotics helped relieve symptoms of psychosis and improve quality of life. But what if you weren't psychotic?

When did I lose contact with reality? After Evens died or before? Since I didn't recall having *murderous urges*, as the psychiatrist stated, I didn't know. Was that proof I had them?

And my dreams. Were they delusions—hallucinations caused by depression? I had no idea, but one thing was certain, Dr. Griffith had no interest in helping me.

11

Self-appointed psychiatrist to the stars, she treated physicians, judges, and professionals from various spheres of industry. But I found her methods suspect. She seemed overly interested in—

"Julia, you coming?"

"Yes, Momma. Be right there."

In the kitchen, Momma prepared breakfast while Daddy consumed eggs, bacon, and toast. Trudging across my mid-century home, I plopped on a seat at the dining room table. Breakfast didn't appeal to me. I prepared it every morning for Evens. But since his death...

"Good morning," Momma said, glancing up from the stove where she scrambled eggs. "Want some?"

"No, thank you." I slouched down in the chair across from Daddy.

A large, arthritic hand squeezed mine as he kissed my cheek. His rough, dry fingers were strong and warm.

"You should eat something. It's going to be a rough day."

Momma joined us at the table with a steaming plate of food and ate.

"I'm not hungry."

"What time is it, honey?" Momma asked Daddy.

Chewing with a mouth full of food, he said, "We've got time."

The smell of fried food made my stomach churn. I wanted a glass of water, but my body refused to move from its perpetual sense of inertia. Meanwhile, my mind ruminated over the death of my only child.

Wiping his mouth with a napkin, Daddy glanced over at me. "After today, you should be able to put this behind you."

My head jerked to attention. "Would you put it behind you if I'd been murdered?"

Tears welled in his eyes. Chastened, I threw my arms around his neck. How could I forget how much he had lost with the death of his only grandchild?

"I…I'm sorry. I didn't mean it." Sobs mixed with my words. "I'm sorry, Daddy."

He rubbed my back and kissed my cheek. The scent of his cologne soothed me.

"I know, baby girl. If someone hurt you… God help me."

I kissed his cheek. At the kitchen sink, I attempted to wash away my tears, but instead, I hovered over it. Similar to Ophelia, except instead of mourning a prince, I grieved Evens' death, weighed down in a marsh of depression. A bit theatrical—but I simply adored Hamlet. I laughed out loud.

Momma frowned as my moment of mirth petered out. I resumed staring into the sink.

"Good morning," Camile said, heading for the coffee maker while addressing my parents. She touched my shoulder. "Better?"

My shoulders rose and fell, but I remained silent.

She filled a mug and turned toward the table. "What time does court start?"

"Ten," Momma said.

Camile sipped coffee. "What time should we get there?"

"Nine," my parents said in unison. Momma was a former office manager, and Daddy had served in the military. In our family arriving early was obligatory.

After collecting the plates, Momma brought them over to the sink. "Go into the bathroom and wash up, Julia," she said, pointing me in the direction of the bedroom.

On the way to the bedroom, I saw Thaddeus in the living room, seated in front of the glass wall of windows overlooking the backyard. Braids extended past his shoulders, and a suit hung loosely on his thin frame. He grew up with Evens.

13

I had become his surrogate mother when his biological mother became *indisposed*—which occurred frequently.

Thaddeus arrived on Saturday. His mom gave permission for him to attend the court proceedings. I thought it would be overwhelming, but he insisted. I prayed he would be okay because I knew I wouldn't. Without addressing him, I retired to the bedroom.

By the time I re-entered the living room, my parents had finished breakfast and sat around the coffee table with Camile. Thaddeus continued staring outside. Something in the recesses of my mind told me I should speak with him.

The mental morass I dwelled in left me with no idea what to say. His curly black hair reminded me of Evens. Shoulder length. Wait… No. Evens kept his hair cut close. Why was it down to his shoulders? Had it grown longer since his death? I blinked rapidly, removing the medication haze obscuring my vision. The shoulder-length hair belonged to Thaddeus. He glanced up at me for a second before returning to the windows.

Instead of joining him, I stood next to Camile's chair opposite my parents, who sat beside each other on the couch. Momma conversed with someone over the phone.

A stack of retirement home brochures rested on the table where I had placed them a week prior. I promised my parents to review them, but I had forgotten. For several minutes, I gazed vacantly down at the table.

Cognitive dysfunction could occur with selective serotonin reuptake inhibitors. Did the medication prevent me from thinking clearly? It could be a defense mechanism, internally shielding myself from pain.

I drifted over to the sliding glass doors, a foot away from Thaddeus. He hadn't stirred. My gaze flowed over the yard. Despite the beautiful Goleta weather, I hadn't been outside all summer. Usually, I bar-be-qued. In summer, Evens played in the yard with his friends. There were parties and sleepovers. Soccer games where the kids challenged the adults.

Emotion choked my throat. Though I needed to cry, no tears flowed. Maybe my body couldn't produce them anymore. Had I depleted my supply of sorrow?

Hairs on my arm raised. Evens turned toward me.

A second later, I detected Thaddeus approaching. From the corner of my eye, Evens slipped away. I reached forward.

He whispered, "I miss him so much."

My chest ached as I slowly nodded.

"I wish… I wish I could've been Evens' brother."

I didn't respond. Evens' voice sounded like Thaddeus. I looked over and saw Thaddeus standing beside me. Salty lines covered his cheeks. Where had Evens gone?

He's dead, Julia. Your son is dead.

But Thaddeus lived, and he mourned. He needed comfort, assurance everything would be fine. I should have reached out to him, but I couldn't. Thaddeus was hurting, but I couldn't address his pain. Every part of my dull body screamed to respond to him, but I didn't.

His head lowered, and Thaddeus walked away. I let him leave.

"Time to go," Daddy said, using the arm of the couch to stand.

Time. There never seemed to be enough while Evens lived. Now, I had nothing but time to reflect upon the past and what wouldn't be.

Momma continued her phone conversation, picked up her purse, and raised her head toward him.

Camile headed for the garage. "I'll drive."

At the rear of the procession, I considered what was about to happen. Doubt plagued my mind—too pragmatic to believe justice would occur today. But I had to attend. Perhaps Daddy was right. Maybe after today, I could move forward.

But what if I didn't receive justice?

CHAPTER 4

As Camile traveled down Highway 101, nestled between the Pacific Ocean and the Santa Barbara mountains' peaceful scenery, I considered the prosecutor's case. Would Evens' murderer finally be held accountable? Justice deferred was seldom satisfactory.

Today, the legal system would mete out due process, but justice? I was skeptical. Despite what occurred in the courtroom, I would still return home without my son.

Like an automaton, I climbed the half dozen steps and entered the courthouse. Inside, I exhaled. The room failed to live up to expectations. Television and cinematic melodramas depicted courtrooms with rich walnut walls reminiscent of stately buildings crafted at the dawning of our democracy.

Deprived of natural light as the room lacked windows, large fluorescent bulbs gave this hallowed hall of justice a dull-yellow illumination. Judge Donaldson presided over a bench more Ikea than classical American architecture. With a bang of her gavel, the proceedings commenced.

Hours passed.

Buttoning his suitcoat, Mr. Henderson, the district attorney, strode up to the bench and delivered his summation.

Uncomfortable on the hardwood bench, I readjusted my position, careful not to cause a disturbance. A lot depended upon the outcome. Whether from impatience or nervousness, my foot tapped repeatedly against the linoleum floor. I rested my hand on my knee to stop it.

The walls, likely manufactured with asbestos, reflected the tragedy of 1950s construction remodeled in the 1970s. Those originally white walls had grown dingy from the sweat and tears of unfortunate people trapped inside this rectangular space. Forlorn hope and desperation tainted the paint.

Behind the prosecutor, I sat on the left side of the room, sandwiched between Camile on my left and Momma on the right. Daddy sat on the other side of Momma, near the end of the pew, beside the central aisle. His military-hardened gaze zeroed in on Mrs. Copeland, the defendant, and her attorneys.

For her part, Mrs. Copeland faced forward, her wide blue eyes feigning remorse. She never glanced at her family seated on the pew behind her—or at me. In the many months since Evens' death, she failed to exhibit one act of contrition or apology.

Ramrod straight, my spine never slackened. Because I sat behind the prosecutor, I received a lot of scrutiny. Reporters stared at me; court artists sketched my portrait. Evens couldn't represent himself, but I would.

I had let him down once, but not again. Though the hardwood pew taxed my patience, I remained steadfast. Desperately, I wanted to move—to get up and stretch, go outside, and breathe fresh air. I stiffened my resolve and refused to yield. Evens had been strong, and so would I.

Six months had passed since the district attorney officially charged Mrs. Copeland with vehicular homicide. However, she hadn't spent one night in jail. Apparently, her husband's money and family's influence precluded any such inconvenience. No, Evens' murderer had been allowed to roam free until the antiquated wheels of justice finally brought her to trial.

The path had been arduous. I couldn't recall a time since that horrible day when a police officer informed me of Evens' death when I didn't feel pain. Since I heard those words, misery had been a constant companion, anger a close second. In nightmares, the police officer's face repeated those agonizing words again and again.

Pain and death surrounded me daily. As a pediatrician, I sewed up lacerations and medicated sore ears, heard the wails of immunized children, and the lamentations of pregnant teens. Death had never been a stranger. I informed parents their children had cancer or newborn babies had died mere minutes after descending from the precarious birth canal. Death didn't surprise me. But I hadn't fathomed mortality would visit *my* son in the dawning of his young life.

A jury wouldn't deliver justice in this courtroom today. The lawyers for Mrs. Copeland chose to have a judge determine her fate. When the district attorney informed me of this decision, the corner of my left eye twitched—for even then, I suspected something was awry.

My gaze fastened on Mrs. Copeland's profile. Seated feet away from me, she refused to look in my direction, to see me, and to acknowledge what she stole in killing my son. Clenching the edge of the pew, I glanced down at my fingers, directing them to relax.

Hold it together, Julia.

Warmth crept up my chest—a hot flash, maybe hatred. I could no longer make the distinction. Like Daddy, I stared at the murderer. Dressed in a pricey, buttoned-down tailored suit, Mrs. Copeland stared straight ahead.

The judge retired from the bench to consider the testimony. While we waited for her return, I closed my eyes and practiced my breathing exercises. Perhaps I shouldn't have spit out my morning pill.

Minutes elapsed. People stirred. My eyes flew open, glancing around the room.

Adjacent to the judge's bench, courtroom staff poured inside from an open door. The gap allowed me a brief glimpse inside the judge's office. She spoke into a cellphone, laughing.

"All rise," the court officer said, slipping a pen into the shirt pocket of his tan uniform.

Everyone stood as the judge entered, hurriedly zipping up her robe. Before the trial, Mr. Henderson explained that despite Mrs. Copeland's intoxication, he couldn't charge her with first-degree murder.

"Why the hell not?", I had asked. As a repeat offender, this had been her fourth incidence of injuring someone but the first homicide we knew of. Who knew how often she drove drunk and had *not* been arrested?

The district attorney had stated the strictest sentence possible would be manslaughter. My heart ached. Even before the trial, I'd been robbed. If Evens had been a flaxen-haired child riding a tricycle, could the legal system have done better than manslaughter?

Unprofitable thoughts, Julia. Focus on the trial.

Hope rested with Judge Donaldson. A mother herself, I prayed she would deliver the harshest sentence allowed.

Behind the bench, the judge adjusted her robe while exchanging papers with the bailiff. My stomach lurched. Bile stung the back of my throat. The stenographer's hands perched above the dictation machine. Sweat rolled down my spine. I sequestered my hands beneath my thighs to prevent them from squeezing my knees. The tightness in my jaw made my teeth ache. *Hurry up and read the decision.*

Large spectacles peered at Mrs. Copeland as the judge addressed the defense team. "The defendant will stand."

How long would this murderer go away for killing Evens? In the fog of my mind, the words blended together. I lost track of who spoke. Internally, I heard what I wanted. Guilty, the defendant would be remanded to prison for the duration of her natural life.

Get out of fantasy land and listen.

"Mrs. Copeland," Judge Donaldson said, reading from a sheet of paper, "I find you guilty of vehicular manslaughter."

The courtroom exhaled a collective sigh.

The judge continued, ignoring the spectators' response. "My decision was predicated on this not being your first offense."

My heart fluttered, and my chest relaxed. The judge understood the prosecutor's argument. This had not been a first occurrence. Mrs. Copeland deserved a severe penalty. Pressure inside my stomach lessened.

"Therefore, I am sentencing you to fifteen…"

Tension in my jaw released. Fifteen years in prison—not a life sentence but the maximum allowed under the statute. My shoulders slumped. Was this how justice felt?

Like a rocket, the prosecutor sprung to his feet. "I object, Your Honor. This sentence is not appropriate."

Confused, I became disoriented. People stirred. The hum of conversations grew around the courtroom like an approaching swarm of bees. I forced my mind to attend to the proceedings. Why would the DA object to fifteen years in prison?

Chaos sucked air from the room. Daddy shouted toward the defense table, his fist pumping in the air. On the other side of him stood Thaddeus—his mouth gaping. Things appeared incorrectly. Why was the prosecutor objecting?

Murmurings throughout the courtroom overwhelmed the prosecutor's voice. Judge Donaldson banged her gavel, which echoed against the walls.

Spectators, my family, and Evens' friends overruled the gavel. The prosecutor's objections were swallowed by the tumult of the gallery. People joined Daddy in gesticulating at the defendant. Others directed their ire toward the judge. I didn't understand. What had I missed?

Mr. Henderson slammed his hand on the table, pointing at Mrs. Copeland. "Your honor, fifteen months in jail is nowhere near enough for a repeat offender. She killed Evens Toussaint."

My head swooned. Seconds passed as I fought to comprehend how the judge sentenced a murderer to fifteen months in jail—not even prison. Slightly over a year for killing Evens.

Because my vision blurred, I strained to view the defense table. Heat bloomed across my tingling skin. To keep my balance, I clutched the pew, determined not to faint. What influenced lady justice this time, money or privilege?

A smile played across the defense attorney's mouth as she rose to address the court. Mr. Henderson preempted her comments and verbally sparred with the judge, demanding a stiffer sentence.

Bang, bang, bang!

Judge Donaldson shouted. "Sit down, Mr. Henderson, or you'll be sanctioned."

"Oh, I get sanctioned for demanding justice for Evens Toussaint, but you let the defendant—a serial criminal—off with a slap on the wrist." Veins popped out the sides of his neck.

People shouted in agreement. Daddy started toward the defense table. Momma reached around Thaddeus to grab his arm, pulling him back into the row.

Boisterously, the crowd voiced their discontent.

Bang, bang!

Pointing her gavel at the prosecutor, the judge said, "I understand your disappointment, Mr. Henderson, and will forgive your disrespect—this time."

My gaze bounced from the judge to the prosecutor, whose furrowed eyebrows didn't appear apologetic. As my eyes ping-ponged between them, my face grew numb. Was this the emotional blunting mentioned in the drug side effects leaflet?

The entire proceedings became surreal. As if in a dream, I drifted outside myself. If people moved around me, I didn't notice.

For her part, Mrs. Copeland turned toward the gallery, head down, seemingly oblivious to the jeers directed at her. She grinned at a man seated in the first row behind the defense table. He rose and accepted her hand but didn't return her gaiety.

I presumed him to be the wealthy husband—his spray-on tan as artificial as the justice meted out in this courtroom. He wore a tailored suit resembling his wife's ensemble. The jeweled wristwatch and pinky ring on his hand testified to a life of privilege. His Barbie doll wife rolled over my son with her BMW without stopping. Witnesses recorded her license plate for the police as passersby fled for safety.

Had someone touched my shoulder? It would've been Camile or Momma. Faces enlarged and shrank before my eyes. My vision dimmed, and my head ached. The Alice in Wonderland symptoms portended an approaching migraine.

Resembling an owl, the judge peered at me.

What did she see? Acquiescence, acceptance, anger. I hoped she saw I deserved justice. I tried to frame my face to convey those thoughts. Mrs. Copeland's life for Evens. Equity, not pain.

She cleared her throat. "Mrs. Toussaint, this is a court of law. I will not tolerate this outburst."

There was no understanding. She said nothing else to me. Her gaze flipped to the defense table. "Mrs. Copeland, you have a second chance. I hope you take this opportunity...."

Nothing else penetrated. Judge Donaldson's words disappeared into the ether. The events and surroundings faded away. I walked as if on air.

From the double door entrance at the back of the courtroom, I viewed police officers pouring inside. An officer wielding a baton hauled a spectator from the back row and pushed her out of the exit.

My gaze rolled over to Daddy. Friends restrained him as he tried to reach the defense table. Momma grabbed Daddy, pushing Thaddeus into the aisle.

A swarm of police officers approached.

As if trudging through mud—weighed down with sorrow and anger—I fought to reach Daddy. I'd lost too much; I couldn't lose him too. Fighting against my medicated stupor, I circled around Momma and touched Daddy's arm. Like an electric shock, the intensity of his bearing flowed into me.

I detected an essence return to my body—becoming present in the moment. As I came to his side, Daddy peered over at me. Those dark eyes pooled with tears that refused to fall. My fingers grazed his clean-shaven, staunch face, and I cried—for him.

He brought me to his chest and hugged me. Those solid shoulders slumped, and he released his fury. I absorbed it—took it from him—to protect him.

Momma hugged us both and pulled Thaddeus close to my side. Camile's hand rubbed my back.

Police surrounded us, palms hovering over their weapons. They demanded we leave.

"Leave them alone," Mr. Henderson said, his chest heaving. "They're the victims."

A police officer wearing riot gear scowled at us. For a tense moment, I thought he would ignore the district attorney. The officer's finger clenched around the butt of a gun. My breath caught as I drew Thaddeus behind me. Why hadn't I been able to protect Evens similarly? Daddy, Momma, and Camile linked arms.

The district attorney yelled at the officers, and gradually, the army retreated. We huddled behind the prosecution team and exited.

Outside, cold air slapped my face. Cameras clicked. Friends, strangers, and family swirled around. People ascended the courthouse steps seeking justice while others descended those same steps, aware justice was a fallacy.

Unscrupulous, unsympathetic lawyers thrust business cards at me, offering representation in suing the Copeland family. As if money would recompense me for Evens—or punish an unrepentant killer.

By persistence, we crossed the street to the parking lot. The crowd dissipated, leaving us surrounded by close friends. We gathered together, cried, and commiserated. People offered condolences on my loss. In my head, I shouted, '*I didn't lose my son, he was stolen.*' I hadn't been irresponsible. A drunk killed Evens and the legal system condoned the crime. Society failed, not me.

Judge Donaldson's face, Mrs. Copeland, the district attorney. I couldn't distinguish reality from the visions swirling in my head. Again, the courtroom scene flashed across my mind. Armed police officers demanded we leave. The troubled face of the young woman dragged from her seat by an officer in riot gear. And Evens.

His face came close, but the hair was wrong. Too long. Not Evens. Thaddeus. His lips moved, but I couldn't understand the words.

Warmth crept up my body. I flushed. Despite the cool breeze, my skin burned. My heart raced, and my breathing deepened. Figures blurred, faces merged. On sensory overload, my autonomic system shut down. I beheld Camile's face, then fainted.

CHAPTER 5

Eight months had elapsed since I sat in a Santa Barbara courtroom and listened to Judge Henderson deliver her sentence. Since then, newspapers announcing her run for political office have kept her face in the public domain. Folding the newspaper, I dropped it on my office desk and gazed out the window. Note to self: cancel home delivery.

Unfortunately, the medical center windows didn't open. Otherwise, the cool Pacific Ocean breezes would refresh my face. Noughton Medical Center in Goleta was located along the rugged coastline not five miles north of Santa Barbara. Often, I spent the lunch hour striding along the beach, meandering among tourists enjoying California's rendition of the Mediterranean Riviera. Salty air would scratch my nostrils as chirping birds hopped up and down the grainy sand.

Now, empty boxes occupied most of the available office space. Since I'd decided to leave, a sudden nostalgia gripped me, weighing me down with uncertainty.

My fingers clicked along the keyboard, regurgitating the history of present illness before I forgot the parent's complaint. The medical center encouraged physicians to document in the EHR, electronic health record, during office visits, but I failed to master the ability to chart in front of patients. It distracted me from the physician-patient relationship to type into a computer as someone conveyed their personal medical concerns.

I tried it again today but failed miserably. Generally, I wouldn't care, but today it mattered. Redoubling my efforts, I directed my attention to charting.

Knock, knock.

My brow creased at the interruption. Determined to finish charting, I ignored them and typed faster. Unfortunately, the knocking persisted. Because I refused to respond, they opened the door and peeked inside.

"Dr. Toussaint, everyone is waiting," Javier, my medical assistant, said.

"One minute. I'm almost done." My eyes stayed glued to the computer.

He stepped inside and glowered over at the desk. "No, you're coming right now. We want to say goodbye to our favorite doctor."

A contrite retort hovered over my lips. When I peered up into his face, I swallowed the comment and allowed myself to be parted from the desktop. I understood what he meant.

My resignation had not been well received by the department *nor* the medical center. Noughton and I maintained a long, mutually productive relationship. Over many years, I worked with the administration to build a robust, solid pediatric department well regarded in the community for our medical care and patient outcomes. For their part, Noughton allowed me the independence to manage the department—and, when needed, time to mourn.

Once we completed our residency training, Jean wanted to return to Florida, where his family lived. I refused. His family were good people, but I didn't care for Florida's tropical weather. Our discussion was moot because Jean's neurology fellowship brought us to California.

We settled along the central coast. Goleta looked different when we had first arrived, less congested. Gentrification and rising home prices changed everything. Jean hadn't experienced those changes. Cancer had claimed his life while the neighborhood retained its natural, cultural heterogeneity. Evens grew up during the city's expansion. Goleta managed to retain its charm, and I hadn't imagined living anywhere else until murder tainted its beauty.

Four months after receiving a cancer diagnosis, my beloved Jean died. After a time, I moved forward, caring for our son alone. Evens and I comforted each other, supported by family. With a career I appreciated and colleagues who respected me, I pieced together a comfortable existence for us.

After completing high school, Evens started at the university. In his first year, he made the Dean's List. Home for summer break, he had decided to bike around the neighborhood.

On our journey to the conference room for my farewell luncheon, Javier threaded his arm with mine. "I'm going to miss you." He hugged me to his side and whispered, "Come back—soon."

Smiling into his hazel eyes, I nodded, appreciating the sentiment. Javier and I had worked together for many years. I battled the insurance company for approval of his gender reassignment surgery. In turn, he endured my emotional roller coaster of loss and grief, buffering me from unsympathetic patients and staff alike. Javier would miss me, and I him. However, I stood by my decision and had no intention of returning.

Down hallways with painted walls of colorful cartoons, we arrived and entered the conference room. Javier stood back and allowed me to enter first. A loud roar of applause rang out.

Inside the room, I intermingled with friends and associates. People I admired and some I hated. In all, they constituted the community in which I had labored for over twenty years. A fellow physician offered me a cup of juice. Though I accepted it,

I didn't drink. My stomach remained queasy over my decision to leave.

Because I desired a fresh start after Evens' murder, I resigned my position as chief of pediatrics and applied for a transfer to a different campus. Noughton managed five campuses in Central California, three of which included a major hospital. Goleta had been the first campus and remained their flagship medical center. Twelve years ago, when I became chief, I also became the first African American woman leader of any of their medical departments.

Once I resigned, there would only be two African American department chiefs in the organization. With my departure, Noughton's diversity demographics sustained a major blow. The chief medical officer personally called me and requested I rescind my resignation. He'd been displeased when I declined, refusing to accept that I would leave a position as chief and transfer to a smaller satellite campus. As such, this perfunctory event had been thrown together within a week.

Around the room, I glided, mechanically thanking people. I mentally calculated how many uncompleted charts remained before afternoon clinic started. Tomorrow would be my last official day.

My head nodded in reply to someone's question about my departure.

"Thanks for the party. You didn't have to do this."

"Of course we did," they said. "You've been at this clinic longer than any other doctor. We couldn't let you leave without saying goodbye."

Eyes slightly narrowing, I regarded my colleague. The comment didn't sound complimentary. Eavesdropping, I overheard tidbits of another conversation. Seconds passed before I recognized the female voice.

Dr. Lena Harris had been temporarily appointed chief of pediatrics following my resignation. Clearly, she wanted the designation to be permanent.

"I can't believe our department has to pay for this," she said. "This money should come out of the general fund. It's bad enough we had to shut clinic down early. I could be seeing patients instead of pretending I care about Julia leaving."

Plastering a fake smile across my face, I pivoted around and said, "Well, thank you, Lena. That's mighty—"

"Julia," Camile interrupted, "come here." Her long arms opened wide as she approached.

The surly comment dried on my lips. I cocooned myself in my best friend's warm embrace, returning the hug. She kissed me once on each cheek.

"It's good to see you. I didn't know you were coming."

She glanced over my shoulder. I turned around and watched Lena slink away.

"What did she want?"

"Nothing. Fomenting trouble."

"Humph." Camile hooked an arm around my waist and led me away from the crowd. She rubbed my arm, a slight smile in her studying gaze. "All good?"

A half laugh escaped my mouth. The awkward sound made me snap my lips closed. Half a minute elapsed before I said, "Yes, I'm fine."

Doubt clouded her face.

My shoulders slumped. "It... It's been difficult, but I think—no, I know it was the right decision."

Camile's scrutiny continued. Her piercing brown eyes surveyed my movements. I fashioned my mouth into a grin, hoping to appease and settle her mind.

"No more bad dreams of the policewoman?"

For months, a recurring, haunting dream of the police officer who notified me about Evens' death kept me awake. In the dream, the officer arrested me while I pled innocence. She glared at me and repeated, "You let Evens down." Night after night, her face plagued my sleep, accusing me of neglecting my son until I couldn't take it anymore and—

"No," I lied.

Her scrutiny hardened as if she attempted to read my mind. "So, you're okay?"

"I am." Again, I attempted a smile.

She leaned toward me. "I think you should see the psychiatrist again. You stopped the medication without consulting her."

"I didn't need her permission. The side effects were intolerable. I couldn't focus."

"Are you seeing the therapist?"

Frowning, I took a deep breath. "I'm fine. Better each day."

A moment passed before Camile smiled. "Fine. And remember, you can always come back."

I shook my head. "Once I stepped down as chief, there was no coming back—not to work under Lena."

Camile's chin rose. "Don't worry about her. You've worked in Goleta for over twenty years, the past twelve as chief of pediatrics. If you want to come back, we'll deal with Lena."

Smiling, I side-hugged Camile. "No. I need a change. It'll be good to work around people who didn't know Evens." My eyes grew damp. Choking back my sorrow, I avoided the gentle eyes of my friend.

She gripped my hand and mouthed the words, "I understand."

I kissed her cheek. Though I loved Camile, I had to be careful. She knew me better than anyone. If I wasn't careful…

Once the trial of my son's murderer concluded, I avoided public places. Lawyers assailed me for months, seeking to represent me in a civil suit, which I knew would be futile. Aware of her alcoholism and repeated DWIs, Mr. Copeland distanced himself financially from his wife. He had segregated their funds years prior—probably after she injured the woman now living in an assisted care facility suspended in a persistent vegetative state. Nevertheless, money would do little to assuage my desire for vengeance.

Besides work, I didn't go anywhere. In the days and weeks after the sentencing, I repeatedly watched footage from the court proceedings, studying my countenance while exiting the courtroom. The weeping woman on the screen looked vague, as if in a trance. At that moment, had the footage captured my thoughts?

Camile's dark eyes continued observing. Not simply my best friend, she was an internist and would notice any relapse.

Be careful, Julia. Change the topic.

"Did I mention the movers are coming next week? If you're not busy, want to help pack?"

She laughed. "Fat chance."

Two nurses approached and interrupted our discussion. "Come on, Dr. Toussaint. We only have you for one more day." They dragged me away from Camile.

For the next hour, I socialized with colleagues and staff. All the time, my mind returned to the decision to leave. Goleta had been my home like forever.

Our once-thriving home became a mausoleum. Ghosts of Jean and Evens tormented my steps. Shadowed memories from each corner of the house teased my mind. Pain pierced my heart night after night as every inch of our home screamed their absence. I had to leave or surrender my sanity to the ecru walls of my mid-century house.

Work offered little solace, suffocating me in sorrow. At the medical office, well-meaning people shared stories of Evens. They spoke about his laughter and intelligence and how much he resembled Jean. I had to escape.

Laughter brought me out of my remembrances as someone laid a hand on my shoulder. I fought the urge to shake it off, recalling I was at a party.

The Chief Medical Officer, Dr. Trevor Madison, laughed. "We're gonna miss you, Julia. I'm sure you know you can come back anytime. Right, Lena?"

With a bird-like titter, Lena said, "Of course." Despite those words, a slight sneer curved along her lips.

Delighted at her discomfort, I grinned. "Maybe I will."

Lena's blanched face made the lie priceless.

When the party ended, I returned to my office. While Javier roomed patients, I sorted office items collected over the years. Some clutter, others memorable. An entire wall had been dedicated to my patients' artwork and photos. Careful to remove each piece, I wondered if I could make them into a collage. My diplomas had to be chiseled from the wall. All afternoon, staff members helped load boxes into my car.

Before seeing my last patient, I removed the items Evens made. I had kept everything he ever created. Delicately, those items were separated into their own container. The final item off the wall was his high school graduation photo.

Clinic patients stopped by to say goodbye. I finished charting with time to spare. At the end of the day, Javier, his face waterlogged with tears, came into the office. I hugged him so tightly our bones creaked.

Pushing him gently away, I said, "Call me if you need anything."

He nodded. "I will."

"Go on. Finish up so you can go home." I hurried him out of my office before I cried. When I left home that morning, I vowed not to cry. The staff had seen enough of my tears.

With a box under each arm, I departed the clinic. I would leave an impression on this office with my absence, like the blank space on the wall where Evens' picture had hung.

Outside, I breathed a sigh of relief with one final glance at the medical center before I abandoned the past. The future depended on understanding my history—discerning the motivation for the actions I took. Above all else, there would be no more deaths.

CHAPTER 6

By habit, I awoke before the alarm. Warmly snuggled under blankets, I teetered on the edge of sleep and wakefulness for several minutes. In the hazy morning, an image of the female police officer arose. Glowering, she shouted, "Where were you?" In a flash, her face dissolved into Evens'.

My breath caught. Instantly, I sat up, and the apparition disappeared. Swinging my legs over the side of the bed, I waited for my nerves to settle.

Despite the disturbing apparition, I slept well. It would be improper to arrive late on my first day at this new office, so I hastened to prepare.

Damn. Forgot to call my parents. They sent me a new list of retirement homes to review.

This is going to happen no matter how long you delay.

Why did they have to leave the home they loved? Because I wasn't ready to move back to North Carolina and care for them. From the moment I relocated to California with Jean, my life belonged here. But now he and our only child were gone. Why did I stay?

The places we visited as a family brought joy and sorrow. Ghosts of Jean and Evens prevented me from finding solace in the home we shared. To escape the past, I relocated to a city I didn't know. A place far from friends.

Cut it out. You'll be late for work.

Thirty minutes later, I parked in the visitor lot and entered the San Marguerite medical facility. Since the office didn't open for another thirty minutes, I strolled around the medical office complex and adjacent hospital. This was my second time here—the first was during my interview.

Drab gray walls and mismatched flooring complemented the dingy art plastered along the hallways. An overwhelming scent of bleach wafted into my nostrils. I tried not to imagine the origin of stains etched into the peeling linoleum floors.

Noughton shouldn't have such a desultory, outdated facility. This place reminded me of the military hospitals of my childhood. How had I not noticed that before? Because my grief was raw. The interview remained a blur—like most of the past year.

This medical center differed significantly from Goleta. I had grown accustomed to working in a first-class facility with a modern design and updated décor. The renowned hospital attached to Goleta's state-of-the-art medical center attracted visitors not only from other parts of California but from around the country. In contrast, this decaying hospital left me dispirited. With a sigh, I retraced my steps and returned to the pediatric clinic to await the office manager.

Heavy with claustrophobic sadness, the atmosphere made me reconsider the transfer. Perhaps I *had* been hasty. This facility provided distance—which I desired—but proximity to Camile in case I needed help. However, the milieu was far from heartening.

The pediatric section of the hospital was also wanting. Children should experience a welcoming atmosphere when they visited the doctor, not this. The medical care, hopefully, would prove more modern—and the staff more hospitable—than the surroundings reflected.

Along the floors, clacking echoed, growing louder in my direction. Down the beleaguered halls, I perceived a familiar face approach. For a moment, I thought I saw...

My skin tingled, and my heart raced. Why would the police officer appear here? Was this an omen?

My chest relaxed when I recognized the office manager. We met during the interview. I dared not look beyond her, afraid of seeing an apparition following me from Goleta. At least the office manager was on time—one point in the medical center's favor.

Folders clutched to her chest, Mrs. Marsha Conroy hurried along. There was no seating in the hallway, so for the past fifteen minutes, I'd stood against a wall.

As she approached, I scrutinized her appearance. Two-inch heels identified her as non-clinical personnel. I doubt she would have chosen those shoes if she chased children around a clinic all day. I remembered to smile, straighten my posture, and prepare to shake hands.

Dressed in a knee-length pencil skirt and blazer, Mrs. Conroy walked with purpose. Her pace increased as she extended a long, doughy hand. "Hello, Dr. Toussaint. I hope you haven't waited long."

Discombobulated, a strained smile aged her appearance. Perhaps my early arrival disturbed her morning routine. I shook her hand.

"Hello, Mrs. Conroy. No, I arrived a few minutes ago."

"It's good to see you again. Welcome to Noughton Reicker Healthcare San Marguerite. Come into my office. I have some forms for you to sign."

A bustling key ring dangled from her purse. She opened the door into a room of disarray. The folders rested precariously in her hand while she rearranged clutter.

"Have a seat while I gather your paperwork. And please, call me Marsha."

"Thank you," I said, appreciating the gesture.

"Well, today you'll have a short schedule." She continued moving items around, clearing space for me on a chair beside her desk.

I effaced myself before one of two windows, attempting to disappear and give her an opportunity to compose herself. She seemed to appreciate my gesture, continuing to search desks and cabinets, I presumed, for the aforementioned documents. Placing my cellphone on vibrate, I recalled Camile's text from last night.

Remember to call back, or she'll worry.

In the intervening minutes, I studied the room. Being an organized person myself, the untidy space reflected negatively on Marsha. First impressions. Trained to question patients and parents in order to diagnose illnesses, my occupation required astute observation. I found it difficult not to be critical. However, I didn't want to be judgmental. My gaze fell over her expensive shoes and polished, long fingernails.

Stop it, Julia.

"Got it," Marsha said, moving quickly to collate the documents. She collapsed into a chair and turned on a computer. An inch-thick stack of papers lay before her on the desk. "Okay, here we go."

I retrieved a pen from my purse and prepared for the endless parade of signatures.

Marsha requested a copy of my medical license, diploma, NPI number, and an assorted list of other documents attesting to my qualifications. Always prepared, I searched inside my binder and provided each item requested. I intended to put my best foot forward. Organization, in my experience, guaranteed success in whatever you undertook. It also maintained my sanity when visions made me doubt my abilities.

Next, Marsha directed me to stand in front of a white square in the center of one of the walls. After the obligatory picture for my identification card, she dismissed me for lunch. I needed a break. Two visions of the police officer in one day left me skittish. If those horrors followed me here, where could I go to escape?

***

Because I already worked for Noughton, I only attended a half day of the new physician orientation conducted in the hospital's large first-floor classroom. I surveyed the room, scrutinizing the other participants. Some were glassy-eyed, while others listened with rapt attention. It didn't faze me as I'd heard it all before.

The moderator shared the usual propaganda about how Noughton delivered the best medical care in the region, superior to their competitors. I hated the politics of medicine, where medical providers exaggerated their own importance. Hospital systems should work together in caring for patients. Childish competition belittled the importance of our work. I noticed several participants glued to mobile devices, oblivious to the hype.

Although I should appreciate a break from clinic duties, I preferred work. It provided a necessary mental distraction, which I craved. When the orientation concluded, I returned to Marsha's office.

More relaxed than this morning, she invited me to be seated while detailing my activities for the week. "I need you to sign this form to receive your keys, and the second form is for your ID."

As I signed the documents, she slid a square plastic badge with my picture across the table. Clipping the plastic identification to my lapel, I watched her retrieve a large purse from a desk drawer.

"I have a meeting in an hour," she said, "but I have time to show you around your wing of the pediatric unit. I know you're familiar with Noughton, but we probably do things differently in San Marguerite, so I started you on a graduated patient schedule."

Internally I shrugged, unconcerned as long as I could see patients. Dormancy gave me too much time to reflect on things I preferred not to remember. Medicine had become a necessary distraction—an extension of myself occupying time and providing satisfaction. I welcomed the emotional dynamics of the doctor-patient relationship.

At San Marguerite, I could establish a new patient roster, form relationships, and work with people unfamiliar with Jean or Evens. There would be no more comments about Evens' murder. Here, I would find a comfortable environment to restore my sanity and abandon those unhealthy habits I acquired in Goleta.

Adjacent to each other, Marsha and I entered the patient waiting area of the pediatric clinic.

"This is where the front staff are located. Three wings lead off to a central waiting area." She waved to the registration clerks, and they returned her greeting.

A key card flicked across the wall reader, and a heavy security door opened. The tour continued into the back offices and exam rooms. Like Vanna White revealing letters, Marsha motioned with her hands, pointing out the bathrooms and break room. We passed the station for the medical assistants and nurses.

"This is Dr. Toussaint," she announced to the staff. "She starts seeing patients tomorrow."

I shook hands all around.

"Behind the desk is the trauma room where medications are stored. The access code should be in your paperwork," she said.

Following behind her, I gave the room a quick glance, noting the medicine and supply cabinets.

Finally, she proceeded down a long hall, which ended at a locked door.

"This is your office key." She placed it in my hand. "Here's the packet from this morning. You'll find directions on how to log on to the EHR. If you have any questions, call IT."

Marsha checked her watch. "I've gotta run. Call or email me if you have any questions."

The last words trailed behind her as she trotted away. She couldn't run in those heels.

Once inside my office, I closed and locked the door. I hung my purse on the door handle and removed a container of disinfectant wipes. For the next half hour, I cleaned every surface in the room—including the chair. OCD came in handy—whether removing dirt, fingerprints, or DNA. After confirming the chair seat cushion had dried, I sat down at my new desk.

Someone lightly tapped on the door.

"Come in," I said, unlocking it.

A woman with thick, shoulder-length black hair entered. With a large smile and dark eyes to match, she proffered a small ceramic baking dish.

"Hi, I'm April Powell."

We shook hands.

"Julia Toussaint. I'm sorry I don't have a chair to offer you."

"No problem. I wanted to welcome you to the clinic."

I accepted the dish and placed it on the desk. "Thank you," I said, hoping she'd leave, which she didn't.

Leaning up against the wall, she asked, "Aren't you going to taste it?"

"Maybe later—when I get home."

"Go ahead, try it. It's homemade." Her eyes danced with eagerness.

Irritated by her insistence because I wasn't hungry, I peeled back the aluminum foil. A fork and spoon lay beside the dish. Spices tickled my nose. It smelled delicious. My stomach rumbled in anticipation. Maybe I was hungry. I forked a piece of meat, and my mouth exploded with flavors of pork and chilies.

"Umm hmm. This is delicious." I took another bite. "What is this?"

She laughed. "I confess, it's from the Soulful Café."

Frowning, I considered the name. "Is it southern soul food?"

April walked farther into the room. "Some new fusion place. Good, right?"

"Yes, it is." After taking another bite, I wrapped the dish and set it aside to finish later—when I was alone. "Well, thanks again."

"You can treat me next time. Maybe we can go shopping together. I heard you recently moved here."

"I don't live in San Marguerite. I bought a house in San Luis Obispo."

"That's not far. You'll need to purchase things for the house. I bought a new home too. I'd love to have someone to shop with."

"I don't—"

"You're not going to be like everyone else and give me some lame excuse about being busy, are you?" She grimaced.

It *had* been my intention, but as I regarded those large dark eyes… Evens had beautiful dark eyes with a sleepy peace to them. I adored those eyes. He also possessed a gentle kindness, which allowed him to easily socialize. A new job required making new friendships. I relocated for a fresh start, right?

"No, I'm not going to be like them."

"Good. Since we're going to be neighbors, we should be friends."

In answer to my questioning eyebrow, she pointed to the wall. "My office is next door."

A medical assistant hovered at the door. "Dr. Powell, your patient is waiting."

"Right." April exited but pivoted on her heel. "I'll call you, and we can set up a time to go shopping. We'll start with antique stores." Without waiting for a reply, she left.

I rose, prepared to shut the door. But as April turned left down a hallway opposite her office, I heard her speak to someone.

"Hi," she said. "How are—"

"Fuck off."

Startled, it took me a moment to appreciate what occurred. Recognizing the voice as male, I rushed to the hallway, concerned about a hostile patient situation. Violence in medical offices had become common. By the time I arrived at the corner, April entered an exam room, and an unknown male proceeded down the hall.

Before April shut the exam room door, I asked, "You all right?"

Her forehead creased. "Hmm. What?"

"I heard someone curse at you."

"Oh, it was nothing." She closed the door, leaving me there gaping.

Unsure of what happened, I listened at the door to make sure she was fine. Not hearing any disturbance, I returned to my office.

Beside the desk, a window looked out over the visitor parking lot. With my identification badge, I would be able to park in the employee lot going forward. I intended to check it out before I drove home.

Satisfied I wouldn't catch some pathogen from the keyboard, I adjusted the chair, brought up the EHR, and reviewed my patient schedule for tomorrow. Since I generally saw twenty-five to thirty patients a day, a schedule with five patients would be easy.

With a yawn, I stretched, extending my feet under the desk. How should I decorate this space? I removed a picture frame from my handbag—my favorite photo of Evens.

Its silver edges sparkled under the overbearing overhead fluorescent light. His somber face shone back at me. He never resembled his father as much as he did in this photo. I positioned the frame at an angle where I could view it as I typed.

In my former home, I could still smell his scent—hear him call from his bedroom. Perhaps he'd been more fortunate than Mrs. Copeland's other victim, who resided in a skilled nursing facility suspended in a vegetative state. If a person had brain activity but could not eat, talk, or engage in any meaningful pursuits, were they alive?

Since Evens' murder, such thoughts had troubled my mind. I posited the question to Camile one evening after imbibing an entire bottle of wine. She accused me of reading Albert Camus's essays again. True. I found them enlightening. However, I refused to believe Mrs. Copeland did me a favor by killing my son immediately instead of confining him to a nursing home.

One phrase in Camus' essays struck me as particularly poignant. "Life can be lived all the better if it has no meaning." I probably hadn't interpreted the sentence as he intended, but at the time, it answered a question in my mind. How would I have felt if Evens survived and remained bed-bound, fed by tubes, and unresponsive? Would I have taken the steps I had to seek justice?

Moot point since I had no regrets. But I did endeavor to do things differently going forward.

Snapping pictures of the office interior with my cellphone, I planned the office décor. As I appraised the room, my gaze wandered outside. Across the street, a uniformed police officer stood in the middle of the sidewalk. He couldn't be looking at me, could he?

For several minutes, I observed him. Staring at the building, he didn't move. Alarmed, I rushed toward the window for a better view, but suddenly, he disappeared. Was he real or another apparition?

My pulse soared, pounding in my chest. The relief I had felt moments before vanished. I shut the blinds. *What did I see?*

In a flurry, I gathered my purse, keys, and badge before fleeing the office. On the way to the parking lot, I tried to recall the police officer's face. It wasn't the same officer haunting my dreams because this person had been male. Still, he looked familiar. For minutes, I searched my memory, but I couldn't be sure.

Since I stopped taking the antipsychotics Dr. Griffith prescribed, my memory had returned incrementally, but gaps remained. Organization helped somewhat.

Tiny hairs at the base of my neck raised. Hurrying inside my car, I secured the lock and scanned the area for police officers—real or imagined. None appeared, but I sensed someone watching me. Half a minute elapsed before I drove home.

I thought I'd taken the first step in a new direction. After the losses I'd experienced, I deserved a fresh beginning. But those demons pursued me here. How would I ever be free?

CHAPTER 7

Seated on an empire chair, April waited for me to catch up. "Ready?" She lifted the chair and carried it up to the furniture store register.

A miniature metal bicycle caused a memory of Evens and I biking around Carmel to flash in my mind. A gentle breeze had propelled us along the jagged coastline.

"I'm going for a quick ride around town. Practice for our trip to Monterey next month," he had said, securing the bike helmet over his crew cut. "Bye, Mom."

It took a moment for my mind to focus. Sweat trickled down my brow as I lifted the cocktail table.

"Wait a minute," I said, maneuvering along the overcrowded aisles of the antique shop. "I'm too old for this."

She smiled. "Not old, just out of shape."

"Thanks, friend."

April preceded me up to the checkout register. This was the third antique furniture store we had visited this weekend. While the cashier rang up our purchases, I mopped perspiration from the back of my neck.

"After this, I'm done for today."

"You need to get back in shape. When did you stop working out?"

My brows raised. "How did you know I used to work out?"

"You have the arms of a swimmer, and your calves aren't bad either."

In tandem, we exited the store.

"Have you been checking me out?" I asked, loading items into the rear of her SUV.

"You're not my type." She reversed out of the parking spot and exited the lot. Without signaling, she executed a left turn at the light.

"I jog. When did you stop exercising?"

By habit, I hesitated, reticent about sharing anything with anyone. Miles down the road, gazing out the side window, I said, "Evens and I biked a lot."

April nodded.

"In Goleta, I built a home gym in one of the spare rooms."

The traffic light turned red as her SUV entered the intersection. A car honked. Oblivious, April swung into my subdivision.

"Are you building another home gym?"

"Not likely."

"Think about it." She parked in the driveway before glancing at me. "You don't want to let yourself go." Her laugh, rich and throaty, sounded like a finely tuned instrument.

"Watch it."

At the house, I removed my furniture from the SUV.

"Come on, old lady. I'll help you carry it inside."

"Careful. What I lack in strength, I make up for in ingenuity."

Her eyes rolled. "Whatever."

She grabbed one side of the table and I took the other. Inside, I collapsed onto the couch. April rested in a recliner.

"Whew. The table's heavier than it looks." She adjusted the recliner and extended her legs on a footrest. "Let's order pizza."

I stretched along the leather couch. Minutes elapsed as neither of us moved. "One of us needs to order food."

"I'm on it."

While the pizza restaurant kept April on hold, I prepared utensils and plates along the kitchen island. Although this small house had a generous great room, it was less than half the size of my home in Goleta. Perfectly suited for one person.

April completed the order and joined me in the kitchen.

"How long have you been at San Marguerite?" I asked, offering her wine.

"Two months. Before that, I worked in Paso Robles. I wanted to transfer to the Goleta office, but nothing was available."

"Jobs there rarely become available." I handed her a napkin.

"I can't believe you left. If I knew you were stepping down, I would've applied for your position."

With a wine glass in hand, I sank into the couch cushions. "They didn't fill my position. Our department already staffed more pediatricians than necessary."

She swore.

"What's your interest in Goleta, other than the gorgeous weather."

"It's closer to my family—in LA."

"There are physician jobs in LA."

"Yeah, but not with Noughton."

"They pay well."

"True." April gazed past me into the yard beyond the sliding glass doors. "And I could use the money."

Frowning, I asked, "Student loans?"

"Family obligations."

"What obligations? You don't have any kids."

"No, but I have a mom and sisters." She rose and sauntered out to the backyard.

Our pizza arrived, and we settled on the patio. April plopped down on a chair across from mine.

Marinara sauce dripped down my chin. I licked at it without success. "What's up with your patient?"

"Who?" April asked, frowning.

"The guy who cursed at you the day we met?"

Seconds passed. April stared distantly into the sky. "Oh. He wasn't a patient. It was Ken."

"Dr. Brady?"

She nodded.

"He curses at you?"

"We have a history."

My gaze widened, but April didn't immediately satisfy my curiosity. At least five minutes elapsed. She refilled her wine glass, and we both returned to the living room.

"I knew Ken when I worked in Northern California right after residency. To make a long story brief, I reported him for having a sexual relationship with a medical student. Of course, he said it was consensual."

"Can't be."

"Exactly. There was a clear power imbalance. He supervised her in an outpatient clinic. After an abbreviated investigation, the medical center sanctioned Ken. He quit a month later. When I applied for a transfer, I had no idea he worked for Noughton—and in San Marguerite."

"Didn't you interview for the position?"

"No." April placed her plate in the sink with the wine glass. "They had a vacancy, and I wanted to be closer to LA. Besides, it didn't matter who I worked with."

"Until now."

She sighed. "It doesn't bother me."

My forehead creased.

"I'd prefer Ken behaved like an adult instead of—"

"A jerk."

"An ass."

"What're you going to do?"

"Nothing." She inhaled deeply. "I wanted to be closer to my family, and now I am. Screw Ken."

I raised my glass. "To family."

As April cleared away the remaining pizza boxes, I remembered my parents asked me to review Charlotte nursing homes. The idea of them leaving their home irked me. They'd worked hard, carefully crafting a beautiful house and desirable life. But old age had changed their circumstances.

In California, I, too, created a stable life. Until disease consumed my husband and a drunk murdered my son.

Beep. Beep.

Expecting to see a message from my parents, I answered the cellphone. It was Dr. Griffith.

We need to meet.

No way would I trust her again. I deleted the text.

April was wise to move closer to family, but fate might suddenly rip them from your life. Proximity didn't provide security.

This time, my phone rang. Camile. I knew what she wanted to discuss, but I was spending the day with April and didn't want to be bothered. The call went to voicemail.

Eventually, I would need to address the situation with Dr. Griffith. Tonight, however, I chose to hang out with my new friend.

CHAPTER 8

Located on the first floor of the medical center complex, the pediatric department had three separate wings. Morning clinic in B wing started slowly and became worse. A week had elapsed since I'd joined San Marguerite. On my first day, Marsha, the office manager, asserted things functioned differently here. Each day brought further appreciation for her statement. I spent the first week educating the medical assistants on properly rooming patients.

The computer clock read 11:30 a.m. A medical assistant finally roomed my 11:00 a.m. patient. Another late lunch.

I donned my white lab coat, laced the stethoscope around my neck, and trotted to the exam room. Grazing my coat pocket to check for the portable fan, I smiled and entered the room.

Fifteen minutes later, I exited the exam room and noticed the department chief, Dr. Ken Brady, down the hall in front of the medical assistants' workstation, speaking with Marsha. He waved.

"How's it going, Julia?"

"I'm well, thank you." I slipped the stethoscope into my coat pocket as he approached. "Anything wrong?" He worked in A wing.

Together, we entered my office. I hadn't furnished the room yet, so I remained standing as there were no seats available for guests. It felt rude to sit while he stood. Marsha offered chairs from the lobby, but they were ugly and uncomfortable.

Ken's nose twitched. Scents from the cleaning products clung to the air.

"Marsha's arranging a staff meeting. Are you on your way to lunch?"

"No, I brought food."

Stretching his neck forward, he inspected the room. "There's a cafeteria downstairs. Did Marsha show it to you?"

"Yes, she did." Memories of the tiny, dark, unappetizing cafeteria halted my growling stomach.

My face must have betrayed my thoughts because Ken chuckled.

Bright-blue eyes sparkled above his wide smile. I tried to reconcile this person standing in my office with the person April described.

"Believe me, the food is better than the place looks. Let's go."

No reason to alienate myself from the boss, so I accepted his invitation. Minor gastric upset could be forgiven to establish a good rapport with the department chief. It also provided an opportunity to formulate my own impression of Ken.

We exited the clinic, conversing on various subjects concerning the medical center. During the walk, I studied him. A hint of gray dusted the edges of his sideburns, contrasting against his slightly tan complexion. Although not handsome, combined with an affable manner and decent physique, some women might consider Ken attractive.

The cafeteria looked as dreary as I remembered. We placed our orders, paid, and collected our meals. When a group left a table beside the windows, we bustled into the vacant seats, sitting opposite each other.

For a moment, I gazed out the window, admiring the grassy square dotted with tables. People huddled under shaded umbrellas. Others gathered on stone benches shrouded by trees.

My attention returned to our table, and I tasted the burger. I grimaced and set it aside, unsure how a vegetable burger could taste worse than the actual vegetables.

Ken devoured his salad, spearing a tomato. "What are your intentions here?"

Taken aback, I readjusted the chair and evaluated his blank face. "What do you mean?"

"Come on, Julia. You were chief of pediatrics in Goleta." He smirked. "Did you come to take over my department, or did the administration send you to check up on me?"

"I came here to practice medicine. I have no ulterior motives."

Neither of us spoke. Seconds later, Ken returned to his salad, eyeing me between bites. I scrutinized his expressionless face. The silence wasn't hostile, but tension altered the dynamics of our lunch. I allowed my gaze to wander out the window again.

Finished eating, Ken smiled. His manner, similar to his blue eyes, brightened. "Good. I believe we'll get along fine."

I reconsidered the lackluster burger, eager to silence my grumbling stomach. A tiny nibble required considerable time to break down those petrified vegetables.

"I'm sorry about your son," he said.

Surprised by his abrupt comment, I swallowed the stale burger with a slight cough. Where did that come from? Perhaps he had noticed the picture of Evens on my desk.

Tired of repeating the obligatory "thank you," I remembered what my Mississippi mother said about good manners being made for those times you wanted to be bitchy.

"Thank you." Disgusted with the sandwich, I draped a napkin over the plate. RIP.

"I heard the woman who hit him died from an overdose. Cruel justice, right?" Ken swallowed the remainder of his cola.

Before my jaw dropped forward, I froze. Not a muscle twitched. The hairs at the nape of my neck bristled at the innuendo. His eyes remained soft, and his square jaw steady. I couldn't determine whether he meant to be malicious. Was he suggesting...

You're overly sensitive, Julia.

The ringing of his cellphone broke the impasse. While he answered the call, I rose, discarded the meal, and returned to the clinic. Lunch hadn't transpired as expected.

Ken didn't interview me for the position at San Marguerite, and consequently, I hadn't met him before. Perhaps I should've asked questions about the chief before accepting the position.

Afternoon clinic ended without incident. While completing charts, my cellphone vibrated. A glance showed it was an unknown number. I hit the red button, ending the call. Besides the awkward moment at lunch with Ken, the day had been decent.

My apprehensions about leaving Goleta started to lift. I'd made the right decision. Santa Barbara retained too many memories—most good—but the bad ones were horrible. I'd made a new friend and begun establishing my place in this practice. As the computer shut down, I glanced out the window.

"What?" My shoulders stiffened.

Across the street, in the middle of the sidewalk by the visitor parking lot, stood a man. People traversed around him as he remained inconveniently positioned in their path. Again, I thought he looked familiar but couldn't remember from where.

Time slowed until a memory exploded in my brain. On my first day in the San Marguerite clinic, he had stood in the exact spot, except he had worn a police officer's uniform.

Perspiration erupted across my forehead. My heart galloped. I flew up, grabbed the curtain drawstring, and shut the blinds. *Ten, nine, eight...* With closed eyes, I counted backward, breathing in through my nose and out my mouth like the therapist instructed.

Should I call Camile? No. If she detected anxiety in my voice, she'd insist I schedule an appointment with Dr. Griffith. I refused to see a psychiatrist again—or at least not that one. The medications she prescribed made me drowsy and confused. Despite what she said, I knew those drugs caused my dreams. Besides, Dr. Griffith displayed a disturbing interest in my urges—as she called them. Bullshit. I didn't—

A ping preceded my cellphone vibrating. The screen displayed Dr. Griffith's office number. The demon herself. I declined the call and peeked outside around the blinds.

The man had departed.

See, Julia, everything's fine.

Why would a police officer surveil me? He was probably waiting for someone. I led a blameless life—or had until...

I was the victim. My son had been murdered.

Before the man returned, I grabbed my purse and left.

Shadows shouldn't wander but keep to the corners and recesses of their tombs. At least, I hoped they would.

CHAPTER 9

Disturbed by the man's appearance, I bustled across the employee parking lot, anxious to jump in my car and head home. Unfortunately, five yards ahead, that same man smoked a cigarette, leaning against a tree beside my car. Pressure mushroomed in my chest.

He watched as I approached but made no effort to speak. Noise from my pounding pulse hammered in my ears.

Cars motored nearby. Reassured by being in a public area, I advanced with the car keys in my left hand while palming a can of mace in my right.

Ten feet from the car, he pushed off the tree with his foot, tossed the cigarette on the ground, and proceeded in my direction.

I flipped the lid off the mace and held it alongside my thigh. Before I unleashed a torrent of capsaicin, his hands raised in a sign of surrender.

"Dr. Toussaint?"

The can rose incrementally higher.

"I'm Detective Jack Pruitt with Santa Barbara Homicide. I need to speak with you."

The can dropped in my purse as I continued forward. "About what?"

He stood beside the driver's side rear door, blocking my path.

"Not what, who. Mrs. Copeland."

For the moment, I didn't trust my voice. Police officers were adept at detecting verbal cues and reading people. Instead, I observed.

His demeanor—wide stance, hands at his side—was cautious. Face blank, he dressed casually. When I didn't speak, he removed his identification. Mentally, I recorded his name and badge number but remained silent.

"You remember her, I'm sure." He smirked.

Did I remember the woman who murdered my son? Moron. "What do you want, Officer?"

"Mrs. Copeland died from a morphine overdose, but there's a possibility her death might not have been an accident."

Immediately, my finger rubbed my wedding band. Not wanting the detective to notice any nervousness, I gripped the car keys harder.

"I had no idea. If you'll excuse me."

Since he wouldn't move, I maneuvered around him and climbed inside the car.

He stepped aside. "I thought you might be interested to know I'm looking into her death."

Unsure of his motivation, I slowly reversed out of the parking spot. With the car idling, I observed him ambling over to the visitors' lot. I pulled forward into the parking spot again and rested my head on the steering wheel. Sweat pooled at the base of my spine. It took a moment for my heart rate to moderate.

As I lifted my head, an object moved in the bushes beside the parking lot fence. Because my hands were shaking too hard to drive, I decided to investigate.

Movement came from what appeared to be a heap of brown-mottled clothing. At least... On closer inspection, I recognized two frightened eyes peeking up from the mass. It stirred, and I recognized the object was a dog.

Emaciated, the creature froze. Flies buzzed around its head. With a light tap, I prodded it with a shoe. I detected a slight rise in its torso accompanied by a noxious, pungent odor. I returned to the car.

After locating a blanket inside the trunk, I donned gloves used for pumping gas.

"You better not bite me," I said, approaching it.

Cautiously, I wrapped the blanket around the dog. It whimpered and laid its head down. The gaunt creature relinquished whatever fight it possessed and curled into my arms.

I had never owned a dog or any other pet. Using my hip, I pushed open the rear door and deposited the dog onto the back seat. Its dry black nose peeked out of the blanket. Once it settled down, I offered it my lunch. It sniffed the food, licking around the sandwich before devouring it. Since I didn't have a bowl, I formed my hands into a small well and poured water inside for the dog to lap up.

Satisfied the mutt wouldn't bite me, I rolled down all the windows—the dog reeked. I searched on my cellphone for the nearest vet. From the rearview mirror, I checked on the dog while exiting the lot. It laid down its head and closed its eyes. Once the signal light turned green, I headed for the emergency vet.

During the drive, my thoughts returned to Officer Pruitt. His arrival portended trouble. Right after Evens died, I obtained a leave of absence from work. How could I feel happy for new parents with beautiful, healthy babies when my child had been murdered?

I couldn't promise their children would live to accomplish their dreams. Should I warn them a murderer could upend their carefully woven lives? The acute pain from Evens' death prevented me from focusing on patients. In addition, I feared my demeanor might betray my thoughts.

Two hours later, I arrived home after entrusting the dog with the local vet. The homicide detective's allegation required verification. If the authorities *had* opened an investigation into Mrs. Copeland's death, I needed to know.

CHAPTER 10

Before collapsing into my office chair, I peeled off the sweaty lab coat and flung it on the desk. Morning clinic had finally ended. Menopause had not improved my disposition. Lack of sleep and an irritable bladder frayed my patience. I switched on all three fans.

Under the desk, I kicked off my dress shoes and slipped into sneakers for a walk around the hospital. I briefly considered reading the horror book I'd brought from home, but I needed air—and exercise. Right as I clicked off the computer browser, the door swung open. A medical assistant entered.

"Dr. Toussaint, would you mind seeing a patient for Dr. Dickerson?"

With a deep sigh, I removed my sneakers and slid back into dress shoes. "Sure. Which room is the patient in?"

"Right now, her patient's at the nursing station."

I found a woman waving her hands erratically in front of the staff. Careful not to be struck, I strode up beside her.

"Excuse me. My name is Dr. Toussaint. I would be happy to see your child."

She thrust a form in my face. "I need this completed for school. My daughter can't play basketball without it."

I accepted the form. "What room are you in?" Expeditiously, I concluded the visit, spending the majority of the time calming down the mother. After completing the form, I started to depart when she summoned me back.

"Yes?" My question came as my stomach grumbled.

"What's your name again?" She stuffed the form in her purse.

"Dr. Toussaint."

"Humph. I can't pronounce that. Are you taking new patients?"

Lucky me. "You can speak with the front staff about changing your provider."

"I'll call the help desk. They're better than the stupid people in this clinic." She left with her child.

Relieved, I returned to my office, pulled on my sneakers, and departed. Steps from the door, someone called.

"Julia."

At first, I pretended not to hear. After two steps, I turned around and discovered April jogging toward me.

"Wait up."

"Who's the old lady now?" I smirked.

"You are."

I smacked her arm, and we exited the clinic side by side.

Early spring air refreshed my senses. I pulled the cap snugly down onto my head, angling the rim to shield my eyes.

April used her hand to block the sun. "It's nice to get outside. I've missed running. If I'm not working, I have stuff to do around the house."

"How's the yard coming along?"

"Fine. I hired someone. Unlike you, I'm not a gardener. We should take a day trip somewhere we can run."

"I don't run."

"If someone was chasing you, you'd run."

"No, I wouldn't. I'd stand my ground and whoop their ass."

Her laugh was infectious. She tilted her head back and smiled up into the sunshine. She kneaded me in the side with her elbow. "I needed a good laugh."

"Me too." When was the last time I laughed?

And this time, it was appropriate—not cringy.

During our hike around the medical center, my cellphone rang. Dr. Griffith. If nothing else, she was persistent.

"How was your morning?" April asked.

"Fine, until I had to see a patient for Bryce."

For a second, April's gaze widened, gradually drifting over the street. "Be careful. She's tight with Ken."

"Really?"

Her brows rose slightly, but she didn't answer. I glanced at my watch. The lunch hour was almost over, and I had a patient scheduled in ten minutes.

"I need to head back."

Neither of us spoke—me because I was panting, hurrying back to clinic, and April… Something was bothering her.

At the clinic door, I said, "Anytime you want to talk."

"I don't," April said before entering her office. She shut the door, and I didn't follow.

At my desk, I exchanged sneakers for dress shoes and drank a bottle of warm water.

Knock, knock.

"Come in," I said, reading patient charts.

A blond head poked around the door, followed by a tall, athletically built woman. "Hi. I'm Bryce Dickerson."

"Yes. We've met."

"Oh, right. I'm too busy to remember everyone." With a smile full of Osmond-white teeth, she entered, speaking in a resonant voice. "Thank you for seeing my patient this morning. It was only a physical, but I appreciate it. Did you get to eat lunch?"

Brown roots betrayed Bryce's actual hair color. Her braying voice grated on my ears. Irritable due to missing lunch—not to mention a leaky bladder screaming to urinate for the fourth time today—I swiveled the chair around to face her.

"No, I did not. But I did get outside for some exercise."

She tossed her head, sending cotton candy thin hair swirling. "Oh, well. Missing one meal won't hurt you."

Did she suggest I needed to lose weight? My jaw tensed, but I resisted the temptation to reply.

"Thanks again. Maybe one day I'll repay the favor." She vanished.

From the corner of my eye, I noticed on the computer screen my next patient had been roomed. As I rose, my cellphone rang. This time, the screen read Camile.

"Hey, lady," I said. "I'm about to see a patient. I'll—"

"Don't hang up," she said. "This is more important."

"What's wrong?" I sank into the chair. "No one's hurt?" Images of Evens' fractured body swirled in my head.

"We're fine. You're the problem."

"I am?"

"Dr. Griffith said you're ignoring her calls."

"She's no longer my physician."

"Julia, she's worried about you."

"Why? Because I've returned to work and am functioning well without her?"

"Are you?"

Silence drifted between us. I struggled not to slap back. I realized Camile was worried. Given what happened after Evens' murder, she had reason to be. But she didn't understand what I'd experienced and how Dr. Griffith made it worse.

Unless a person lost their anchor, the one thing mooring them to this world… How could I explain? Emotional scars are invisible to those unafflicted.

The transfer from Goleta had been difficult. Some mornings, I still couldn't believe I left. But it *had* become necessary. Evens' spirit permeated the hallways of Goleta's medical center. Staff—though kind—wouldn't let me forget his murder. Patients expressed sympathy, not realizing their comments tore the bandage off my wounded heart. I couldn't move forward when daily sorrow dragged me backward into a pit of despair. Dr. Griffith didn't care about my mental health. On the contrary, she fed off my misery.

When Mrs. Copeland died, I thought the pain would lessen or subside into a dull ache I could ignore. It hadn't. People expected me to rejoice at her death, but I felt no happiness. Evens hadn't miraculously rejoined the living.

Emptiness filled my life, accompanied by guilt. I trusted Dr. Griffith to help me process those emotions. Instead, she compounded my grief, plunging me into a drug-induced stupor where I couldn't discern reality from illusion.

Once Evens died, I was no longer a wife *or* mother. I had to redefine myself and establish a purpose. The transfer to San Marguerite became the first step in a new life.

In Goleta, I'd been the department chief. I set the practice's tone, answering only to the medical director. The chief medical officer of Noughton Healthcare entrusted me to care for *his* children. On this new playground, I had to learn the players and study their game.

"Yes, I am. Better than I ever was under Dr. Griffith's care."

"Talk to her. Don't you believe she deserves that much?"

Hell no.

Julia, be careful.

Old habits were difficult to abandon, and I didn't react well to being challenged. Deep breath.

"Camile, I am working, eating, and sleeping like normal people do. My internist is treating my depression. There's no reason to speak with Dr. Griffith."

"She comes highly recommended."

"The physician-patient relationship depends on mutual respect. I don't care for her treatment process. I'm not going back."

Half a minute elapsed.

"Fine. But I'm still concerned."

"I know."

Careful, girl. Don't slip and reveal your secrets.

CHAPTER 11

A crisp breeze wicked sweat from my brow as I cycled around the street corner. My gaze shifted from the traffic snarl to foamy ocean waves breaking against the sandy Carmel beach. My body soared with energy. Unencumbered by the petty complexities of life, cycling made me feel like a bird flowing over roads, down hills, and along trails. I hadn't ridden like this since—

"Wait up."

From a distance behind me, I heard April call.

"What's wrong? Is the old lady kicking your behind?"

"Next time, we'll run along the beach and see who kicks whose butt."

Up ahead, I spotted a small cul-de-sac. I pulled off to the side as April cycled up next to me. She wiped her forehead with the back of her hand.

"It's magical."

"I love it. This was always one of Evens' favorite places for biking." A dull ache grew behind my sternum.

April's eyes softened but she didn't inquire—for which I was grateful.

"Is that the Frank Lloyd Wright house?"

Careful of the traffic, I steered my bike forward as pressure mounted in my chest. "I believe so. We should be getting back. Didn't you have a call to make?" Aware my breathing had increased, I worried about a panic attack.

"Let's turn around at the point. I'll send my sister a text."

We mounted our bikes and did as she suggested.

On our return to the hotel, I hastily excused myself and returned to my room. I needed a shower and wanted to decompress. Biking along the coast refreshed tender memories of Evens *and* Jean. Right then, I preferred to be alone.

Stepping out of the shower, I toweled off and glanced in the steamy mirror. Unable to see clearly, I started to wipe the mirror when Jean's face reflected back at me. Startled, I jumped back. The towel slipped off my shoulders.

"Um, so beautiful."

"Jean?"

"Why are you standing there? Come here."

I walked toward his open arms. My leg bumped against the bathroom cabinet. Instantly, Jean's reflection disappeared. For a second, I gawked at the mirror, trying to discern where he went.

"Jean! Come back!" I collapsed on the bathroom floor, sobbing.

"You promised you wouldn't leave me."

***

An hour later, we journeyed down Highway 1 South. April stared out the side window.

"Everything okay?" I asked.

She smiled. "It's so beautiful. Thanks for inviting me."

"Did you enjoy the weekend?"

"Absolutely. Monterey was nice, but I liked Carmel more."

"Maybe next time we'll visit Napa."

"Is it as nice as Carmel?"

I grinned. "Well, you'll have to see for yourself. If you want, we can take Highway 46 and visit Paso Robles."

April chuckled. "No, I'm good."

Craggy coastline tumbled past us. Again, April stared out the window, lost in the scenery.

"Have you tried talking with Ken?"

"And say what?"

What could she say? Leave me alone, you adulterous abuser?

"Work out some understanding. Tell him to back off, or you'll file a complaint."

"Oh, no," April said, aggressively shaking her head. "That's why I'm in this situation." She shifted in the seat, repositioning to face me. "Medicine touts this big rigmarole about standing up and reporting abuse. And when you do, they ostracize you."

Glancing at her, I nodded. "Yes. There's definitely an inconsistency."

"There's no justice." April frowned, gazing out the front window. "The best you can do is carve out a small sanctuary for yourself and your family."

"Sometimes, we have to make our own justice."

The right side of my face warmed from April's glare. Conscious of her observation, I controlled my breathing. Could she read my sins in the wrinkles along my forehead?

Calm down. No one knows. Well…

Ninety minutes later, we arrived at April's house. She thanked me for playing travel guide and hugged me tightly.

"Thanks for the ride. Next weekend, we go jogging."

"Doubt it. Bye."

"I'll call you later."

Waving, I reversed down the driveway and headed home. A mile down the road, my cellphone thrummed. Because I didn't instantly recognize the number, I started to let it go to voicemail but recognized it was the vet. I pulled over into a parking lot and answered.

"Hello."

"Is this Mrs. Toussaint?" a female voice asked.

"Yes. Is there something wrong? Did the dog die?"

"Oh, no. She's fine. We need to know when you're coming to pick her up?"

"Pick her up?"

"Yes, she's your dog.

"No, I found her on the street. She's not mine."

"We can't keep her. You have to pick her up."

"Can't you give her to someone or take her to an animal shelter?"

Raising her voice, the woman said, "If you don't come and pick up your dog, we'll charge you $50 a day."

"What? I can't keep it. I don't know anything about dogs."

"When are you coming?"

I hit the mute button and uttered a trail of profanities I'd learned from my Navy vet dad. With my composure restored, I unmuted the phone. "I'll be there in thirty minutes."

After the long drive from Carmel, I was exhausted. Once I arrived at the vet's office, I decided to find the nearest animal shelter and dump the dog. It wasn't a good time for me to take care of a four-legged furry creature.

A bell chimed as I entered. At the desk, I met the rude woman from the phone call. She spoke with the same short barks. "We charged your credit card for her treatment *and* boarding."

My jaw clenched. "I hadn't been informed about additional charges."

She handed me a billing statement. "The dog required IV fluids, antibiotics, and deworming medications. Her hair was too matted for washing, so we had to shave her."

My gaze skimmed the bill. "Would you explain these other charges?"

Her body slouched, and her eyes narrowed. "Which charges?"

"If you aren't prepared to answer my questions—"

"I can explain the bill." Another woman entered from a side door. She directed the barky woman to attend to something else. Once we were alone, she smiled.

"Sorry about that. What questions did you have?"

She explained the bill and eventually brought out the dog. "Have you ever had a pet?"

"No." I couldn't tell her Evens had always wanted a dog. Each year I promised him a dog the following year. Always next year until there were no more years because he'd been murdered by a serial drunk driver.

Breathe.

"It's easy." She rubbed the dog between the ears. "Treat her like you would want to be treated. She's already house-trained. We gave her the required vaccinations. Feed her…"

My head throbbed with the information she provided. I felt like a parent of a newborn being given a pamphlet on how to care for their new arrival. Cautiously, I accepted the rope from the woman and led the dog outside to the car.

The poor thing had no hair—nor fur—left. But she appeared more alive than when I had found her in the parking lot. Her tail wagged endlessly, and her nose looked moist.

Inside the car, I applied my seatbelt and looked into the rearview mirror.

"Listen, dog, I don't know how to care for you. If things don't work out, I'll drop you off at the shelter. But I'll try. That's all I can promise."

It—she—barked.

Unsure what the dog meant, I turned on the ignition and drove home. What would've happened if I had bought Evens the dog he'd always wanted? Could a dog have saved his life?

In the rearview mirror, I observed the dog sitting up straight, panting. How would this animal affect my life? Was I ready to have another living creature in my house? My last two living companions died. Perhaps I functioned better alone.

CHAPTER 12

Once I completed patient messages, a familiar name popped up on my schedule. Thaddeus Frye. Months had passed since our last visit. I should've called him, but I'd been preoccupied. But was I? Thaddeus stirred up conflicting emotions, both pleasant and sad.

On a similar morning at the Goleta pediatric clinic, Javier had informed me that Thaddeus had been hospitalized. In a panic, I fled the clinic—disregarding my patient appointments—and rushed over to the inpatient pediatric floor, where a nurse informed me Thaddeus had been transferred to intensive care.

In the PICU, I had found him hooked up to intravenous fluids with a nasal cannula looped under his nostrils. Thaddeus teared up when I entered the room. Tonya, his mom, clutched tissues, dabbing at her dripping nose. Sobbing, she explained what her fiancé did to eight-year-old Thaddeus.

Recalling the incident made my fists itch. Buried memories resurfaced, flooding my mind with unhealthy thoughts.

Don't dwell on the past, Julia.

With a hand towel, I mopped my brow. The computer browser closed down, and I headed for the exam room.

"Hello, Thad—" His name froze on my tongue as I entered. Grasping the knob, I scanned the room. No Thaddeus. My shoulders slumped as I greeted Tonya. "How are you?"

We hugged and exchanged pleasantries. A moment later, I sat on a stool, scrutinizing her heavily made-up face.

"What brought you all the way from Goleta?" Eager to see him, I'd forgotten my fan. No hot flashes, I warned my body. "Where's Thaddeus?"

Tonya smiled. "We missed you, and I wanted to see your new office."

My thumb rubbed up against my wedding ring, a habit I developed after Jean died. The cool gold band reminded me of Jean's love and calm demeanor. Touching it settled my nerves. Was I nervous? Worried more correctly explained my emotions.

Since I transferred to San Marguerite, several former patients had visited or transferred their children to this new office. Tonya, however, survived on a precariously fixed income. She'd only started a full-time job with a decent salary in the last six months. I knew this because I got her that job.

Driving to San Marguerite in the middle of a workday couldn't have been easy for her, nor financially responsible. I feared she'd been in trouble again. Or did something happen to Thaddeus?

I slid the stool closer to Tonya's chair. Her fingers blanched, gripping the purse straps. She saw me looking at them.

"Is Thaddeus okay?"

Her head nodded as if bobbing for apples. "Yes, he's fine. He's in school."

"Good."

The corner of her right temple twitched. Could she be using again?

"Then what's wrong?"

A childish giggle proceeded the jiggling of her clip-on ponytail. "Nothing, Doc. I—I just wanted to see you." A smile revealed corroded teeth, remnants of her bout with

73

methamphetamines. Those dull-brown eyes looked too clear for her to be high.

Unsure there wasn't a problem, I sat up straighter and smiled. "Thank you. It's nice to see you. Are you enjoying the new job?"

She released the death grip on the purse strap. "Yeah, I'm doing real good. My boss said he might give me a raise. Thaddie said he was proud of me."

"You should be proud of yourself. Clean and holding down a job. I knew you could do it. But *you* had to believe it."

"I couldn't have done it without you."

"Tonya—"

"Doc." She leaned forward. "I forgot to thank you."

My eyes narrowed as I studied her. "I didn't do anything a doctor isn't supposed to do."

"You did more than that."

A trickle of sweat slid down the center of my back. "What are you talking about?"

Chair legs scraped across the floor as she moved closer, our faces mere inches apart.

"How you got rid of him?"

Slowly, my head tilted right as I scrutinized her. "Who are you talking about?"

"My fiancé, Kevin. I know—"

"Know what?" I scowled, crossing my arms. "You're delusional—again. Remember when you were in withdrawal and thought the government poisoned you?"

Tonya frowned and retreated into the seat.

"Why are you thinking about him? Have you forgotten what he did? Your *fiancé* went to prison for assaulting your son."

Tonya's head lowered. "I know."

I paced around the room. "Maybe you remember *I* helped you find a job after he died. *I* arranged for Thaddeus to attend a private boarding school when you went into rehab. And who assisted your social worker and legal aid to make sure you regained full guardianship of Thaddeus after he spent six months in foster care?"

"You did. But I..." She clutched the purse tighter. Large, droopy eyes regarded me as she asked, "Who else would want to kill him?"

"How about the drug users he associated with? Perhaps one of the women he strung out on drugs and trafficked in prostitution."

Tonya's weepy gaze fell. Tears poured down her cheeks. "But he loved me. Why did he have to die?"

With a deep sigh, I went to her side. "He put Thaddeus in the hospital. Your fiancé was not a nice man. He sold drugs—used them and people. He kept you addicted, pimping you out to his friends. Why would you be surprised someone killed him?"

A pack of tissues tumbled out of Tonya's purse. Her hands shook as she wiped tears from under her heavily mascaraed eyes, loosening one of her fake lashes. It floated like a leaf beside her eye each time she blinked.

"I miss him."

"Do you miss the beatings?" I knelt down beside her chair, gazing up into her tear-stained face. "Do you remember how he broke your son's ribs? Beat his face so badly Thaddeus couldn't see out of his swollen eyes."

Tremors racked Tonya's body. "He didn't mean it. He... He loved me."

Too many words leaped to the end of my tongue at once. Prudently, I kept quiet. I wanted to remind her about the abuse she'd suffered—gang rapes, solicitation charges, humiliation when her fiancé impregnated a teenager—but it would be cruel and pointless.

Tonya required help; she needed me. I had been the one to move away. Worried about my own problems, I had forgotten the wounded families left behind, people who relied upon me. Wrapping my arms around her shoulders, I pulled her close. She collapsed on my shoulders and sobbed.

The exam room door opened, and a medical assistant peeked inside. "Dr. Toussaint, your next patient—"

Scowling, I inclined my head toward the door and signaled for her to leave. After the medical assistant departed, I helped Tonya wash her face and reattach the wayward lash.

I grasped her about the shoulders. "Listen to me. You are worth more than any man's attention. You have to love yourself. Thaddeus deserves better, and so do you."

She gave me another hug. "I'm sorry. I wanted to see you."

"I'll come down for a visit, promise. I needed time to get settled, but I haven't forgotten about you and Thaddeus."

"Thank you."

With my hand on her back, I led her out of the room. "Tell Thaddeus I'll come by soon."

Before she left, a thought came to mind. "How did you get here?"

Tonya's eyes enlarged. She stammered. "I... He... I have to go." She fled.

Something was wrong—very wrong. I started after her, then noticed the medical assistant vying for my attention. Though concerned about Tonya's visit, I had patients waiting and hurried to the next exam room.

Thirty minutes later, I returned to my office. In the middle of writing a patient assessment, someone knocked on my door.

"Come in."

April read over my shoulder as I typed.

Glaring at her, I asked, "Do you mind?"

She laughed and ambled over to the door. "Did you forget about the meeting?"

"What meeting?"

"Business meeting, once a month."

"When is it?"

"Now."

Dammit. I saved my work and headed upstairs to the fourth floor with April—remembering to bring along my pocket fan. In the hallway, we joined Kim and Juanita.

To no one in particular, I asked, "What's the meeting about?"

Kim shrugged. "Who knows? At least we get a free lunch."

"And an hour away from our computers," April said. "I have incomplete charts with a full schedule of patients this afternoon."

"How many patients did you have this morning?" Kim asked.

"Fifteen."

"Must be nice to be popular," Kim snickered.

In the conference room, people lined up for boxed lunches arrayed on a long table against the far wall. On a second table were desserts and beverages. I bypassed the boxed lunches and grabbed water. In a seat next to Juanita, I opened a water bottle and chugged.

Juanita opened a boxed lunch. "Aren't you hungry?"

With the back of my hand, I wiped a dribble of water from my chin. "I brought lunch from home."

"Humph." She munched on a pickle. "Do you like soap operas?"

"No, why? Am I about to see one?"

She nodded. "I don't know what business meetings were like in Goleta, but here…" Juanita grinned. "You'll see."

People hurried into their seats as Ken and Marsha stood at the front of the room before a large whiteboard. With a clicker in his right hand, Ken presented a slide show while Marsha explained statistical analyses of the pediatric clinic patient demographics, appointment scheduling, and clinical outcomes. The information, similar in content, was presented differently to what I'd become accustomed to in Goleta, but it came down to the same thing—how many patients were seen and the amount of revenue generated.

While she droned on, my thoughts trailed off to personal matters. Specifically, Tonya's erratic behavior. A full day off work to visit me and her continued mourning of an abusive boyfriend—fiancé—created a problem.

However, Thaddeus was one of my favorite patients. No, he meant significantly more to me than a simple patient-doctor relationship. I truly cared for him. Since the moment I saw Thaddeus seated on Tonya's lap during his infant wellness exam, he captured my heart. Would our relationship have differed if I hadn't fostered him?

Smart and gentle, he was pleasant to everyone—amazing given the circumstances of living with a drug-addicted mother. Tonya's proclivities included shacking up with the worst men. What those men did to her had been terrible, but what they did to Thaddeus? Monstrous.

"What do you think, Julia?" Ken asked before taking a drink from a soda can.

All eyes pivoted in my direction. I hadn't heard what he asked, but I had learned a long time ago how to get a person to restate their question. I didn't like admitting I hadn't been listening.

"What specifically would you like me to address?"

He grinned. "How did your department in Goleta room patients?"

Before answering, I considered whether he wanted my input or was testing whether I paid attention to the presentation. In under a minute, I provided a quick synopsis of how the Goleta clinic functioned. Without further discussion, he moved on to someone else. Like I suspected, he wanted to test whether I was listening.

"Any other comments about how to improve patient scheduling or rooming?" Ken asked.

Like a schoolboy, Carter Reynolds, another pediatrician whom I'd already met, raised his hand to speak.

Ken nodded, and Carter said, "I believe you're doing a great job. Each year, the medical director commends the pediatric department for our performance, and it's due to your leadership."

A squelching noise followed his comment. Juanita puckered her lips and made a kissing gesture. I bit the inside of my lip to keep from laughing. A blushing Carter glared at her. I turned aside as my body shook. Muffled laughter peppered the room.

Ken feigned ignorance and continued the meeting.

Juanita whispered, "You've met teacher's pet."

I followed her gaze to the front of the room where Carter sat. His flaming red hair made him difficult to overlook. His obsequious attitude toward Ken brought a new meaning to the term brown-nosing. I watched him fiddling with his phone—another one of my eccentricities was studying people.

As soon as the meeting ended, April sprung out of her chair and bolted from the room. At a moderate pace, I returned to the clinic. My thoughts returned to Tonya. Why had she come? I doubted she missed me that much.

Better check on Thaddeus.

While I waited for the medical assistant to room my next patient, I called Thaddeus' boarding school. The dean's assistant stated Thaddeus was in class, but they would have him call me later. Restless, I considered speaking with April but recalled she was busy charting.

In the few months I'd been at San Marguerite, April and I had developed a nice friendship. I found her refreshing. She didn't question me about Evens or Jean. April discussed family, work, and her personal interests. She failed to mention any romantic relationships. Interesting, because she was such a social person.

"Dr. Toussaint?" a medical assistant asked, standing in the doorway.

"My patient ready?"

"Yes."

I scooped up a stethoscope and went to work. Once I finished with clinic, I'd figure out what was going on with Tonya. Something was behind her visit. I needed to figure it out. Our relationship was one of my weaknesses.

CHAPTER 13

Flat, dry Central California scenery drifted away as I sped down the highway, bypassing Los Alamos for the Santa Barbara mountains looming ahead. Like a tourist, April snapped pictures as we traveled alongside Gaviota State Park. She remarked about the train's proximity to the beach.

"Can we stop and take pictures? I'd love to walk along the tracks."

Traffic was heavy. I didn't mind playing chauffeur as we toured California, but it remained my prerogative when and where we stopped.

"I wouldn't recommend it. People have been killed standing on those tracks."

She frowned. "No way."

I shrugged, eager to arrive in Montecito and leave the traffic behind. Because April wanted to ride bikes along the Santa Barbara coast, I'd agreed to drive down on a Friday night. Chugging along Highway 101 in bumper traffic, I wondered why.

After April failed to find affordable accommodations, I contacted Camile, who consented to hosting us. Camile lived south of Santa Barbara in Montecito. Unfortunately, I'd miscalculated the intensity of Friday evening traffic. In the backseat next to April, the dog stared out the side window.

"Did you give her a name yet?" April asked, petting it.

"Nope." I exited the freeway, turning left onto Hot Springs Road.

"I thought about getting a pet," she said, rubbing the dog behind its ears.

"Evens always wanted a dog," I murmured, glancing at the dog in the rearview mirror. Why hadn't I given him one? Had I selfishly wanted all his attention?

"I can't believe you left this place voluntarily."

"Not here, but in—"

"Santa Barbara, Goleta, Montecito—it's the same thing."

"Humph." I snorted. "Property values differ by thousands of dollars."

"Seriously?" She pouted and rolled down the window.

To fill the void, I conversed about Montecito, listing celebrities living in the area. Winding roads spread before us as we climbed further into the hillside. Like a child at Christmas, April gawked at the rugged landscape.

"If I owned a home here, I would never leave."

"Even if it meant working with an ass like Ken?"

The shadow darkening April's brow made me regret my question.

"Perhaps," April said, gazing out the side window.

"When we visit Napa," I said, hoping to cheer her up, "you might change your mind about Santa Barbara."

"Doubt it."

In Camile's driveway, I tapped the horn and parked beside the garage.

While April hauled our overnight bags out of the trunk, I released the dog. She trotted alongside me to the front door. Camile greeted us and shook hands with April as I made introductions.

Inside, children swarmed around the dog. The last thing I saw was a tail beating rapidly against the tile floor. I escorted

April out to the patio deck.

"Oh my goodness," she gawked. "Camile, you have a lovely home—and the mountains. What a view. It was worth the drive."

"Speak for yourself." I collapsed into a cushioned recliner.

Lupita inserted a glass of water in my outstretched hand and kissed my cheeks. The chair groaned as I rose to embrace her. She greeted April.

"Should we eat on the patio or inside?" Lupita asked.

"Oh, please," April asked, "may we eat outside?"

"Of course we can. You're our guest." Lupita returned inside.

The kids giggled and romped outside with the dog. They threw a small toy back and forth for the mutt to chase.

Relaxed in the chair, I closed my eyes. In the distance I heard happy cries, reminding me of summers in Goleta where Evens and Thaddeus played outside with the neighbor kids. Though younger and less athletic, Thaddeus kept up with Evens. Other than minor skirmishes over toys, they never fought. In time, would they have grown closer or drifted apart?

Despite living on campus, Evens came home often. We considered Camile's place our third home and my parents' house in North Carolina our second. Grief and depression made me flee the house in Goleta.

Here, now, surrounded by people who loved me, I felt safe—not like with Jean, but no one would ever make me feel like he had.

Jean kept my secrets. To him alone, I revealed my fears and desires. Or at least until Camile brought me to Dr. Griffith, who characterized them as urges. As more time elapsed since our appointments, the more I doubted I ever had any urges or impulses. Simply another hazard of her overzealous treatments.

Jean didn't judge me. As a neurologist boarded in neurology and psychiatry, he understood—

Bang! Crash!

"What happened?" I asked, rushing into the kitchen.

"A glass fell," Camile said, sweeping aside the shattered remains.

"Go outside," Lupita said, herding the dog and the children out the sliding glass doors.

"Sorry about the dog." I helped Camile dispose of the larger glass shards.

Lupita sniffed and turned aside to stir a pot on the stove. "Next time, warn me. I would've bought a leash."

"I have rope in the car," I said, moving toward the entrance.

"The dog's fine," Camile said, rubbing her wife's arm. "Lupita had a difficult day at work."

"Our stupid manager—"

"Either report her or stop complaining," Camile said, pouring wine into a long-stem glass. "I'm tired of hearing about your micromanaging boss."

"How irritating," I said, nibbling on crackers.

"Well, I told Lupe to report her or quit." Camile drank long and deeply from the wine glass. "There's only so much a person can take."

"Tell me about it," April murmured—but I doubt Camile or Lupita heard.

"I had the same problem when I started with Noughton," Camile said. "They thought because I was a woman and had a family, I wasn't ambitious."

"But you proved them wrong," I said, giving her a side grin.

"*We* quickly set them straight." Lupita spoke while filling an enormous bowl with chili.

"It's not easy," April said.

"Nothing is," Camile said, refilling her glass. "But life shouldn't be miserable."

April thrust her chin forward. "Circumstances differ."

"Exactly," Lupita interrupted. "This is a state job, not private sector. The rules are different."

"This is America." Camile swallowed before continuing. "If you don't like your job, find another one."

Together, Lupita and I gathered utensils and carried the food out to the covered deck. April eventually followed. Play ceased. The dog stopped frolicking, tilting her head to the side with her tongue hanging out. Minutes elapsed as everyone washed up, gathered bowls, and found places to eat.

"Come, dog."

I set a bowl of ground meat and vegetables on the ground, and the dog devoured its contents before I returned to my seat. Conversation grew slowly and steered clear of anything concerning jobs or bosses.

A half hour into dinner, Lupita asked, "Where're you from April?"

"LA. After residency, I moved to northern California for work. Eventually, I ended up at Noughton's Paso Robles campus."

"Oh, nice," Camile said, slipping a piece of steak to the dog. "Did you like it?"

"Not really. There wasn't much to do." April wiped her mouth but didn't say more.

"Where does your family live?" Camile asked, tossing the dog more pieces of food.

"They're still in LA," April said. "But it's difficult."

"No?" Lupita asked, spooning chili into a bowl for one of the children.

"They don't understand that not all doctors are rich."

"Most aren't," Camile said.

"We had similar problems with Camile's family," Lupita said, studying April with her dark eyes.

"They don't understand." April's gaze rested on the mountainside.

Minutes passed, then an hour.

"It's getting late." Lupita picked up a sleeping child curled around her feet. "Come on, April. I'll show you to your room."

She and April departed, with the former herding the children away like cattle.

Camile cleared the table and returned inside to the kitchen. From the table, I gazed across the yard and up the mountainside. A desert oasis juxtaposed against Camile's lush backyard. Contrasts. Like my memories of Jean. His confidence in me *and* his concern. Wait? Was he worried about me? But why?

Without food, the dog glanced over at me, raising one ear and an eyebrow.

"You can't be hungry."

Woof.

She stretched her limbs and trotted onto the grassy yard.

Something shiny winked at me from the ground. An earring. I scrutinized it. April's. I'd return it to her tomorrow.

Though we'd talked about different topics, April and I hadn't discussed finances in any great detail. Did she feel obligated to support her family? Had they suggested it or insisted?

In the recliner, I sank between the pillowy cushions and drifted off to sleep. Movement near my head made me snap awake.

"Hey," Camile said, tapping my arm. "We need to talk about Dr. Griffith." She scooted a chair over to the recliner. My shoulders tensed.

Listen, Julia, and don't react.

"Okay."

"You *are* better, but it's still best to consult a professional. For a long time, you were seriously ill. I... We considered committing you."

Does she think I'd forgotten? I recalled everything from the moment a police officer notified me about Evens' death. Up until Dr. Griffith prescribed a cocktail of anti-psychotics, which sent me into a dazed stupor. I remembered—

"Julia?" Camile stared at me.

Lost track of time—again.

"I heard you, and we've had this discussion before."

"Wait—"

"No. I'm seeing a therapist—a professional."

"You're not willing to reconsider?"

"Why should I?"

Time passed. In the yard, the dog chased a bird. I swatted away a fly while observing Camile's icy glare. She exhaled deeply before kissing my cheek.

"Okay. But I'm watching you."

"Of course you are."

"Love you," she said before slipping into the kitchen.

From the recliner, I watched her wash dishes.

Careful. Camile's no fool.

CHAPTER 14

The following Monday, I arrived early at the medical center. That morning, I'd found a picture Evens had sketched, and I wanted to hang it in my office. At the time, he was still in high school and considered studying architecture. Though the figures were more abstract than he intended, I admired his ambition. Once college started, he decided to pursue engineering. He'd only completed his freshman year when...

With press and stick Velcro, I attached the picture on the wall next to the window. Not exactly Picasso, but it was my masterpiece.

While on the phone with a parent, someone knocked on my door. I pressed the mute button and opened it.

"Hello," Ken said, striding inside.

With a nod toward the nearest chair, I unmuted the phone and continued my conversation.

In apparently no hurry, Ken sauntered around the room for several minutes before taking a seat. His crystal-blue eyes scanned the room. Was he admiring the décor or searching for something in particular? His curious manner irritated me, and I hastily terminated the call. I pivoted around to find him standing beside my bookcase.

"Please, have a seat."

The tip of his aquiline nose twitched slightly, reminding me of a rabbit or a rat.

"I see you've made yourself comfortable."

"Since I spend as much time here as at home, I should be."

With his left index finger, he pointed at my desk fans. "Menopause?"

I nodded.

"My father had a problem with his prostate. The doctor prescribed hormones. After that, his air condition bill soared." Ken grinned and continued surveying the room. "I wanted to see how things were going. It's been three months. For new hires, I have to complete a probation evaluation. Of course, you've been with Noughton twice as long as I have." A laugh twinkled in his eyes.

Whether an acknowledgment of a simple truth, mockery, or sarcasm, I knew not. I accepted it as a statement of fact. "I'm adjusting to San Marguerite's routine. Everyone's been helpful."

He pointed at the wall above my head where Evens' high school graduation photo hung. "Your son?"

"Yes." Tears threatened to pour down my face, but with effort, I kept them at bay.

"Was he interested in medicine?"

"No." Though I didn't intend to reply so abruptly, I had no desire to discuss Evens' personal goals—especially not with Ken. The incident in the cafeteria was the last time we spoke in person. Frankly, I wouldn't mind if it became the last.

Despite his charming manner and outwardly calm demeanor, I detected an ugly undercurrent. Given his hostility toward April, I judged it best to maintain a healthy distance. The impulse of impending danger heightened whenever I was alone with him.

Conversation stalled as Ken stared at me. If he waited for me to elaborate, he'd wait in vain. I left the moment open for him to proceed, having no interest in explaining how Evens saw his father and I work long hours, interrupted during piano recitals and soccer games to answer Mommy calls or ER physicians. We missed school events to admit patients to the hospital, had our sleep interrupted to explain how to clean a baby's nose, and devoted endless hours to maintaining our board certifications.

We hadn't discouraged Evens from becoming a doctor but were delighted he chose a different path—at least I was. Jean died before Evens entered high school.

Ken's folded hands rested on his lap. "Any questions or problems?"

I scooted away from the desk and stood. "Nope. I'll let you know if I need anything. If you'll excuse me, my next patient is ready."

He rose. "Oh, by the way, good work with that dermatomyositis diagnosis."

It took me a moment to recall the patient he referenced. If I recalled correctly, the child was ten or twelve years of age and had suffered from chronic rashes and intermittent joint pains for years. A different physician diagnosed and treated her for atopic dermatitis. Frustrated with her daughter's lack of improvement, the mother insisted on a second opinion.

Upon review of the girl's growth charts, I noticed her weight had declined over the past year. On examination, she appeared cachectic. Abnormal lab work, combined with the history and exam, led me to refer her to rheumatology, where they confirmed a diagnosis of dermatomyositis. Because she wasn't my assigned patient, I hadn't followed up with the family.

"I'm surprised you were able to make the diagnosis."

My left brow rose. "Why would you be surprised? I'm a board-certified pediatrician with over twenty-five years of experience."

His grin evaporated. Wrinkles multiplied across his fore-head. He was gauging how to respond. Again, the tip of his nose quivered.

Interesting. Should I relieve his discomfort? Under different circumstances, I would let him flounder, but I had a patient waiting.

"I've treated dermatomyositis before."

He visibly exhaled. "Well, that explains it," he said before fleeing.

Clearly, Ken underestimated my competence. Perhaps I should buy him a copy of Dr. Tweedy's book, *Black Man in a White Coat: A Doctor's Reflections on Race and Medicine*. Although I attained the status of chief of pediatrics in Noughton's flagship medical center, he doubted my intellect. Not surprising.

Oh well. Being underestimated by people—especially men—often worked in my favor. After securing the office door, I hurried to the patient exam room.

At the end of the appointment, I escorted the family to the nursing station and returned to the hallway of physician offices. Halfway down the hall, I spied Carter skulking away.

It would be reasonable to presume he was looking for the restroom at the end of the hallway. However, the pediatric offices were situated in three separate wings. This was B wing. Carter worked in C wing with Juanita. Why was he here?

To see someone? But we were all busy with patients. Quickly, I inspected each office and found them closed or locked—except April's. She'd left her door open. I glanced inside. Nothing seemed out of place.

"What's wrong?"

Startled, I swung around as April approached. She entered her office, and I followed.

"You should lock your door."

"Why? There's nothing worth stealing." April pulled the chair away from the desk and gasped.

"What?" I asked, hurrying forward.

A hairy dildo had been draped across the chair. Disgust hampered our words. I rallied, though, and retrieved a garbage can. With my foot, I kicked it into the trash, depositing the can in the hallway.

In a daze, April said, "Who did this?"

"Ken."

Tears clouded April's eyes. I steered her onto a side chair.

"I know he hates me, but this… This is so juvenile."

"And again, Ken fits the mold."

April shook her head, flinging aside tears.

"This can't be happening."

"Why not?" I perched on a corner of her desk. "It's not such a big stretch from manipulating sexual favors from subordinates to sexual harassment."

For half a minute, I regarded April's weepy face.

"Oh, damn!"

"What?" April half rose.

"We should've taken a picture of it on the chair before we moved it." I popped into the hall and snapped a quick picture of the dildo in the trash can. "Doesn't matter. We can show this to Human Resources. It's still proof."

"Proof?" April gawked. "Why?"

Enunciating each word as if April didn't understand the language, I said, "Sexual harassment."

April flew off the chair. "Oh, no. Not again." She rushed forward, pushing me out of the room. "No way."

"You don't have a choice."

"Yes, I do." She reached down and ripped the bag out of

the trash can. Tying off the bag with a knot, April ran into the bathroom. A second later, she returned.

"Just because last time—"

"They made my life a living hell," April said, chest heaving and her eyes wide. "I did the right thing and paid for it with my career."

Lightly touching her forearm, I said, "This time, I'll be with you. Things will be different."

"Yeah, they will. Because I'm not reporting this."

"You have to."

She shook her head and began to shut the door. "No way."

"I'll do it for you."

"Go ahead. I'll deny it."

I frowned. "Are you serious?"

"You don't understand what I went through."

"Trust me."

"Forget it." She shut the door in my face.

For a moment, my fist hovered in the air near the door. Instead of knocking, I returned to my office and considered what had occurred. Then I pulled out my cellphone and ordered a teddy bear camera off the internet, selecting expedited delivery. I always believed in being overly cautious.

***

Foreboding weighed on me as I crossed the parking lot and entered my car. Generally, I left the clinic early. Distracted by recalling Carter's presence in our wing that morning, I failed to notice Detective Pruitt planted near my car until I clicked the door opener.

His precipitous advance caused me to recoil. On reflex, I took a defensive stance, balling my fists and preparing to fight. He wouldn't know how close he came to being assaulted.

"Did I scare you?" A slanted grin crossed his craggy face, pitted from acne. Tobacco—and probably coffee—stained his teeth a tan-yellow.

My heart raced, and my eyes narrowed. I veered around him, but he adopted a wide stance and squared off in front of the driver's door.

"What can you tell me about Kevin Page?"

The second thing my parents told me—after they gave me the DWB talk—was not to speak with the police without an attorney present. Despite your best intentions, things could sour, and you might become a suspect instead of a witness. Since he blocked my door, I stood there, studying him. The stubble on his chin gave an unkempt appearance. He reeked of cigarettes.

"You know he was robbed and beaten to death. The investigating officers believe a rival drug dealer killed him, but I know differently." He winked suggestively.

My stomach churned—from hunger, not fear. His bluff was conspicuous.

"Mrs. Copeland's overdose wasn't an accident." Leaning forward, his voice lowered. "She was murdered. But you know that, don't you?"

My face remained flat and my tongue silent.

He shrugged, whistling as he ambled away.

Heart racing, I put the car in gear and exited the lot. In my rearview mirror, I saw Pruitt shaking his head. I didn't like it. I needed to get the situation under control—and fast. A rogue cop wouldn't dismantle my life.

As I watched the traffic light, a dour female police officer's face flashed before my eyes. At night, that bitch haunted my dreams, repeating those same words, "Your son was hit by a drunk driver. Where were you?"

Cancer killed my husband. An alcoholic murdered my son. At the time, I wondered if it was a test. A Job-like exam to determine whether I deserved God's love. Clearly not.

Jean had been my first and last love, but Evens' death eclipsed even that pain. The ache in my soul threatened to swallow my sanity. For months, my thoughts teetered between homicide and suicide.

As I drove away from the medical center, similar emotions bubbled up in my chest, threatening to erupt into a full-blown panic attack. I began hyperventilating. Worried I might cause an accident, I pulled over to the side of the road.

Breathe, Julia.

Half an hour passed before I re-entered traffic.

Pruitt's interference wouldn't be tolerated. Mrs. Copeland didn't destroy me, and neither would a scraggly police officer.

My sweaty hands gripped the steering wheel. On the drive, I contemplated various scenarios. I'd always been a planner. Details mattered, especially when your actions skirted the law. As traffic meandered north along the highway, a plan formulated in my mind.

CHAPTER 15

Clinic ran smoothly all day, and I anticipated being able to grab dinner before the medical seminar later that evening. The computer calendar beeped an alert. I glanced at the clock: 5:15 p.m. Forty-five minutes until the seminar began.

Once I'd dismissed the last patient, I rushed out of the exam room and into my office. Half my brain completed the chart, while the other half considered where to grab dinner. I knocked on the wall to see if April had left already. She didn't return my knock, so I sent a text.

DINNER?

THERE'S FOOD. HURRY.

Unfortunately, San Marguerite didn't have any Caribbean restaurants. I enjoyed cooking but had done little of it since Evens died. A chef needed diners. At least gardening was something I could do alone. I needed to train the dog not to dig up the plants, though.

The EHR showed my 5:15 p.m. patient had not arrived. On the computer, I changed their status to no-show. The seminar started at six, and I needed the CMEs. The topic, *Rediscovering the Joy in Medicine*, sounded intriguing. After over twenty years in medicine, I wanted to regain my passion. There was no joy in medical charting though. But it was necessary, so I charted in haste.

With two charts remaining, I glanced at the EHR and noticed the patient I no-showed a minute ago now read as present. Without the luxury of time to track down the medical assistant, I continued working.

From down the hall, I heard steps rapidly approaching. The meeting started at six o'clock, and it was now 5:38 p.m. I didn't want to eat the lousy complimentary meal provided upstairs. If I had to sit through a four-hour seminar after a ten-hour workday, I at least wanted decent food. With the final chart completed, I snatched up my purse from the bottom desk drawer, locked the door, and headed out. Instantly, I collided with a medical assistant.

"Sorry. I'm in a hurry." I circled around her, headed for the exit to purchase Indian food.

"I'm sorry, Dr. Toussaint, but your 5:15 patient finally arrived."

I frowned. "She was fifteen minutes late."

Generally, I saw assigned patients, regardless. However, tonight was different. I had to be somewhere with a strict attendance policy.

"I knew you'd want to see her, so I told the registration clerk to check her in."

The part of my brain ignited by menopause wanted to shout. My introspective self intervened and dialed down my reaction. No reason to cause a scene. It was partially my fault for usually seeing late patients. The medical assistant believed she'd done what I wanted, operating on prior knowledge of how I functioned. Besides, why waste time chastising her when, in the end, I would see the patient?

With slumped shoulders, I returned to my desk.

Kim popped her head around my door. "Are you coming?"

"Not yet." I tossed my purse in the drawer and slipped on a lab coat. "My 5:15 patient arrived late."

In a singsong voice, Kim said, "If you're late, they won't let you in." She departed.

This seminar, in addition to being free and local, offered twenty continuing medical education credits—and I needed them to maintain my state license.

Cursing internally, I rushed into the patient exam room. "Hello. I'm Dr. Toussaint. How may I help you?"

Seated in a plastic chair, the woman squinted through tinted glasses. "Where is Dr. Dickerson?"

My first thought, though unkind, was to tell her if she removed her tinted lenses, she could see I didn't have Dr. Dickerson with me. "What can I help—" I glanced at the EHR, "—Megan with?"

I completed the visit and ran from the clinic, perspiring and panting along the way. I arrived on time, though without dinner. Most of the seats were occupied, but I noticed Juanita's waving hand. I grabbed a water bottle and sat beside her.

She said, "Didn't think you'd make it."

I wrenched the lid off the water bottle, spilling a large amount on the table. "Got stuck seeing Bryce's patient. Someone placed her on my schedule."

"I'm not surprised."

The muscles in my temple twitched. I scanned the room's occupants. "Is she here?"

"Yep."

Juanita pointed at a long table in the front of the room. Bryce sat beside Ken. Also at the table were Carter, Kim, and April. Bryce's bleached-blond hair tossed back as she laughed loudly at something Ken said.

My vision constricted. Heat zoomed up my back as sweat trickled along my forehead. Dammit, where was my fan?

Despite initial interest in the evening's topic, I absorbed little information on how to return joy to medicine. Bryce consumed my attention. Once the meeting ended, I would confront her about seeing that clinic patient.

The seminar concluded, and Juanita and I left the conference room together, heading toward the parking lot. I paced around, waiting to accidentally, on purpose, run into Bryce or Ken—or both. Someone was going to experience my wrath tonight—or so I thought. Despite my slow pace, neither arrived at the lot.

Juanita left. April and Kim waved before they departed. Thirty minutes elapsed. Bryce either parked somewhere else or went inside the pediatric clinic.

A rational person would go home. Instead, I stalked the parking lot. Another five minutes elapsed. Anger overcame hunger, and I returned inside the medical center. Hands pumping in tandem with my legs, I swung the door open, careened into Carter, and knocked him down. The papers he held went airborne, and the collision shook the anger out of me.

"Sorry," I said, more out of obligation than sentiment. I helped him up.

His wrinkled forehead relaxed as he went from surprise to displeasure to calm in seconds. Together, we gathered papers off the floor.

On hands and knees, he asked, "What's the hurry? Aren't you going the wrong way?"

"I wanted to speak with Bryce. Have you seen her?"

"No. I'm sure she's gone." A slight hesitation betrayed his reply. More surprisingly, from the upturn at the corners of his mouth, he knew I recognized the lie. Carter's freckled face lit up with a smile reaching up to his red hairline. For a moment, his face displayed a youthful impishness. For a moment, we held each other's gaze. Then I stood up and returned the papers.

"Sorry about knocking you down."

"No harm done." He moved toward the exit and stepped outside. "Coming?"

"Not yet."

His laughter reached my ears before the door closed shut. Intrigued by Carter's behavior, I decided not to leave—yet.

Inside the pediatric clinic, I headed for B wing. All three wings were identical, with the physician offices located in the rear. After knocking on Bryce's office door, I opened it. Empty. Where was she?

Ken worked in A wing. She might be with him. A single light at the nursing station lit the area. I detected whispered voices. Cautiously avoiding wheelchairs and the weight scales, I proceeded forward, searching inside my purse for a burner phone. Once I located it, I pressed Start and followed the voices.

In a supply cabinet near the staff restrooms, I heard heavy breathing proceeded by a snap. On tiptoes, I inched along the edge of the hallway, recognizing Bryce's deep voice.

"How about dinner?"

Rustling clothes preceded what I knew to be Ken's voice. "Uh, uh. Not tonight. Besides, I already had dessert."

Bryce giggled.

I wanted to vomit.

Footsteps headed in my direction. I searched for a place to hide. The steps came closer. My skin itched, and I knew a hot flash was coming, but hiding took priority.

Hurry, Julia.

In the next hallway, I slipped into a patient room right as they reached the corner. Careful not to be seen, I hovered near the doorway. Kissing noises intermixed with voices.

"I need to get home," Ken said.

"Why?" Bryce asked. "It's not like Nancy cares. All she worries about are those brats."

"Hey. I told you before, don't talk about my kids like that."

Footsteps stopped right outside the doorway. Moving lightly, I retreated farther inside the exam room.

"Well, they *are* spoiled. You're always buying them something or taking them somewhere."

"I don't tell you how to raise your kid."

"She's not mine. And besides, she hates me."

"No, she blames you for the divorce—own it. Try harder. Do special things with her."

"Why create another entitled devil like—"

"I'm not joking. Lay off the kids."

"Okay. Let go of my arm."

"I don't care what you say about Nancy, but don't badmouth my kids."

"I said, okay. Shit. Chill the hell out."

Their voices trailed away. Finally, the clinic door shut. Another minute passed before I exited the clinic and medical building.

In my car, I checked the burner phone. The app was still running. I hit Stop, then Replay. The app had recorded Ken and Bryce's conversation—not bad, given the distance between us.

In California, legally, we're not allowed to record conversations without consent from all parties. Although the tape wouldn't play in court, it provided a new perspective on Ken.

Unsatisfied with the situation concerning Bryce's patient, I now had something more interesting to ponder on the drive home. Ken and Bryce's affair, which I was certain Carter knew about.

Carter's attitude left me perplexed. Was he using the information to obtain advantages from Ken? Or maybe he simply relished knowing people's secrets. I'd have to be careful. A snoop could be a nuisance if you had secrets.

CHAPTER 16

I dropped April and the dog off at Camile's before driving south on Highway 101 toward Ventura, then east toward Thaddeus' boarding school in Santa Paula.

When I called the school about picking him up for spring break, I'd been informed Tonya had left instructions that Thaddeus must remain on campus. I was pissed.

Thaddeus attended the school on a partial scholarship. I paid the majority of his tuition. Students were allowed family visits, but visitors only during special events and holidays.

Tonya had always permitted me to remove Thaddeus from campus. This time, she insisted on speaking with me first. She agreed to meet me at the school tonight.

As I drove onto the campus, the sun began to set. In the main office, the woman at registration informed me Tonya and Thaddeus were in the gathering room.

On the way there, I found Tonya in the hallway. She smiled distantly but accepted my hug.

"How are you doing?"

"I thought I'd take Thaddie home with me," she said, ignoring my question. "We haven't spent Easter together in a long time."

"Sounds fine." Confused, I tried to understand the reasons behind this sudden change. "Tonya, I'm not trying to keep Thaddeus from you. Would you like to spend Easter at Camile's, too? She'd love to have you."

"Oh, no…I couldn't do that."

"What are your plans?" I asked, interested in what lie she would tell.

"Well, I-I thought we could have an Easter egg hunt."

"Don't you think he's too old for that?"

"Well…" She looked around, I presumed, for inspiration.

More concerned with her own needs, Tonya didn't generally spend holidays with Thaddeus. Why now? Something—or someone—was behind this new interest in her son.

Thaddeus hurried in our direction. "Mrs. T," he said, running into my arms with a bear hug.

Squeezing him tightly, I kissed his forehead. "Um. So handsome. What happened to the braids? Who cut your hair? It looks nice."

He grinned and rubbed his scalp. "Thanks. The school hired a new barber. Next time, I want him to put a design in my hair."

I laughed. "The school won't allow it."

He laughed.

"Thaddie," Tonya said, "you're so big."

His face fell. He attempted a short side hug, but she pulled him in close and long.

"Why are you here, Mom?" He frowned.

"Don't you want to come with me?"

When he didn't respond, I said, "Your mom made plans for Easter break. Didn't you, Tonya?"

"Thaddie, if you want to go with Dr. T, that's fine," she said, rubbing his shoulder.

Unsurprised, I accompanied Tonya to the registration desk while Thaddeus retrieved his suitcase. Once Tonya signed him out, we walked outside.

Clicking the car lock, I said, "Thaddeus, wait in the car. I need to speak with your mom."

He nodded and did as directed.

Tonya and I walked over to her car. It was new—well, used but new to her. A sporty sedan, maybe two years old. I hadn't seen it before.

Walking around the car, I asked, "Tonya, where did you get this?"

She grinned. "You like it?"

"It's nice. Who gave it to you?"

"I bought it."

"How? I know how much money you make. There's no way you could afford this."

Her ruby-red lips pouted. "I bought it on credit."

Running my hand over the body of the car, I bent down and examined the tires. "You have no credit. Tell the truth."

"I am!" she shouted.

People exiting the school turned in our direction.

A moment passed as I allowed the tension to dissipate. I went over to Tonya. "I'm sorry. It's nice."

She grinned timidly.

"Why did I have to meet with you before taking Thaddeus out of school?"

Her arms folded over her chest. "You forget, he's my son."

So do you, I wanted to say but didn't. "What did you want to discuss?"

Lowering her voice, she marched up beside me. "I need you to trust me."

My brows wrinkled. "About what?"

"About Kevin."

I stared.

"My fiancé." Because she leaned in close, I felt her breath

on my face. "I won't tell anyone, but I need to understand why you killed him."

"Tonya—"

"I trust you with Thaddie."

"Except this time."

"I wanted to talk, but you've been avoiding me."

"I've been busy." I slipped a form out of my purse. "Oh, don't forget to sign this. It gives me permission to bring Thaddeus back to campus."

She scribbled her signature where I directed without reading it—as expected. Folding the paper, I secured it in my purse.

"Anytime you've needed help, I've been there. How many times have I bailed you out of jail? When your fiancé beat you up and threw you out of *your own* apartment, I paid for a place for you to stay."

"I appreciate everything you did."

"Oh. And this is how you say thank you? Repeatedly mentioning the bum who assaulted your son."

"You always talk about the bad times. Kevin loved me." Running into her car, Tonya gunned the engine and sped away.

For a moment, I watched her drive off, then joined Thaddeus in the car. Tears brimmed along the edges of his eyes. I held his hand.

"It's okay."

"Why did she have to come? She ruins everything."

Under different circumstances, I would've tried to justify a parent's actions. But Tonya pissed me off. Clearly, she understood the control she wielded over me when it came to Thaddeus.

At a moderate pace, I followed Tonya down the hill and back onto Highway 126. The road merged with Highway 101 North, and her car blended into an endless stream of vehicles.

It was late when we arrived at Camile's house in Montecito. Thaddeus was excited to see the dog. He and the kids played outside under the patio lights.

Camile handed me a margarita. "You need to give the dog a name."

"Any ideas?"

"No, but I'm sure the kids could come up with something."

Sipping the cocktail, I licked the salt off my lips. "Delicious. Where's Lupita?"

"She and April went to see a movie."

"And left you alone with the kids?"

"Funny," Camile said, smacking my shoulder.

Together, we walked out to the backyard. Seeing Thaddeus and Camile's children playing with the dog made me smile. They looked so happy. I rested in the recliner, sipping the margarita. Tired from driving and Tonya's nonsense, I dozed off.

"Okay?" Camile asked, shaking me awake.

"I'm exhausted." I finished the cocktail.

She frowned. "Tell me what's going on."

Not this again. "Life. Things are difficult at work but getting better."

"Are you adjusting?"

"Gradually."

Pulling her chair closer to mine, Camile said, "But you aren't the same person. Julia, you still aren't yourself."

I sat bolt upright in the recliner. "My husband died after a protracted illness from cancer, and my son was murdered. I'll never be the same."

The children stopped playing. All eyes regarded me. I hadn't realized I was shouting. The dog came over and licked my hand.

Patting her head, I said, "I'm a different person. I hope you can learn to love this Julia."

"I will." Camile leaned over and kissed my cheek. "I already do."

"Thanks. Besides, the problems at work don't involve me."

"Oh."

"April's having problems with the pediatric chief."

"Let's talk about it later." Camile called the children inside. "Come on guys, time for bed."

Lying on my back, I stared up into the dark sky. Camile loved me, but she couldn't love me like Jean had. He loved me not despite my flaws but because of them. He understood and kept me grounded. We shared everything. And most importantly he kept my secrets. As a neurologist, he would have understood impulses, dreams, urges—any aberrant behavior.

I searched my memory but failed to recall us discussing urges. Surely, if I harbored murderous thoughts, he would have noticed. Jean was an astute clinician. Wouldn't he have detected murderous tendencies in his wife? Maybe he died before he could.

The patio lights flickered off. I went inside, locking the sliding doors. Lupita and April came in from the garage door, laughing and discussing the movie. We gathered in the kitchen. While we conversed around the kitchen island, she mixed more cocktails.

I hadn't eaten dinner and didn't trust myself with more alcohol on an empty stomach. Additionally, alcohol wreaked havoc with my hot flashes. After declining another cocktail, I slid onto a stool as Lupita and April explained the movie.

April accepted a glass from Camile. "You need to see it, Julia. It's good."

I nibbled on chips, dropping a few on the floor for the dog. "Maybe later."

Patting my hand, April said, "You better hurry, old lady. You don't have much time left." She laughed.

"Ooh!" Camile and Lupita teased.

"We'll see how old I am the next time we go biking."

Waving her hands dismissively, April said goodnight and retired to her room.

Winking, Camile said, "She pretty."

Sliding off the stool, I refilled the dog's water bowl. "She's not my type."

"Really. I always thought you were bi-curious."

Seeing the wicked grin curling at the edge of her mouth, I said, "April is a beautiful woman, but since Jean died, I'm asexual. And quite content."

"Things change," Camile said wistfully before she and Lupita exited the kitchen.

I retired to the guest bedroom. After shutting the door, I heard whining and scratching.

"Sorry." I let the dog inside. "I need to give you a name."

Bark.

"I will. Promise." Unzipping my purse, I removed a device I acquired quite a while ago. Santa Barbara had one of the most well-stocked spy stores I'd come across. Once the Start button turned green, a small red light popped up on the screen.

Like a snail, the red light crawled along a map, detailing Tonya's travels. The tracker would help me locate her if necessary. There was a reason she suddenly started talking about Kevin, and I intended to find out. Both our lives depended upon it.

CHAPTER 17

The stool wobbled as I tried to balance while ignoring the sweat pooling around my waist. Damn menopause.

"Mrs. Jenkins, I have the lab results," I said, perched precariously on a seat too small for my wide ass.

Tamesha, a shy seven-year-old girl, sat patiently on the exam table while I faced her mom.

"The Depakote levels are low again, too low to be effective. When does Tamesha take her seizure medication?" Peripherally, I watched the child for any reaction.

"I give it to her every morning before school like the doctor told me," Mrs. Jenkins said.

The little girl's eyes widened slightly. Her mother had lied.

In the EHR, Mrs. Jenkins was listed as a single mother of three children. Tamesha was the oldest. Thin with a head full of microbraids, Mrs. Jenkins looked older than her reported age. Upon reviewing the chart, I noted the family often arrived late for appointments—at least to the ones they kept.

Dr. Carter Reynolds was Tamesha's assigned provider. Mrs. Jenkins sent a medication refill request to him, but since he was on vacation, I responded. After reviewing the chart, I insisted the mother come in for an office visit before approving another refill.

At first, she refused, calling the triage nurse to complain. When the neurologist refilled the anticonvulsant three months ago, she requested Mrs. Jenkins take the child to the lab for a serum drug level. Mrs. Jenkins only took Tamesha to the lab this morning at my insistence.

While studying the mom, I tried to gauge her motivations. She acted concerned about the child, but why didn't she keep their appointments? Why didn't Tamesha receive her medication as prescribed? Questions required answers.

"Tamesha has missed several neurology appointments. Are you having problems with transportation?"

"We go to all her scheduled appointments," Mrs. Jenkins said, her mouth puckering.

As her mom shifted in the chair, I noticed Tamesha's small body involute. Her large brown, sleepy eyes resembled Evens'.

"Tamesha has not seen the neurologist in two years. You only contact the doctor for medication refills. And the child hasn't had a physical exam in *three* years." I paused. Her turn.

As her right foot jostled up and down, she glared at me. Her fingers gripped the edge of the chair. "I didn't know about those appointments. I can schedule a follow-up with the neurologist today. But I'm in a hurry. I need to get back home. My boyfriend is watching the kids, and he needs to go to work soon."

"Where does he work?"

Seconds passed.

"Walmart."

Her hesitation was a tell. "Mrs. Jenkins, if you need help, we have a medical social worker in the office."

"No!" She leaped out of the seat. "I don't need a social worker. I can remember my appointments. Are you going to give me the medication or not?"

Rocking slightly back and forth, Tamesha remained on the table, her head cocooned between her arms.

"Please have a seat. I'll write the prescription after I complete the exam."

Though attentive during the exam, the child's conversation sounded forced, rehearsed. Despite several questions about her interests and school, she peered around me for visual cues from her mom.

I washed my hands and requested Mrs. Jenkins step outside the exam room. She didn't seem inclined to leave, but I assured her Tamesha would be safe. I gave the child a container of crayons and a picture to color. Her eyes sparkled when told she could keep the crayons and paper. For a few seconds, I watched her coloring—she was left-handed like my son.

Outside, I escorted Mrs. Jenkins down the hall and into my office. At her request, I left the door cracked so she could see the exam room door where Tamesha remained.

"Mrs. Jenkins, I'm concerned about Tamesha's health," I said, draping my exam coat over the back of the chair. "She has to follow up with the specialist and keep *all* scheduled appointments."

Mrs. Jenkins straightened her back. "I know. I… She'll get to her appointments. I'll make sure."

I held her gaze. "Why has she missed so many?"

"Sometimes I can't get the car to drive her. My boyfriend works."

Another excuse involving the boyfriend. "I can arrange with the social worker for transportation."

This time, when she jumped up, she fled the room. "I don't need help."

Before she could return to Tamesha, I rushed forward.

"I know something's wrong. You can either tell me now, or I'll find out from the social worker."

Her wide-based nose flared. "I told you; I don't need help."

"Yes, you do. I don't know if it's abuse or neglect, but something is keeping you from bringing Tamesha in. If I check the medical charts of your other children, I'm sure I'll find the same pattern."

Her eyes became slits. "You have no right to look at my other kids' charts."

"I'm a mandated reporter. I have to report any suspicion of abuse or neglect to child protective services."

She shrank from me.

Blocking the door with my arm, I whispered, "Let me help you. I promise. I won't be like the others. Give me a chance."

The purse slipped down her slumped shoulders. Tears pooled in her eyes. "I—I can't lose my kids—not again."

We re-entered my office. As her leg jostled, Mrs. Jenkins gave me a short synopsis of her history with social services. Due to her drug use, social services had been involved after the birth of each of her children. She feared they would take the children away permanently if they discovered the situation with her present boyfriend—who was not the father of any of the children.

"Does he use or sell drugs?" I asked.

"Nothing dangerous, only steroids." She hurried to explain. "He works out a lot."

My jaw clenched. I felt tired—tired of the same pathetic excuses. Sighing, I deferred giving a lecture about the side effects of anabolic steroids, allowing her to simply relate her story.

She tried to leave him before, but he found her and beat her up. No, he didn't physically or sexually abuse the children, she stated. But she admitted he terrorized them, which was why she didn't like to leave him alone with the kids. The younger children were presently with a neighbor, but if she was late returning home, her boyfriend might go pick them up.

Leaned back in the chair, I listened, evaluating her sincerity despite the half-truths. "What do you want?"

Her damp eyes regarded me as if I were an alien. "What?"

"From life, for yourself, your children?" I recalled Tamesha's innocent joy over simple crayons.

Blinking rapidly, she scanned the room as if for inspiration. She cleared her throat. "I want to feel safe and take care of my kids."

"I can help. Will you trust me?"

A large sob escaped her throat, and she cried. Rocking gently, I hugged her. Minutes passed before she mopped up her tears, smearing her make-up.

Handing her a box of tissues, I explained what needed to happen. "I have to call social services."

Her dark eyes bore into me. "You said you'd help."

"I will." After detailing my plan, I escorted her back to the room where Tamesha had finished the picture.

"Very nice. May I have it?"

The child gripped the paper. Conflict brewed behind those intense brown eyes.

"How about this? I'll keep the picture until you find a permanent home for it. Okay?"

The child's face went from a question to joy in a split second. She didn't understand what I meant, but she was content to understand she would one day receive the picture back. I assured Mrs. Jenkins the medication refill had been sent to the pharmacy.

Hopping off the table, Tamesha followed her mom to the door.

Before she departed, I squeezed Mrs. Jenkins' hand. "Trust me."

With a nod, she left.

Late for my next appointment, I didn't call social services until the end of morning clinic. Exhausted, in my office, I peeled off the damp lab coat, turned on my desk fans, and sopped sweat off my face and neck. Perhaps I needed to reconsider taking hormone therapy. The side effects couldn't be worse than what I currently experienced.

Over the phone, I explained Mrs. Jenkin's situation to the social worker and my concerns for the safety of her and the children. The social worker promised to call me before they made a home visitation. Ten minutes later, the call ended. Not content to trust the family's safety to bureaucracy, I made my own arrangements.

My mind wouldn't rest, though. Once clinic ended, I grabbed my purse and left. I needed to make sure my patient was safe.

***

Thirty minutes later, I pulled into a neighborhood that hadn't seen better days in decades. Abandoned stripped-down cars hugged broken, chipped sidewalks.

Squinting against the sunlight, I scanned house numbers. Once I found the correct location, I slowed down and scrutinized the house.

The pale-pink brick home looked as despondent as its neighbors. A neglected yard and cracked driveway showed no one had cared for this home in years.

A half minute later, I continued down the street, observing the surroundings and searching for security cameras. A long, narrow alleyway extended behind the homes. One block away, I turned around and parked several houses down from where Mrs. Jenkins lived with her boyfriend and three children.

Fifteen minutes elapsed before I spied a multicolored van approaching the house. Lettering on the side of the van read

SOS, *Saving our Sisters*. Pictures covered the entire side of the van depicting women of different ethnicities standing with fists raised in protest. Brakes screeched as the vehicle parked in front of the pink house.

After Tamesha and her mother left the office, I called Anjelah, a friend who runs SOS, a non-profit helping abused women. She promised someone would stop by to pick up Mrs. Jenkins and her children. Concerned, I came by to make sure they arrived before the boyfriend returned. Years of experience taught me not to rely on social services. To protect my patients, I became personally involved—often too much.

Anjelah, a tall woman with a thick ponytail trailing down her back, exited the van, knocked on the door and disappeared inside. Two minutes elapsed before she exited the house with Mrs. Jenkins and three children, one I recognized as Tamesha. Once everyone entered the vehicle, the van pulled away.

Idling next to the curb, I continued to observe the house. Thirty minutes later, a Camaro shot up the driveway. Loud music blasted from the car as the driver waited for the garage door to scroll up.

I cruised past the house, viewing the prince Mrs. Jenkins allowed to beat her and torture her children. Disappointed—but not surprised, I found him lacking. Snake tattoos encircled his biceps. Those didn't bother me as much as the tiny pencil mustache, goatee, and the patterned fade on the sides of his head. Hastily, I noted his appearance—for future use.

CHAPTER 18

The morning started out gray and stormy. Although people in California couldn't drive in the rain, they came out in droves to see their doctors in poor weather. Varied seasons was one of the few things I missed about living back East. North Carolina might not receive a lot of snow, but enough to signify when winter arrived.

Due to traffic, my last patient came late. Behind schedule, I careened into Ken while hurrying to an exam room. "Excuse me," I said, circling around him.

"Hello, Julia. How're things?"

"Busy." Running into my office, I picked up a book I wanted to share with a patient family. Unfortunately, Ken followed, talking as if oblivious to my plight.

"Looks like it. When you can, I need to discuss your quarterly review. It won't take long, but it's required."

"Absolutely," I said, shutting my office door. "Let me know, and I'll place it on the calendar."

While we spoke, April exited her office.

"Hello, Ken," she said.

Ken's lips shut. Before stomping away, he said, "Fine. I'll email you."

April dashed after him. "Ken, please. We need to talk."

"There's nothing to talk about. I placed the quarterly review on your desk. Sign it and get it back to me."

"We have to discuss what happened."

Spluttering, Ken's face went florid. His paltry mustache wriggled like a caterpillar. "No, we don't." He leaned into her face. "You cost me one job. It's not going to happen again. Now, stay the hell away from me."

Ken started to leave but swirled around to face her again. "Better yet, why don't you get another fucking job." He stomped off.

I joined April. "Listen—"

"Not now, Julia." She strode off.

For a moment, I considered following her. *Never mind.* I rushed into the exam room.

***

Clinic ended as I completed my last patient chart. I reached into the bottom desk drawer to get my purse when April entered. With a sigh, she collapsed in a chair next to the door.

"Bad days get better," I said, observing her downturned lips.

"This situation with Ken... It won't work."

"Don't forget, you have options."

She inhaled deeply and blew it out. "I know, but none of them good."

"I checked with my former CMO. There aren't any openings in Goleta."

"Figures."

We both rose and exited. While I locked the door, she asked, "Are you driving down to Montecito this weekend?" Her hound-dog droopy eyes begged for a positive response.

"No, I have things to take care of around the house."

She leaned against the wall. "Too bad. I was hoping to get away."

"April, you can visit Camile and Lupita without me. They're your friends, too."

"Really? I-I wasn't sure. They're nice, but that's because of you."

"They wouldn't pretend to like someone—believe me." Removing the cellphone from my purse, I said, "I'll text you Camile's number."

"Thanks. I desperately need an escape."

"How's the family?"

"Same." She turned aside. "My mom wants me to move to LA so we can share a house, and my sister wants me to cosign on a car loan."

"She can take the bus."

April laughed. "Yeah, right."

"Or get a better job."

We headed for the parking lot.

"Why doesn't your sister get a place with your mom?

"Because she doesn't want to."

Not three yards ahead of me, sitting on a bench beside the bus stop, I saw Detective Pruitt. In one hand, he held an umbrella over his head—it wasn't raining as much as misting—and in the other, a cigarette.

My steps slowed. I considered returning inside, but he might simply wait. Swallowing my apprehensions, I continued toward the employee parking lot. April and I parted.

When I reached where he sat, he dropped the cigarette under the bench and stood, blowing smoke in front of me. Deviating around the death cloud, I continued toward my car.

Falling in step with me, he said, "Dr. Toussaint, you have a sec?"

Without answering, I crossed the street. He followed.

"Did you know Kevin Page worked for me?"

Feigning disinterest, I mentally recorded everything he said.

"As an informant." He removed another cigarette from his

118

pocket, lit it, and took a long drag. "It upset me when he was brutally murdered *and* robbed."

This time, he blew the smoke aside. "These things are gonna kill me."

Or someone irritated by the smoke.

He coughed and spit. A minute passed. "That's how I met Tonya."

I clicked the car door open.

His hand with the cigarette flew up, directing me to stop.

"I won't be long, and I'm sure you'll want to hear what I have to say."

Silent, I stood ramrod straight and regarded him.

A large smile crossed his face. "Tonya is an interesting woman, talkative. Especially when you give her something to drink."

Control your breathing, Julia. Don't let him see you stressed.

"Tonya led me to you. Then, I learned about her son. What's his name, Thaddeus?"

He tossed the cigarette on the ground. I watched the smoke curl upward and disappear. Now, if he would simply disappear, too.

"It seems Page beat the boy up pretty bad. Put him in the hospital. Weeks later, Page gets killed. A coincidence?"

I regarded his stubby nose and considered punching it closer to his smoke-stained face.

He advanced. "I don't like coincidences. After his death, I spoke with Tonya. Back then—when she was clean—she didn't talk much." He snickered. "But her sobriety didn't last long."

Because I stepped forward, he inched backward, blocking the door with his leg.

"I looked into your past and found another death," he said, the words coming faster. "Mrs. Copeland. A chronic alcoholic and drug user who died from a morphine overdose."

Not a muscle on my body flinched. I listened and made mental notes. He was right-handed. Potbelly, so probably not in good physical condition.

"Huh, not talking? You're a tough cookie. But I guess you have to be to kill two people."

My teeth gritted. Obviously, Pruitt believed he knew the truth. No reason to contradict him. I recalled a quote from Dame Christie's *ABC Murders*: "…speech is an invention of man's to prevent him from thinking." There was no profit for me in talking.

Someone entered the car beside mine. Momentarily distracted, Pruitt turned aside. I took advantage of the moment to hop inside the car.

As I locked the door, he knocked on the window, bending down so his face was level with mine.

"For the right price, I can forget what I know. Otherwise… Who knows what a good detective could do with your connection to two murders."

Checking my rearview mirror, I reversed out of the parking spot and drove away. As I neared the exit, I watched Pruitt head toward the visitor's parking lot.

You need to figure out what's going on. What is his relationship with Tonya?

Right then, I felt like the protagonist in Chinua Achebe's *Things Fall Apart*. An unseen force acted upon my life, leading me to what? Self-destruction. I had no intention of succumbing. But first, I had to understand my adversary.

By executing three left turns, I returned to the parking spot. Removing a latex glove from my purse, I retrieved the cigarette butt Pruitt discarded. It might come in handy.

The sky was a clear, faded blue. We paid extraordinarily high taxes for those tranquil skies. I closed my eyes, letting the sun warm my skin—at least before a hot flash started.

When did I last call my parents? Suddenly, I missed them. Things got out of hand after Evens died. I lost control. On cue, my parents flew across the country, offering compassion and support.

If Camile hadn't insisted, I would've ended my treatment with Dr. Griffith sooner. That monster poisoned me with a cocktail of psychotropics and hallucinogens. Her treatment protocol bordered on malpractice, but I couldn't prove it.

It's over, Julia. Move on.

True. I had eliminated her from my life.

When Evens died, I fell apart. I didn't eat or sleep. All day, I sat in his room and cried. I needed to breathe him in to keep him alive and present. The scent on his clothes, the remaining warmth from his pillow.

My parents stayed with me, but I-I couldn't get it together. Camile said if I didn't see a psychiatrist, she'd look into having me admitted to a psychiatric unit. I'd lost a dangerous amount of weight and avoided mirrors because I feared the gaunt woman glaring back at me.

After prescribing me anti-psychotics, Dr. Griffith encouraged me to record my thoughts. She said I could use an app, but I feared it could be compromised. Instead, I went old school and recorded my thoughts on a tape recorder.

The voice on the tapes sounded foreign. I didn't understand what the person said, ramblings and disparate comments without a cohesive thought. The person on the tapes didn't resemble me, not my voice, diction, or ideas.

Despite asserting the medication caused these incomprehensible communications, Dr. Griffith refused to prescribe an SSRI or something with less potential for hallucinations and delusional thoughts. I needed an anti-depressant. But Dr. Griffith insisted I was psychotic and manifested signs of an anti-social personality disorder. She lied.

I never felt compelled to kill. My interest in forensic medicine led me to imagine different ways to kill people as a mere exercise. Jean and I would discuss those ideas. Though morbid, it remained an innocent game.

Then Jean died, and I felt alone—angry. Not long after I buried my husband, the boy I adopted into my heart and raised alongside my son was brutally assaulted. Sorrow combined with outrage. Innocent, kind Thaddeus had been abused and hospitalized. If those two events hadn't occurred at those precise moments in my life...

Anyone can kill if properly incentivized.

CHAPTER 19

After loading the dog in the car, I headed for the nearest pet store for an unguent to treat sores on her abdomen. The vet promised the lesions were mere remnants of a skin condition and easily treatable.

Other than a rope the vet's office provided, I didn't have a proper leash. The dog never quit my side, though, even on extended walks. However, I wanted to take her to the park without people giving me the evil eye, so I needed a leash.

We entered the pet store, and I located the correct aisle. While I scrutinized the selection of leads and harnesses, a store employee came over.

He said, "You have to leash your dog."

Gazing at him from the corner of my eye, I said, "I know, that's why I'm looking for a leash."

"Didn't you have one when you came in?"

"No."

With his help, I managed to find a leash that didn't look too uncomfortable. I didn't want to strangle the poor creature.

Before he walked away, the employee asked, "What's her name?"

"I don't know. She's a rescue."

"Well, you have to name her." He chuckled and walked off.

"Did you have a name before?" I asked the dog.

Woof.

"I'll take that as a yes. Since you can't tell me what your name was. I'll have to come up with a new one. Okay?"

Woof.

We made our way to the dog food aisle.

"Which one?"

She sniffed around the different bags. I selected the one she rested her paw on.

"Well, at least it's not the most expensive brand. Let's go find snacks."

Along the aisles, I noticed other items—a heavy chain, poop scooper, and bear spray.

Ping.

A text from Momma reminding me to call about those senior living facilities. Quickly I texted back.

Forgot. Call later.

At checkout, I paid for the items. Once the cashier rang them up, I leashed the dog. Apparently, I blocked the exit because a woman leading a small poufy dog cleared her throat loudly.

She said, "Would you move."

I scooted to the side. "Sorry. I'm trying to adjust this leash. I wouldn't want anything to happen to the dog."

Looking down her nose, she said, "Not a great loss. You could always get another mutt. Peaches is a papered purebred." She bent down and picked up her dog.

"Nice. Are you papered too?"

Not appreciating my wit, she stomped off. The cashier came over and assisted me with the leash. She scratched the dog behind her ears.

"What type of dog is this?" she asked.

"A good one."

The dog's ears perked up, and we departed.

Talking to myself—and the dog, I supposed—I said, "Not a nice lady. Bragging about her pedigree dog."

Woof.

On the way home, I recalled a story by Alice Walker titled *Am I Blue.* I wished I had remembered it while I was in the pet store and shared it with that obnoxious shrew.

"We'd rather be free mutts than captive purebreds. Right?"

Woof.

I was starting to like this dog. But once I named her, she belonged to me. Became part of my family. Could I handle losing someone else I loved? Peripherally, I eyed the dog. "You better not die on me."

She barked, her tongue lolling out her mouth.

At home, I unloaded our items and stowed them away in the kitchen pantry.

"Are you hungry?"

Bark.

"You want dog food or people food?"

Two barks.

"Good. People food it is." Shutting the pantry door, I started removing items from the fridge—eggs, bread, milk, and butter—to prepare a frittata.

Glancing at the dog, I sized her up. "I guess you're my dog now."

Bark.

A warm smell of browned butter scented the air. I whisked eggs with spices, added vegetables, and poured the mixture into a sizzling frying pan coated with olive oil and a tab of butter. As I watched the edges of the eggs firm up, I considered dog names.

Evens always wanted a dog. I didn't feel I could manage a pet *and* a child. Now, I had no husband or son. Simply me and an abandoned mutt—dog.

"Sorry," I said to the dog. "Mutt is insulting. I-I didn't expect to have to take care of an animal. I'm having enough trouble managing my own affairs."

She barked.

Sprinkling cheese on the surface of the eggs, I placed the pan in the oven. Once I washed my hands, I regarded the dog.

"What name seems appropriate for you?"

Her head tilted once to each side, her ears flopped down, and her tail wagged.

From her response, I presumed it meant this was my problem. "Evens liked to watch the cartoon Clifford, but I believe that dog was red and male. You're more of a tan brown. What's a good dog name? Scooby?"

Two barks and a growl.

I grimaced. "Fine. Don't get an attitude. I'm new at this."

Once the frittata was finished, I placed it on a plate and chopped up pieces for the dog, leaving a large portion on a plate for myself. After setting her plate on the floor, I sat at the glass table in the kitchen nook. "There you go, Lady."

Bark.

"Oh, you like Lady. Cool. Lady's a decent name."

Woof.

We ate in silence. When I stood up to boil water for tea, my work cellphone beeped. Dammit. Should've turned it off. Usually, I automatically switched it off at 6 p.m. on Friday evenings. The phone screen read Ken. Double damn. After a few deep breaths, I answered.

"Hello?"

"Hey, Julia."

Instantly, I noticed a change in Ken's voice. Humility, sadness? My skin prickled.

"Sorry to bother you, but I need someone to cover my weekend shift. I have an emergency. Could you cover tonight or Sunday?"

Freeway noise blared in the background. Plans to work in the yard slowly evaporated. I didn't respond right away.

"Are you there?"

"Is everything okay?" I glanced over at Lady licking around her plate.

"My father had a stroke. I'm going home to help my mother."

"I'm sorry. How are the kids coping?"

"They're okay. Thanks for asking. They're coming with me."

"Well, I'm sure your mom will appreciate having you and Nancy there."

He huffed. "No, Nancy's staying home."

Shocked by his comment, I didn't say anything. What could I say?

"I'll let the staff know you'll cover for me tonight. Thanks again." He rung off.

A second after Ken hung up, my eyes drifted over to the senior living brochures on the living room coffee table. As an only child, I felt guilty living so far away from my parents. Soon, they would need help. In fact, they wanted it now.

Call them.

Why couldn't I move back to North Carolina? What kept me tied to California?

For once, I empathized with Ken. This was the first time I heard anything close to compassion from him. But his comment regarding Nancy sounded more like the jerk I knew. He was taking his kids to comfort his mother but not his wife. Weird.

Since I agreed to work the evening shift, I decided to shower and get some rest. In bed, I reflected on my parents' living situation. Visions of nursing homes and bingo games danced around my head. I wasn't sure when, but I fell asleep.

An hour before clinic, ringing woke me up.

A text from Anjelah.

JENKINS BOYFRIEND AT IT AGAIN.

Damn.

CHAPTER 20

California summer heat beat down mercilessly, day and night. The state essentially had two seasons: rain and drought. At six in the morning, I jumped in the car and turned on the air conditioner. Anjelah expected me at seven. Earlier, Momma called to inquire about me moving back to North Carolina.

Thirty years after he joined the military, Daddy returned home to Alabama. Momma tired of living near his extended family, so they had relocated to North Carolina. I couldn't imagine living in Alabama, but maybe in North Carolina. I promised Momma to decide soon.

Down the street, a woman pushed a grocery cart along the sidewalk. A city bus stopped at the corner as she rambled across the crosswalk.

The dashboard clock flashed 6:55 a.m. Five minutes early. I requested a morning meeting. Menopause required I work before the blistering heat of the California summer became unbearable. I parked in the vacant lot across from the shelter. Shaded by the building, I pushed a buzzer next to the huge steel door and waited.

The bus continued on, its tires kicking up litter and debris. The odor of trash hung in the air. By midday, it would become intolerable.

Scratching noises brought my attention back to the door. A tiny window slid back, and two glowering eyes regarded me. As required, I provided the security guard with my name and identification. The window closed. Locks turned. The door swung aside, and I entered.

Wiping sweat from my brow, I said, "Hello, Sharon."

She retreated, tilting her head in the direction of the administrator's office.

I'd known Sharon for years. She took her position with SOS seriously. Former military, she brought the same prowess she demonstrated on the battlefield to protecting women at the shelter. I doubted many people at SOS knew she had her own small brood of children. As their pediatrician, I knew them and Sharon's universal undying affection for children.

She resigned from a corporate job in San Francisco to accept this position. However, security wasn't her official job. Instead, she functioned as chief operating officer. I presumed the regular guard was late, and she'd stepped in to assist.

I knocked on the administrator's office door and heard, "Come in." Inside the sparsely furnished room, I felt the intensity of its occupant. Enormous brown eyes greeted me.

"Julia." Anjelah stretched her arms wide and embraced me. "Hello."

"It's so good to see you."

Tension evaporated from my shoulders as I sheltered in her warm embrace. I was among friends. My collaboration with the organization increased after Evens' murder, keeping me busy. Listening to mothers detailing their abusive relationships allowed me to focus on something other than the woman who murdered my son. These women had taken a dangerous step toward protecting their children. Did my love for Evens justify the actions I had taken?

Arabica beans scented the air as I noticed a small percolator in the corner. Posters hung on the walls demanding independence for women and their bodies from government overreach.

"How's Mrs. Jenkins?" Straight to business, otherwise I'd socialize all day.

She pulled out a chair for me and resumed her seat. "Relax. She's fine. Nervous, but she's ready for change."

My gaze drifted over Anjelah's family pictures.

"The kids were asking about you the other day. They watched a movie the other night, which reminded them of Evens."

Tension shot up my spine. Not now. It was impossible to visit Anjelah without discussing my son, which was why I didn't visit her often. Memories were like daggers to my soul. Evens grew up with her children. My finger grazed my wedding ring.

"Give them my best."

"Why don't you come by and tell them yourself? We miss you, girl."

I managed a slight smile. "I can't stay long. I adopted a stray dog, and she's adjusting to the house."

"Good for you. I always thought you were a dog person."

Was I? Were dog people good?

She poured coffee into a large mug—she knew I didn't drink it so she didn't offer any—and together, we left the office.

We approached a large space with cold concrete floors. The community room held half a dozen tables. Inside were two groups of women conversing separately in hushed voices.

At a smaller table in the far right corner, I spied Mrs. Jenkins seated alone. I presumed her children were in one of the game rooms. The staff at SOS tried to shield children from legal transactions involving their mothers.

Waving as I walked over, I got her attention. She met me halfway to the table.

"Dr. Toussaint," she said, "I-I'm so glad to see you." Tears cascaded over her sharp cheekbones.

Her anxiety concerned me. Had she changed her mind? Would she return to the abusive boyfriend?

Leading her by the arm, I escorted her back to the table. "I told you I'd come."

Anjelah accompanied us. With a glance, I signaled her to lead.

"Have you decided what you want to do?" she asked Mrs. Jenkins.

Picking at her fingernail polish, Mrs. Jenkins glanced around the room as she chewed on a nail. "My kids were in school—a good school. That's one of the reasons I put up with…" Her head lowered.

"I want them to stay at their current school. A good education is worth putting up with Craig. I appreciate your help, but I can't stay. We need our own place. I—"

"Can you work?" Anjelah asked. "Do you have any skills?"

Over the next half hour, we obtained information from Mrs. Jenkins about employment, education, and convictions. We formulated a plan to get her stable and independent.

"We'll get you a job," Anjelah said. "Not a great job, but it'll be a start. You have to be patient and work with us."

Leaning forward across the table, I said, "I'll help you get an apartment."

"What if he comes after me?" Mrs. Jenkins shivered.

Anjelah and I exchanged a glance. She sighed. "Have you called him since you arrived?"

Mrs. Jenkins' eyes drooped. "Yes."

"Did you tell him about this place?"

"No!"

The frown across Anjelah's brow showed she doubted Mrs. Jenkins' veracity. I knew what she was thinking. Mrs. Jenkin's presence could be a liability for the other women.

First rule at SOS—the most important rule—was not to disclose our location. Cellphones could be tracked with GPS.

"Does he own any weapons?" Anjelah asked.

"Yes, but he never threatened me with a gun or anything."

No, he simply beat her with his fists. Watching their mother being physically assaulted was almost as bad—maybe worse— as being threatened with a weapon. We hadn't discussed the incident involving Tamesha since the evening at the ER.

Police had been contacted, and the boyfriend, Craig, was arrested. Once more details emerged, the authorities released him. According to witnesses, Mrs. Jenkins and Craig were having a heated, though not physically violent, argument outside *his* house.

Believing he was at work, she'd gone to the house to retrieve some personal items. During their argument, Tamesha started hitting Craig, and he pushed her aside. The child fell, striking her head. The ER staff disagreed on whether the child suffered a seizure or a concussion. Because Tamesha had a known seizure disorder, the judge didn't apportion any fault to Craig for the child's injuries.

Anjelah placed a hand over Mrs. Jenkin's. "We'll explain how to protect yourself and get a restraining order. We also offer self-defense classes."

Mrs. Jenkins goggled. "I can't fight! How am I supposed to protect my children? I-I shouldn't have left, and now I can't go back. He'll kill me!"

As her voice raised, other women in the room gawked at us. Anjelah tried to quiet her, but as expected, it didn't work.

"I... This was a mistake. I have to go." Mrs. Jenkins fled. She ran down the hallway, checking doors, presumably looking for her kids.

Anjelah and I pursued. Fortunately, Mrs. Jenkins headed toward the entrance instead of the game room where the children congregated. She was in no state to see them, and they would've been terrified at her appearance.

Sharon came out of her office as Mrs. Jenkins reached the front door. Realizing she had gone the wrong way, Mrs. Jenkins turned around and smacked into us. We encircled her, pleading with her to listen. Sharon returned to her office. I stood aside—not wanting to crowd her—and allowed Anjelah to speak.

"You can't go back," Anjelah said. "Let us help you."

Her chest heaving, Mrs. Jenkin's gaze oscillated between us. Her body trembled. Over several minutes, Anjelah explained the SOS process.

"Give us a chance," I said. "Let's sit down and discuss a plan."

While Anjelah retrieved forms inside her office, I escorted Mrs. Jenkins back to the community room. We didn't speak until we were seated. I waited while she nibbled at her nails.

When I felt she'd calmed down enough to hear me, I said, "This *will* work. Believe me. SOS has helped many women." I stared into her face and held her gaze, telegraphing my sincerity.

She nodded.

I held out my hand, and she placed hers in it. Tears dribbled from her eyes. We silently waited until Anjelah returned.

Although I knew I shouldn't make promises, Mrs. Jenkins couldn't return to her abuser. Tamesha might not survive another incident.

Collapsing into a chair, Anjelah placed the forms aside and spoke with Mrs. Jenkins. Her brow creased. "You can't call your boyfriend from here again. We'll get you settled into a women's shelter."

"I don't want—"

"I'll find a place for you and your kids, but don't contact your boyfriend. We can't protect you if you don't follow instructions."

The intensity of Anjelah's gaze scoured the side of my face, but I watched Mrs. Jenkins. A minute elapsed before anyone spoke.

"Okay," she said.

We left her in the community room to complete paperwork.

Once we returned to Anjelah's office, she slammed the door. "You shouldn't pay for an apartment, Julia. She'll become as dependent on you as she was on the boyfriend."

Nodding, I took several deep breaths. "I know. But it'll be for a short time."

Anjelah made a face.

"Okay, okay. I won't do it again."

Ten minutes later, after lecturing me about becoming too involved, Anjelah left to retrieve the paperwork from Mrs. Jenkins. In her absence, I sauntered down a side hallway past the psychologist's office.

Employed by the shelter part-time, the psychologist conducted interviews in a square room across from a broom closet. Centered inside was a low table where children sat. The room contained toys, puzzles, puppets, and a whiteboard for drawing. A small camera in the upper corner of the room allowed the sessions to be recorded. Often, the children's revelations proved beneficial in court.

Bypassing the square room, I slipped inside the psychologist's private office where the camera feed led. Presently, the recording equipment was off. Shutting the door behind me, I flipped on the equipment but not the recorder. The television switched on, and for a quarter of a minute, I observed a blank screen.

Static preceded figures appearing on the screen. Across from the psychologist, I viewed Tamesha seated at the tiny table. Turning the volume low, I listened.

"Tell me about your picture," the psychologist said, handing Tamesha a crayon.

The child didn't answer but continued drawing, selecting a different crayon from the one the psychologist offered. About five minutes later, she showed the psychologist her picture.

Smiling, the psychologist said, "Thank you for sharing your picture. Who are these people?"

"This is mommy, and …"

I scrutinized the picture as Tamesha described her family on vacation.

"Where is the vacation?" the psychologist asked.

A large grin lit up the child's face. "In a big house. I have a room by myself. And there's a swing in the yard…" She described the home.

"Who lives with you?"

"Mommy and…" she named her siblings.

"Anyone else?"

The child's face scrunched up. "No boyfriends."

"Why aren't boyfriends allowed?"

Tamesha's eyes darted up at the psychologist. With a huge grimace, she shook her head.

Minutes passed. Finished with her drawing, Tamesha leaped from the table and ran toward a shelf containing a half dozen dolls. Asking permission, she removed a black doll with an afro. The psychologist stood to the side as the child played with the doll. While Tamesha tried to place the doll inside a small toy car, the psychologist kneeled on the mat beside her.

She said, "Tell me what the doll is doing."

After maneuvering the doll into the car, Tamesha said, "She's driving away."

"From where?"

"The pink house. She doesn't like pink houses."

"Why not?"

"Boyfriends live in pink houses. And I don't like them."

Over the next half hour, Tamesha explained to the

psychologist what occurred in the pink house. After gaining a better understanding of the situation, I turned off the equipment. Peeking my head out the door, I made sure no one saw me leave the psychologist's office.

Quickly, I exited the shelter. As I crossed the street toward my car, the hairs on the back of my neck rose. My body tingled. Another hot flash? No.

Starting the engine, I surveyed the area. Someone was watching me, but who? No cars idled along the street. No bystanders patrolled the sidewalk. Two cars exited a parking lot down the street. I noticed nothing irregular.

At the stop sign, I checked my review mirror. Three cars idled behind me—a station wagon and two sedans. When I turned the corner, none of the vehicles followed. This was irregular. Because I trusted my instincts, there was definitely someone trailing me.

Instead of taking the highway, I kept to the local streets. The sensation of being observed intensified. Was I having a panic attack? Maybe I shouldn't have stopped all the medication the psychiatrist prescribed. I couldn't drive to San Luis Obispo like this. A half mile from the shelter, I pulled over into a store shopping center. While seated in the car, I surveyed the area.

A man seated in a station wagon lit a cigarette and grinned.

I cut the engine and headed for Pruitt. Before I arrived, he had exited the station wagon and stood in front of the car.

He wore a ball cap and held a lit cigarette between his fingers. "It's nice of you to volunteer at a women's shelter. Is that atonement for your sins?" He took a long drag on the butt.

There was no need to answer him, so I didn't.

After a few more puffs, he tossed the cigarette away. Apparently, he noticed my eyes following the cigarette as it smoldered on the asphalt.

"I know. Dangerous in California with our high risk of fires, but bad habits are hard to break. I'm sure you'd agree." His grin was too toothy to be nice. "Time to pay for your sins, Doc."

Shopping centers have cameras. I kept my back toward the store with Pruitt facing it. Both our license plate numbers would be recorded, but only his facial expressions—if the video quality was good.

Keeping my arms at my side so as not to appear hostile, I said, "There's no debt. My conscience is clear."

An unlit cigarette hung from the rim of his ball cap. He removed it and rolled it along his lips. "If the police discover what you told the psychiatrist—"

In a moment of weakness, my eyes slightly widened.

"Oh, yes. I know about her. Doctor to people of importance with money." He raised his brows suggestively before clearing his throat and spitting.

"Bet Tonya's boy remembers something. Conversations between you and his mom. Innocent, I'm sure. But valuable to someone who understands their relevance."

Now I had confirmation of what I suspected. Pruitt had used Tonya to get to me. Or had he been using her before? He admitted Tonya's boyfriend had been his informant. I remained motionless.

He puffed on the cigarette. "Okay, I'll give you the friends and family discount. Thirty thousand *if* you pay before Thanksgiving. You wouldn't want the medical board to learn about your extracurricular activities."

He dropped the cigarette on the pavement, squashing it with his shoe. A card flicked between his fingers. It stayed there. He tossed it at me, but it floated to the ground. "Well, you know how to reach me. Get the money, and I'll give you the drop location."

As he strutted to the car, he said, "Oh, I found the tracker you placed on Tonya's car. Nice model. More expensive than the one I placed on your car."

With a salute, he climbed into his station wagon and drove away.

Once inside the car, I checked the glove box. A small black metal object nestled in the corner under the car owner's manual. A month prior, I found the tracker Pruitt hid under my Honda wheel well. As long as Pruitt believed he held the stronger hand, I controlled the situation. I wasn't the only one with a tainted background.

Knowledge was like a hand of spades. Keep your cards close and play them strategically. But Pruitt remained a problem in need of a solution. *My plan better work.*

CHAPTER 21

Entangled with a complicated patient requiring admission to the hospital, I missed lunch and worked straight through afternoon clinic. A glance at the clock alerted me to the late hour. If I wanted to leave by six, I had to hurry. Lady needed a walk.

Fifteen minutes later, I completed the last chart. As I bent over to retrieve my purse, the office door crept open. Rude.

Glistening blue eyes shone from around the edge of the door as Ken peeked inside. Without an invitation, he sat in the chair beside the door.

"Hey, Julia. Busy day?"

As chief of the department, Ken had access to all my patient statistical information and demographics. He knew how many patients I saw each day, their ages, diagnoses, and the length of their visits. I recognized his question as a polite prelude to something more substantial.

"Fine." Shouldering my purse, I locked the desk drawer. "I'm on my way out. Did you need something?"

He stood and exited the room. "No, simply checking up on everyone."

I shut and locked the door behind him. "Well, good night." I proceeded toward the clinic exit, irritated to find him traipsing along beside me. For someone who liked getting up close to people, he needed to stop wearing musk cologne. My nose itched.

"Are you heading over now?"

Confused, I regarded him. "Over where? I'm going home."

"You can't. We have a department dinner tonight."

"Have fun. I'm going home."

Ken laid a hand on my right arm. The glare I shot caused him to peel his fingers off.

He didn't apologize but said, "This is a group function, Julia. I expect you to attend."

My left leg slouched to the side. "The email read optional. Is this an official meeting?"

His face slumped. "No, it's informal."

I headed for the exit as soon as he said "No."

Like a lost puppy, he followed. "I still expect you to come."

"If this doesn't involve official Noughton business, I don't have to attend."

Pink bloomed along his jawline. "This is about being part of a team, getting to know each other, and being supportive."

His words might have carried more conviction if I hadn't known his history with April. Oh, and let's not forget the dildo, but who could?

"Ken—"

"No," he said, pointing a spindly finger at me, "I expect you to follow my lead. *I'm* chief here, not you. If I tell my team we're having a dinner meeting, I expect everyone to attend."

His supercilious tone struck me as funny until I noticed several of the medical assistants gawking at our exchange. I restrained the impulse to laugh, realizing this moment would define our working relationship. Although not scared of him, I wasn't prepared to openly challenge his authority—yet. Understanding his masculine ego needed a win, I conceded.

"Sure. I'll be there."

He would regret the tiny grin curling at the edge of his lips.

***

Traffic was heavy. A major problem in the California Central Valley—among many—was the lack of thoroughfares. Highway 101 was the primary, if only, major expressway from Ventura to Paso Robles. After running errands, I made my way to the restaurant to join the clinic pediatricians.

It took five minutes to find a parking spot in the shopping center. The night air had cooled. I parked far from the restaurant, desiring the exercise. I hadn't joined a gym since I moved from Goleta. Biking, running with April, and walking Lady helped, but my body felt neglected. At the restaurant entrance, I vowed to get back on a regular workout schedule and maybe take up kickboxing again.

A mixture of spices danced around my nostrils as I entered the establishment. From a side room off the entrance, I saw Juanita waving me over.

She gave me a short hug. "I didn't think you'd make it." Her voice lowered. "I heard about April and Ken." Her dark eyes questioned me.

Deciding not to respond to her teaser, I asked, "What's good?"

Together, we approached a buffet table covered with an abundance of Indian dishes. My stomach grumbled with impatience. Juanita listed her favorites. I had my preferences, but since I was unfamiliar with this restaurant, I accepted her recommendations. Instead of sampling the spread, I placed a personal order with the waitstaff. Buffet bars clashed with my style—and OCD. We were soon joined by Kim and Carter.

Kim set down her glass. "So, Julia, are you coming to Ken's pool party?"

The multicolored invitation arrived in my email weeks ago, but I hadn't replied. Weekends were precious. I wavered on whether to attend.

Juanita wiped her mouth and tossed her napkin on the table. "It's tons of fun. We get to spend an entire day with our illustrious leader and his spawn."

With his elbow, Carter nudged Juanita, smirking loquaciously. "You love it. Food, games, backbiting..." His list continued.

"I don't mind going," Kim interrupted. "But I hope it doesn't get awkward—like last year." Her gaze cut to Juanita, who looked at Carter.

Seconds passed as I waited for an explanation. Since no one spoke up, I asked the obvious. "What happened?"

They exchanged weighty glances. A nod of Juanita's head signaled Kim should relay the story.

Lowering her voice, Kim tipped her head in my direction. "Ken and his wife got into a *heated* argument."

Juanita shook her head. "No, they didn't. There was no argument. Ken yelled at her for a good three minutes."

"It was horrible," Carter said while chewing on some naan.

"Then what happened?" I asked, frowning. "Did someone say something to him?"

Simultaneously, their bodies slunk from the table. Conversation stalled. I glanced at each of them in turn, hoping for more. They didn't reply.

Carter scrubbed his mouth with a napkin, apparently trying to remove any signs of the conversation from his lips. He pushed his chair away from the table and stood.

"Excuse me, ladies. I plan to retire in five years. I should be going."

I watched him depart. "What was that about?"

Kim scooped up her plate and rose. "It's about keeping our jobs." She headed for the buffet table.

Juanita and I stared at each other for a moment.

She leaned back in her chair and crossed her legs. "Welcome to the coward's table."

"No one said anything. You simply allowed him to yell at her?"

Juanita shrugged. "I can't speak for everyone, but I didn't say anything because I didn't care. If it was one of their kids, maybe. If Nancy tolerates his behavior, why should I interfere? I take care of children, not adults."

"You don't believe spousal abuse leads to child abuse?"

She sighed deeply. "It can, but I've known Ken for years. He dotes on his children. They are well cared for. His wife is a moron. Ken would get one chance to yell at me. I've talked with her before about his behavior. She laughed it off, so I left it alone."

Though I didn't agree, I understood Juanita's position. Over the years, I'd implored women to leave their useless, abusive husbands, baby daddies, or fiancés. *It becomes trying.* As I rubbed my temples, a vision of Tamesha sprung into my mind.

"You're judging us," Juanita said.

"No. I'm thinking about what I would do."

Minutes later, Kim returned holding a plate overflowing with food. Talk returned to discussing patients. As we conversed, I saw April enter. She smiled and advanced toward our table. A noxious odor accompanied her approach.

She paused next to Ken, who was speaking with Carter and another physician. Although I couldn't hear their conversation, I noticed Ken's expression.

Those blue eyes darkened as a scowl creased his forehead. Ken and the other physicians abandoned April, chuckling as they departed.

Whatever he said made her flush. She fled from the room.

"Excuse me," I said to Juanita and Kim, having lost my appetite. I hurried after April but didn't find her in the main section of the restaurant. The foul odor intensified. What was that?

Rushing outside, I caught up with April and discovered the source of the odor.

"Hey." I laid a hand on her shoulder, and she turned around. "What's going on? And what's that smell?"

Tears flooded her eyes. "I can't…" Her body trembled.

"Tell me."

"Someone smeared feces over my car doors and windows." She shuddered. "I had to ask the maintenance staff for rags to clean it. Some probably got on my shoes."

"Did you take pictures?"

"Of course not."

"April—"

"No!" She shook me off and jumped in her car. She sped out of the parking lot burning rubber.

Before I re-entered the restaurant, I sent her a text. Forty minutes later, I departed with a large to-go tray tucked under my arm. Hopefully, Lady would forgive me for not walking her this evening.

April hadn't replied to my texts. I'd call her when I got home. On the way to my car, I noticed Ken standing in the parking lot.

He grinned and lifted his chin in my direction.

Asshole. I accepted his unspoken challenge.

CHAPTER 22

Once the office lights came on, I dropped my purse and started the computer. Another gorgeous day spent working inside.

When the EHR opened, I noticed a follow-up patient on my schedule with a knee injury. Recalling an email where the mom requested a knee splint, I checked the hall supply closet. Unable to locate one, I decided to look in another wing.

Since I had arrived at work early, I didn't expect to encounter anyone. As expected, I heard nothing as I entered A wing. The supply closet was positioned between Ken's office and the bathroom. Unfortunately, the equipment had not been arranged by size. I dove in and searched.

A tiny creak made me freeze. I listened, evaluating the source of the noise. It didn't recur so I returned to my search.

After five minutes, I located an appropriately sized splint and prepared to depart when Ken's office door cracked open. In an instant, I sprinted around the corner and down the hallway nearest the bathroom. As I rounded the corner, I heard his voice and another I didn't immediately recognize because it was so low.

Ken said, "If Howard gets promoted to administration, I plan to be the next chief medical officer at San Marguerite."

"Can you get the votes?" the other voice asked.

I strained, trying to place the voice. It sounded familiar, but—

Someone snorted.

"The medical director isn't voted in," Ken said. "Noughton's CEO and the administration appoints him."

"And you're *sure* you'll be voted in?"

Was that Carter?

"Oh, yeah. I've been negotiating for this position since I got hired."

"I'd like to be chief of peds when you leave."

"You keep helping me, and you will."

Feet shuffled around. From the noises, I couldn't determine who was moving where. Not wanting to be found eavesdropping, I hurried down the hall, turned around and walked casually toward the supply cabinet, hoping it appeared as if I had just arrived. Rounding the corner leading toward Ken's office, I ran into Carter.

"Oh, excuse me."

Carter blushed. "Hey, Julia. Good morning."

"Morning."

He rushed off.

Scatter, you rat. That reminded me to check the teddy bear camera.

***

Back in B wing, I placed the splint on my desk. The medical assistants had already roomed my first patient, so I donned a lab coat and hustled into the exam room.

"Hello, Mr. and Mrs. Tomas."

They returned my greeting as I stepped over children scattered around the floor of the tiny, cramped room. Why did the entire family have to come to the appointment? A two-month-old little boy wriggled on the exam table. After I pronounced the baby healthy, I returned him to the waiting arms of his mom.

The oldest child said, "I'm going to be a doctor."

"Me, too," her sister said.

"Well, I hope you become geriatricians because I will be needing one soon."

The parents laughed as I explained to the girls a geriatrician cared for older people. Though ignorant of the implication, they giggled and danced around the room. They sang out good-byes as I left. The music of a happy family. I missed it. There were many things I had forgotten about being part of a family.

Barely a minute later, my office door flew open, and April hurried inside with wide eyes and her hair in disarray. "Julia, would you please help me?"

In my rush to stand up, I bumped my knee against the desk. "What's wrong?"

"My schedule's crazy. The day just started, and I'm way behind."

"Sit down. Tell me what's going on."

"I can't. I have three patients waiting."

"Why?" My hand absently rubbed my bruised knee.

"I don't know. Someone added them to my schedule."

"Who? Forget it. I'll speak with Marsha."

"No." She took a deep breath and lowered her voice. "Please, just help me?"

"Of course."

"Could you see one of them? They aren't my assigned patients, so the parents shouldn't mind."

In the EHR, I moved two patients from April's schedule to mine. She gave me a quick hug before flying out of the room. At a more tempered pace, I followed.

The morning proceeded in a blur of appointments. I managed to see two of April's patients and all of mine on time. Instead of leaving for lunch, I went in search of the office manager. My hand hovered in front of her office door, but I didn't knock.

What would I say to Marsha? Would it help April or make her situation worse?

Better judgment suggested I figure out who added the patients to April's schedule on my own.

At my desk, I again brought up April's schedule. At the end of the screen, next to appointment time, I located the initials MC, Marsha Conroy. I had my answer. Now I had to decide what to do with it.

Damn. As my hot flashes kicked up, I turned on all the fans. This foolishness had started to stress me out. No, it was seeing the Tomas family. They reminded me of all I had lost.

Deep breaths, Julia. In the nose and out the mouth.

Jean came from a large Haitian family. We met during medical school. He attended state college, and I paid the heftier university price. We met at a social event. He was giving a dissertation on the advantages of some imaging technique—completely boring his audience—and I found his fascination with neurology endearing. He bought me dinner, and I gave him my number. We became a couple that night.

At fifty years old, he had been informed by an arrogant oncologist with absolutely no bedside manners to go home and put his affairs in order. After arranging our finances, Jean spent every possible moment with me and Evens. Chess had been their favorite game. Jean dazzled his son with gory stories about medical school and his neurology practice over the chess board. But there wasn't enough time.

Cancer ripped apart his body, leaving a broken shell where a former vibrant, robust man dwelled. Death sapped his strength, then his dignity. Incontinent and incapacitated, the reaper claimed him by organ system. Bowel, bladder, lungs, brain. When Jean's pained eyes forever closed, I was there holding his hands.

I had no idea how to proceed in life without him. He kept my secrets and understood my weaknesses. But after a time, I *had* moved forward—with Evens.

Like my parents, I had one child. Did they have any regrets? I didn't. Evens was enough. But now he was gone, and I missed him horribly. Tears wet my cheeks.

Minutes passed. I blew my nose and gazed out the window, admiring the families walking to and from the medical center.

Camile had invited me down for the weekend. Initially, I was disinclined to go, but now… Empty and lonely, I ached to reclaim my family. Maybe visiting Camile would improve my mood.

A beeping cellphone brought me out of the doldrums. I checked my personal phone, but the alert didn't come from it. At the bottom of my purse, I retrieved a burner phone reserved for special situations. Fumbling, I managed to answer before the caller hung up.

"Yes?"

"Dr. Toussaint?" Mrs. Jenkins asked frantically.

"What happened?"

Crying, she said, "It's Tamesha. She's in the hospital. Craig hit her."

Without replying, I hung up and rushed to the ER.

***

Automatic beige doors swung aside, and I ran into the ER bay up to the triage desk.

"I'm Dr. Toussaint. My patient was brought in by her mother."

Once she scrutinized my medical badge, the medical assistant directed me to a room at the end of the triage area.

When I opened the door, emotions washed over me. Momentarily, I became dizzy. Faces flittered across my consciousness—Jean, Thaddeus, Evens. Blinking them aside, I forced those memories away and focused on the battered child lying on the stretcher.

Mrs. Jenkins ran over, tears streaming down her face. Choked with sobbing, she explained what occurred. I didn't understand most of what she said. My gaze remained fastened on Tamesha.

The child's bruised face looked pained, her brow furrowed, and her cut, swollen lips downturned. An IV hung in her arm, and an oxygen nasal cannula looped at the bottom of her nostrils. As her mom spoke, I followed the rise and fall of her chest.

Heat flared across my body. Not a hot flash. This fire was internal, primal. Another injured innocent. How long would the blameless suffer at the hands of the wicked?

Assisting Mrs. Jenkins to a stool, I held her hand and promised I would help Tamesha—and I would.

"You over-empathize with others," Jean had said.

"Don't you care?" I asked, closing the bedroom door.

"I do, but you make their problems your own."

"Why is empathy a weakness?"

Jean had wrapped his arms around my waist, pulling me to his chest. I inhaled his cologne, nuzzling his neck.

"I didn't say it was a weakness, but there are consequences."

"Like fostering an abused child." I grinned.

He kissed my lips. "I don't regret bringing Thaddeus into our home. He's a wonderful child."

"Evens loves him like a brother."

"But he has a mother with serious problems."

"We can help her."

"Have you forgotten what happened the last time you helped her?"

151

I had.

As usual, Jean had been correct. But I had done what I believed to be necessary. And he forgave me. Who would forgive me now?

CHAPTER 23

Lush lawns rolled across this suburban neighborhood. I drove cautiously around children playing ball in the street, noting the contrast between this section of town and my own.

Lack of sidewalks deterred unwanted visitors. Posh homes settled far back on expansive lots. Though older, these sturdy homes had individuality unlike the planned subdivision where I lived, which offered five house varieties on postcard-sized lots with drought-tolerant front yards.

I didn't have to check my phone for the address. A line of cars extended in opposing directions from a rectangular mid-century home, signifying I had reached my destination. The unrelenting summer sunshine glinted off my front window. Shielding my eyes by bringing down the visor, I saw April salute as she exited her car. Executing a sharp U-turn, I parked behind her. She waited for me to remove my cake container, and together, we strolled up to the home.

Majestic trees full of leaves and wildlife surrounded the house like a canopy. Birds flitted along the calm skies while squirrels raced along thick tree limbs.

A cake dish nestled in my arms as I scanned the entryway. I wished I could say Ken's house sucked, but it was lovely. A well-manicured lawn framed by opulent rose bushes lined the walking path leading visitors up to the entrance. A kaleidoscope of colors dazzled my eyes. Meaty scents wafted over on the light breeze. I inhaled deeply.

More to myself than to April, I said, "Nice house."

She laughed. "I heard he loves this place. According to Juanita, new physicians are given the *tour*. Maybe he'll take us together."

Shooting her a side glance, I checked to see if she was joking.

She nodded. "It should be interesting."

"Hello." A woman opened the front door before we could knock. She had shoulder-length brown hair with blond highlights pulled back into a ponytail.

I noticed sweat glistening on her brow.

Holding a store-bought vegetable platter, April said, "Hello, I'm April Powell."

"I'm Nancy Brady. Come in, come in." She stepped aside, and we entered.

"I'm Julia Toussaint," I said, following behind April.

Nancy shook our hands and directed us where to deposit our dishes in the kitchen. As they chatted, my pace slowed. I surveyed the home, noticing tired furniture, outdated appliances, and worn dining room chairs. In the living room, a tall silver Coptic cross sat on the fireplace mantle. My eyes searched for and found a weathered Bible on a battered side table. The inside of the home in no way resembled the outside.

Two shrieking kids emerged from a side hallway. They scampered around Nancy begging for her attention and pulling on her arms, pre-teens about ten to twelve years of age.

The girl, who appeared to be the oldest, asked, "Mom, *now* can we go outside?"

Nancy spoke while arranging items on the dining room table. "Did you clean the game room?"

"Yeah," the girl said, rolling her eyes.

Flicking her hands toward the back of the house, Nancy dismissed them. "Go, go—and behave."

Both children yelled, "Thanks, Mom," before running outside.

Large sliding glass doors opened out over the backyard, which was more dazzling than the front. At least thirty people socialized around the spacious yard. Most I recognized as medical colleagues. I added my cake to the dessert table, listening as my hostess and April conversed.

Squealing from outside caught my attention. The yard resembled a domestic amusement park. I stood under a white pitched tent, observing children splashing in the pool.

April joined me on the stone patio.

"I'm going to find Ken and say hello."

Nancy stood beside me on the patio.

"Your home is beautiful," I said, basking in the joy of summer.

Shading her face with her palm, Nancy gazed over the yard. "At least on the outside." She laughed, stepping across the stone paver pathway to the grassy yard.

I followed. "This is a nicer part of San Marguerite. If I knew about this place, I would have bought a home here. I live in San Luis Obispo."

"I know. Ken told me all about you." Her head tilted slightly in my direction. "I'm sorry about your son."

My jaw clenched. I waited for what would come next, hoping it wouldn't be some spiritual platitude. "Thank you." I swallowed and changed the subject.

People dotted the lawn. Some gathered under shaded structures. Others huddled near the pool where children swam, giggling and amusing themselves despite the summer heat. A volleyball set occupied the middle area. A handful of people played. A group of five people, including April, surrounded Ken near a grill where smoke rose into the robin-egg blue sky.

Roasted aromas enticed. My stomach rumbled, but I quickly hushed it. I planned a brief, obligatory visit. If Ken hadn't insisted, I'd be home with Lady, digging around my garden. I caught Ken's eye, making sure he noticed my arrival. Thirty minutes should be sufficient. I had more important concerns than his ego.

Carrying a soda can, Ken abandoned the grill and headed in my direction. With a long face, April followed him for a few steps, hesitated, then joined a group of physicians near the pool. As he got closer, I manufactured a grin.

Behave. This is your boss' home.

Ken's face irritated me. Those gentle blue eyes contrasted with the obnoxious cologne he bathed in. He stirred conflicting emotions. Contrasts.

It reminded me of a couch where a body lay. A hand drooped over the edge. But that hand wasn't male. The fingernails were long and painted—like Dr. Griffith's. But this couch wasn't in her office. And the face. If I could focus. The hair was golden, and the complexion... Crumpled with blue lips. It wasn't me! It was—

"Hello, Julia."

Deep breath. Act normal.

Clenching my fists to stop my hands from shaking, I massaged my gold wedding band. Despite standing in the sun by a grill, not a drop of moisture dampened Ken's brow. Apparently, ghouls don't sweat.

"Good morning."

"I'm glad you could make it."

Fortunately, he didn't try to hug or shake hands. It would've created a scene.

"Come, let me give you a tour."

As we walked between the tents, I asked, "What about April? She'd probably like to see the place."

Ignoring my comment, he led me beside the pool, where he greeted his children and tossed them a beach ball.

"Be careful," he said, smiling down at them.

"Your gardens are lovely," I said, strolling beside him. "Did you do the work yourself?"

"It's my passion. An oasis—and it's cheaper than a vacation." He winked.

Yuck. I shivered.

He led me to the left corner of the yard, where a structure slightly larger than a tool shed stood. Once there, he opened the door and entered. Flicking on a central light, he stepped aside. His hand invited me to enter.

Though small, the building had been converted into an entertainment center. A large television occupied almost an entire wall. A U-shaped leather sofa sat in the center of the room. A dart board and wet bar were positioned against opposing walls.

"Nice," I said.

He frowned and looked in my direction. Perhaps he felt I should be more impressed. Reaching around me, he shut the door. Suddenly, alone with him in this tiny room, I felt claustrophobic. My skin tingled, signaling another hot flash. Needing air, I approached the door, determined to leave.

His hand darted forward but pulled back before making contact. My bent brows and clenched fists warned of the folly of such an action.

"Wait. I wanted to speak with you privately."

Though I didn't fear Ken—I could take care of myself—it would be inappropriate to beat up your boss on his own property. Besides, it would give Camile another reason to refer me back to a psychiatrist. I stepped toward the door for an easy exit if necessary. Folding my arms over my chest, I waited.

"Julia, you're a strong asset for the department. I'd like us to work together—make pediatrics stronger. The best medical center in Central California."

I hesitated. Had I misjudged him? Was he trying to mend fences?

"Sounds good."

His smile resembled a hyena. No, I hadn't been mistaken. The spell broke. I detected a pitch coming.

"If we want a strong department, we have to trust each other. Help each other."

"What do you want?"

"Simply your support. That's all."

My left brow arched.

He chuckled. "Fine. I want to be CMO of San Marguerite. You've got contacts in administration. Help me, and I'll take care of you."

"What about April?"

"What about her?"

"Oh, so, now, you're playing stupid."

His face flushed down to his burnt-red neck. We glared at each other. Before it became awkward, the shed's doorknob twisted. Because he stood behind the door, Ken jumped aside to avoid being hit.

Carter entered. His sun-kissed forehead wrinkled as his gaze fell over me. "Oh, Julia. I didn't know—"

"No problem. I was leaving."

Pivoting around Carter, my foot barely touched the grass outside when Ken said, "Think about it."

Without replying, I returned to the party.

Juanita sat under an umbrella with Kim and others. Glancing across the yard, I noticed April beside the pool, speaking with another physician.

As perspiration trickled down my neck, I slid under the umbrella. "May I join you guys?"

Several people said, "Sure."

From inside my purse, I removed a hand fan. "How are things?"

"Fine," said a beaming Juanita, who introduced me to her six-year-old twins, a boy and girl, and her husband before they trotted off to get food.

Stretching my legs forward, I leaned back into the chair.

Juanita tightened her braids. "I noticed Ken showed you his man cave."

"Umm-hmm."

"Did he ask you to join him in making the pediatric department the best in Central California?" She laughed at my gaping mouth. "I'm not psychic. He did the same thing to me when he became chief."

My head pivoted toward Kim. "You?"

She placed a fruit bowl on the table and finished chewing. "Yes. It seems to be a rite of passage—a privilege for future partners."

"Believe me. It wasn't a compliment."

As the children played, a vision of a youthful Evens speeding across the yard flashed before my eyes. He kicked a ball to Thaddeus. Their game play continued into the setting sunlight. Emotions scratched at the back of my throat.

"Juanita, your kids are adorable."

"They're driving me crazy," she said unconvincingly. "I enrolled them in summer camp to keep them busy."

Conversation became more domestic and personal.

Kim leaned across the table. "Don't tell anyone, but I'm pregnant."

My gaze widened, but I held my excitement in check when Kim's finger flew up to her mouth.

"Congratulations," I whispered. "But why are you keeping it a secret?"

She moved closer to the table. "I'm up for partner in November, and I don't want to blow it with Ken."

"Why would he care?"

"Because he's Ken," Juanita smirked. "And he likes to meddle in everyone's business."

"He's made derogatory comments before about female doctors taking long maternity leaves," Kim said.

"He's an ape." Juanita popped a grape into her mouth.

Over the next hour, Juanita spoke about her family and Kim about her pregnancy. It was refreshing to not have people tiptoeing around me when it came to children. Since Evens' murder, people avoided speaking about their children in my presence. While they meant to make things comfortable, they actually made it worse, highlighting the fact I no longer had a child. With Juanita and Kim, I could relax. Unfortunately, I needed to leave. Lady was waiting.

I hugged Kim and Juanita and returned inside the house. From the dessert table, I removed my cake from the carrier and transferred it onto a paper plate. Ken could have the cake, but I was taking my container home. When I turned around, Nancy hovered behind me.

"Excuse me."

"I'm sorry," she said. "Did I startle you?"

"It's your house." With the container under my arm, I proceeded toward the front door. Nancy remained at my side. "Thank you for inviting me. This place is beautiful."

She sighed. "The outside is. I wish Ken would let me do something about the interior."

"It's not bad."

Cutting her eyes in my direction, she gave me a knowing glance.

I laughed. "Okay, it could look better."

Nancy grasped my arm. "Come. Let me show you something."

As a polite guest, I permitted myself to be led away. We passed a bathroom and continued down a wide hallway. Pushing aside a partially open door, Nancy directed me inside a spacious room.

"This is the kid's playroom."

I entered a child's dream world. Brightly lit from three large windows facing the front yard, the walls were multicolored. A large television screen occupied an entire wall. I noticed a projector centered on the ceiling pointed toward the screen. On the wall surrounding the screen were DVDs and CDs stacked on floor-to-ceiling shelves.

Movie posters adorned the other walls. Fluffy bean bags punctuated the room. Three separate gaming systems and arcade games hugged the walls, along with three-foot speakers.

"This is incredible."

Nancy sat on a chair nestled before the windows. I took an adjacent seat.

Twirling strands of her hair between her pudgy fingers, she said, "Ken doesn't care about the rest of the house. The kids spend all their time in here or the pool—and their bedrooms look like something out of a design magazine. He wants them to be happy every day of their lives."

"What about you? What do you want?"

She paused, staring at me as if trying to understand the question. A minute elapsed. "I want a vacation away from home."

I relaxed back into the seat, interested in Nancy's comment. "Where would you go?"

"A spa." She grinned. "It doesn't matter where—just a place where I could relax and be pampered."

"Sounds nice. I hope you get there."

We sat peacefully, basking in the moment.

Eventually, I rose. "I should go."

Nancy started to rise. "I'll show you out."

Shaking my head, I waved her off. "No, you rest. I know the way out."

"It was nice meeting you, Julia. I hope to see you again."

After our goodbyes, I headed for the front door. Outside on the cement walkway, Ken materialized.

"I wondered where you went."

Damn. I readjusted the cake container under my arm, hoping Lady wouldn't soil the floor before I returned home. Sighing, I shifted weight to my left leg.

"What do you want?"

"I'd like to have you on my side." His deceitful crystal-blue eyes sparkled.

"You're chief of the department. By default, I'm on your side."

He sneered. "You know what I mean."

"What about April?"

"Why do you care about her?"

"She a friend."

"Humph." His nose twitched. "You could do better."

"Why are you acting like a dick to her?"

"Stay out of it."

"Stop harassing her."

His shoulders came to attention. "You and I can help each other."

"I'm afraid not. I'm faithful to my friends." I circled around him and marched away.

Ken's voice trailed after me. "Be careful. If I can't persuade you to help, I'll have to deal with you in another way."

In a fluid motion, I pivoted around and glared at him. A snarl curled at the corner of his mouth. He cackled and entered the house.

At the curb, I noticed April inside her car with her head resting on the steering wheel. I tapped on the window. She whisked away tears before scrolling down the window.

"What's going on?"

Her head trembled. Motioning for her to open the door, I rested on the passenger seat.

"Could you help me transfer to Goleta?" she squeaked.

Sliding closer to her, I said, "Tell me what happened."

"Can you?"

"Vacancies are slim to none. No one gives up a position in Goleta."

"Except you," she said in an accusatory tone.

"What—"

"This is becoming unbearable." Tears teetered on her eyelids.

I held her hand. "You can file a complaint."

"Not without damaging my career—again. It happened at my last job when I reported Ken." Her head slumped. "I might as well quit."

"April, you have to decide. Stay, change jobs, file a complaint… Whatever you choose, I'll support you."

She closed her eyes. Half a minute later, she gave me a tight grin. "Thank you."

"Call me." I exited the car, and she drove off.

From the car's rearview mirror, I noticed Carter standing on Ken's doorstep. A slight grin rested on his lips.

On the way home, I recalled Carter's manner regarding Ken and Bryce. Obviously, he knew about their affair. The teddy bear camera hadn't caught him in my office—yet. But he could've been in April's.

I hadn't decided if Ken had left the dildo on the office chair or Carter. Could Carter be acting as Ken's agent? Perhaps in exchange for considerations like vacation priority or fewer weekend shifts. Or Carter might be acting to assume Ken's position if the latter was promoted to chief medical officer.

What did I get myself into with this place? Too late now. I tossed the cake container on the passenger seat and headed home.

Ken's wife surprised me. Maybe my impression of her had been skewed by Juanita's comments. Nancy wasn't the mousy woman I expected. Clearly, she and Ken loved their children—his one redeeming quality.

Sweat trickled down my neck. I turned up the air conditioner and sped up. Lady expected a walk.

CHAPTER 24

At the top of the staircase, I leaned against the wall, panting. My calves throbbed. I trailed behind April and Juanita.

"Why couldn't we take the stairs?"

"Exercise is good for you." April smirked.

"Not after cycling twenty miles."

"That's what you get for showing off." She opened the conference room door. Monday's monthly staff meeting began in five minutes.

Yesterday had been especially charming. I spent most of Saturday in Santa Barbara. April and I cycled around San Marguerite on Sunday. I hadn't been showing off, just preparing. I needed to get in shape. Besides, Lady adored the outdoors. I hadn't wanted a dog, but now I couldn't imagine life without her.

As I sat down, the burner phone bumped against my thigh. Pruitt had left a note on my windshield with his number and a dollar amount. Presumably, payment for his silence. What did he believe I had done?

He required immediate attention. I reconsidered my plans, worried about bringing Lady along. She could also be of assistance but would pose a slight risk.

In the conference room, people surrounded the boxed lunches. Tables were arranged facing each other in a large rectangle. Ken and Marsha stood at the front of the room talking.

Carter sat near the front as usual.

Since I didn't want to smell Ken's oppressive cologne, I took a seat in the rear. Because of his cologne, I knew he'd been in B wing that morning. In the center of the room, April sat next to another pediatrician. Juanita sat beside me.

The meeting commenced. Ken's monotone voice reminded me of the mumbling, unseen adults in the *Peanut's* cartoons.

Uninterested, my mind drifted. Once, I shared with Jean how when bored, I plotted crimes. Considered the details, measured risks, and assessed potential consequences. It helped pass the time while engaging my mind. Jean would laugh, saying I'd be a good criminal because I maintained laser focus under stressful conditions. It had been a delightful, indulgent sin. But had it ever been more?

Dr. Griffith suggested I had criminal, murderous urges. Had fantasy ever become reality?

There had been a time when I considered taking that ultimate step. When I gazed down at Evens' broken body and when the district attorney explained Mrs. Copeland's history of multiple DUIs, I carefully plotted how to remove the woman who destroyed my life. But I didn't. I mean...I saw a body, but it hadn't been where I intended. It didn't fit with my meticulously coordinated schedule.

And it looked wrong. The hair and face. An afro. No, Evens wore his hair cut close. Thaddeus had fine hair in braids. And this hair was blond. Mrs. Copeland?

"Any questions?" Ken asked.

Snapped to the present, I observed people raising their hands, including April. Ken called on each person except her. As he returned to his presentation, April's hand lowered.

"Ken, you forgot someone," I interjected.

April's hand shot up.

Without saying her name, Ken looked in her direction. "Well?"

"Are you going to address scheduling?"

"I already did." He returned to the whiteboard.

"Not specifically. I'm finding other providers' patients on my schedule."

"We need to help each other. If you don't want to be part of our team, leave." Again, he returned to the presentation.

Without raising my hand, I said, "I agree with April. We're willing to help, but we shouldn't be imposed upon by inefficient providers and overscheduling. I'm frequently asked to see Drs. Dickerson's and Jacob's patients."

Mouths gaped in surprise. A bloom rose from Ken's neck to his forehead. April grinned.

In a half laugh, Juanita said, "Here we go."

After a slight pause, many voices spoke at once. Drs. Dickerson and Jacob protested about the size of their patient panels. Other physicians complained about the volume of patients on their schedules. Ken fought to regain control of the meeting. As the discussion grew more heated, Juanita rose to get a dessert, April quietly watched, and I exchanged glares with Ken.

The hour ended, but discussions continued outside the room. As I entered the staircase to return to my wing, I saw several physicians hurling questions at Ken.

Back in my office, I typed up patient notes. A short knock preceded April's entrance.

She kissed my forehead. "Thank you."

I shrugged. "I didn't do it for you."

"Didn't you?"

Before I could answer, she left. I returned to charting when I noticed on the EHR my patient had been roomed. I started out the door as it opened.

Ken rushed inside, shut the door, and plopped down in a chair.

"I have a patient," I said, draping a stethoscope around my neck. When I moved toward the door, he placed his hand across it.

"Make time."

Though I could've easily left, I didn't fancy the idea of Ken remaining alone inside my office. Outside of physically throwing him into the hall, allowing him to speak would be the quickest way to hasten his departure.

Perched on the desk's corner, I waited. "Well?"

His mustache wriggled. "I didn't appreciate what you did back there."

"All I did was speak the truth."

"No, you did more than that."

"I supported a colleague. Like teams do." I beamed.

Jumping to his feet, he leaned in my direction. "We can't work together if you openly challenge me during meetings."

In a lilting voice, I said, "Oh, you're leaving? Too bad. I'm sure administration can find a replacement."

"I'm chief of the department. *I'm* not leaving."

"Neither am I." Reaching around him, I opened the door.

He whirled around and stomped away. Unfortunately, the stench of his cologne remained.

In short time, I learned a lot about the dynamics at San Marguerite. I had no intention of ignoring Ken's behavior toward April. I wanted to be part of San Marguerite, and team members helped each other. But what could I do if she refused to file a complaint?

Since I was already late seeing my patient, I decided to make a call. Three rings later, the bass voice of Dr. Trevor Madison, CEO of Noughton's Goleta campus, boomed across the line.

"Julia. One of my favorite people."

"How are you doing, Trevor?"

"Fine, fine. Ready to come back?" He chuckled.

"No, not yet." Viewing the medical assistant signaling me, I said, "I need some information."

"Shoot."

"The chief of pediatrics, Ken Brady. What do you know about him?"

"Why, anything wrong?"

"No, simply curious."

"Yeah, right. Well, I've not heard anything bad—nothing good either. Why? You want to take over as chief?" His voice heightened.

"I wanted information about the department."

"Nice try, Julia. You never cared about office gossip unless it served a purpose. I underestimated you. Admin would love it if you took over in San Marguerite. The area is expanding. Noughton wants to dominate Central Valley's healthcare business."

"I see."

"You interested? Tell me what you need. Having you as chief in San Marguerite would be better than having you in Goleta. You could help me extend my control within Noughton."

The medical assistant stood at my door, mouthing the words, "Your patient is waiting."

"Trevor, I may be interested—if you returned the favor."

"Name it."

The medical assistant glared; her hands rose to her hips. I shut the door, resting my back against it.

"A friend wants to transfer to Goleta. I know pediatrics doesn't have any vacancies, but—"

"If you'll take over in San Marguerite, I'll make it happen. Who is it?"

I supplied April's name and information.

Knock, knock.

"Trevor, I have to go. Give my love to Judy and the kids."

This turn of events with Trevor required consideration. Becoming chief of pediatrics had not been my intention. However, things changed. Ken's abuse of his position shouldn't be tolerated.

Something Elie Wiesel, the Nobel laureate and Holocaust survivor wrote came to mind: "Indifference, to me, is the epitome of evil." No one could ever accuse me of indifference—too involved had always been my sin.

Don't go too far—like in Goleta.

Locking my door, I rushed to see my patient. From the corner of my eye, I saw April's open office door. I made a mental note to remind her to keep it closed and locked. I hurried inside the exam room.

CHAPTER 25

During lunch, I alternated between eating my sandwich and charting. From the corner of my eye, I observed Kim pass by the door. Ignoring her, I reviewed patient labs. Suddenly, she peeked inside.

"You busy?"

Startled, I hiccupped. "No, come in."

Kim also worked in this wing; her office was located on the other side of April's. She shut the door and sat down.

Tonight, I needed to walk Lady, or she'd keep me up all night whining. Although she was like a child who would never be toilet trained, I adored my dog. At home, she stayed close as a shadow. On walks around the neighborhood, she responded immediately to my commands. And when it stormed outside, she cuddled on my lap.

Sliding the chair closer to my desk, Kim asked, "Did you hear what happened with Carter's third-year resident?"

"Yes." Not making eye contact, I continued charting. "At least Juanita discovered his mistake before the baby's condition worsened. He's barely competent."

"I know. A third-year resident, and he asked me to look at a newborn's umbilical cord. He couldn't identify a simple granuloma." She glanced at my sandwich and water bottle.

Moving my meal to the other side of the desk, I said, "Not surprising. The other day, he discharged a newborn without noticing her jaundice. The bilirubin level was twenty-one. He blamed it on the child's complexion."

"Ridiculous."

"He's not ready to graduate. I had to supervise him three times this month when Carter had meetings. He needs more training."

"Who, Carter or the resident?"

A side glance revealed a large smile across her face.

"Carter's problem isn't his medical knowledge."

She laughed. "He's just a—" She halted mid-sentence as the door handle jingled.

Knocking on the door as he stepped inside, Ken glanced at Kim. "Am I interrupting?"

Kim jumped out of the seat. "I was leaving." She slipped by him and exited the room.

In the background, I heard her office door shut. Not waiting for an invitation, Ken took the seat she vacated, leaving him uncomfortably close to my desk. My nostrils flared, prepared for the olfactory assault of his cologne.

He leaned an elbow on my desk. "I wanted to speak with you."

His tone didn't allow dissent. I didn't bother explaining this was my lunch break, and besides trying to eat, I needed to complete charts, patient labs, and messages. I swiveled away from the keyboard and faced him.

"Yes?" I exhaled, relieved he'd either changed cologne or stopped bathing in it.

"It's about the resident evaluations."

Resident evaluations were due each quarter. Since I had already completed mine, his presence seemed unnecessary.

"Okay."

His scraggly mustache twitched. "I wanted to discuss your nomination for resident of the year."

"Dr. Lima."

"Reconsider. She's a problem resident and not right for our organization."

The part of my mind cogitating the amount of work I had to complete before afternoon patients arrived told me to shut up. But the spirited, pugilistic side of me asked, "What do you mean?"

He glowered. "The staff complain about her attitude. She's aggressive and haughty."

"Not true. Dr. Lima is direct—maybe blunt—but she expects people to do their jobs. She's very involved with patients and cares about the service they receive. I haven't noticed any haughty attitude."

"Well, other people have," he said dismissively.

"I don't agree. She's intelligent and confident."

"She's arrogant, mean, and bossy."

"If she reminds the staff to complete their work, she's doing her job."

"She's aggressive."

"That's a cultural misconception. When an intelligent, assertive African American woman is in an authoritative position, she's often misinterpreted as mean or bossy. A white man exhibiting the same behavior would be considered a confident leader."

Engorged blue veins laced across Ken's temples. Sitting up straighter in the chair, his hands gripped the edge of my desk. "Are you calling me a racist?"

Where did that come from? "I didn't say you were. I said it's possible Dr. Lima's behavior is viewed negatively because of inherent bias."

"So, you're saying because the medical assistants complain about her nasty attitude, they're biased, and we're all racists?"

Me doth think he protests too much.

Deep breaths, Julia.

My fault for broaching a sensitive topic when I was tired and busy. Ken was already in a snit when he entered my office. Now he was pissed, and I'd wasted valuable time.

"I apologize—"

"You better." He sneered.

Heat mushroomed from the core of my body. Not a hot flash this time—I wish it were. In a rush, I stood up and slammed the office door shut.

With a widening gaze, Ken stood.

"I don't know who you think you're dealing with," I said as my finger darted in his face, "but let me make something clear." I stepped toward him, my chest heaving. "Don't come into my office disrespecting me. Don't yell at me, and don't play your macho mind games here. I can break your sorry ass as easily as snapping a twig."

As my temper cooled, I returned to the desk, giving Ken an easy berth to exit. Instead of leaving, he glared. Reflexively, my hands balled into fists. I thought I might actually use my kickboxing skills.

Maybe half a minute elapsed before I noticed his countenance change. Similar to a slow summer swell, his lips crept upward. Like a maniacal clown, he grinned, his lips pulled back, revealing his perfect teeth. He acted happy, possibly excited.

Disgusted, my face scrunched up as if I smelled something rotten.

He chuckled. "We're a lot alike, Julia—own it. We could work well together. As CMO, I could appoint you chief of pediatrics. We could run San Marguerite." Departing, he spoke over his shoulder. "Let me know."

I rushed toward the door and locked it. In a daze, I wandered around the office. Books, photos, and magazines streamed before my eyes, but I didn't register them.

Stumbling to the desk, I pulled up the DSM, a diagnostic and statistical manual on mental disorders. In the months immediately following Evens' murder, I checked it often to compare my emotions against the criteria for depression. Now, I reviewed it for the characteristics of narcissism and antisocial personality disorders. There should be a classification for self-obsessed racists.

Sociopath or psychopath—I couldn't remember the distinction. Both were listed under the umbrella term anti-social personality disorder. Laypeople often used them interchangeably. It didn't matter to those they hurt.

Psychiatry was my least favorite rotation in residency, but I understood antisocial personality disorders—especially since my psychiatrist suggested I suffered from psychosis. Dissatisfied not to find a picture of Ken under narcissists, I closed the browser.

Minutes passed. Despite Ken's demand, I had no intention of changing my resident evaluation, but I would be more cautious about discussing cultural diversity around him. What was I going to do about Ken's offer?

Trevor wanted me to assume the position of chief to solidify his control within Noughton. Ken had similar aspirations. Two men trying to use a woman to achieve their goals. Neither truly cared what I wanted—or what would be best for me. Jumbled thoughts made my head throb. I needed time to consider the options.

My cellphone beeped. The screen read *Anjelah*.

"Hello."

Her voice came fast and at a high pitch. "Julia, Mrs. Jenkin's boyfriend showed up at the kids' school. I asked Sharon to pick them up. Mrs. Jenkins is frantic."

With thoughts on Ken, I said, "We knew this might happen, but she insisted on keeping them in the same school."

"I thought you'd want to know."

Quickly, I said, "We'll transfer them to the apartment tonight. It's not fully furnished, but it's safe. Tell her not to contact him again."

"Oh, you can bet your ass I did."

After discussing arrangements with Anjelah, I hung up. My hand reached for the sandwich when a glance at the EHR reminded me a patient had been roomed.

Tonight, I would help Mrs. Jenkins. The simplest way to deal with Ken would be to become chief. However, it would take time and effort to remove him. Today, he got to me. Bad mistake.

According to *The Art of War*, one of the five dangerous faults which may affect a general is a hasty temper, which can be provoked by insults. Once Trevor approved April's transfer to Goleta, Ken lost his leverage.

Grabbing my hand fan, I put on my lab coat and headed for the exam room.

CHAPTER 26

A yellow-orange streak of sunlight glowed across the darkened sky. Despite the insulated winter coat, my body shivered. November was not an ideal time to sit outside in a cold car, but I needed to verify Mrs. Jenkins' story about her deadbeat, abusive boyfriend.

For the past month, she and her children had been living in an apartment SOS maintained for emergencies. When I spoke with her last week, she claimed Craig stalked her, often parked outside the apartment complex, and had tampered with her vehicle. She'd replaced two tires in as many weeks and discovered explicit photos of women—usually naked and brutalized—taped to her car windows.

Anjelah encouraged her to file a restraining order, which Mrs. Jenkins had done and received. It made little difference, though. When her tires were slashed, the police requested proof that her boyfriend had committed the vandalism. Of course, she didn't have any. She was busy working overtime, caring for her children, and trying to piece together a life independent of violence and drug abuse.

Thus, I sat in a cold vehicle, trying to confirm her story. I considered drinking more lukewarm tea. My bladder tightened, vetoing the idea. Squirming, I tried to placate my back, which whined its disapproval of the uncomfortable seating arrangements. My watch read 5:30 a.m. As I reconsidered my decision to babysit Mrs. Jenkins and her children, I spotted movement in the parking lot.

A shadowy figure slowly crept between the cars. Head low, the individual wore a ball cap and oversized jacket.

I watched as a gloved hand reached out and grabbed the door handle of Mrs. Jenkins' car. My bladder clenched. I sat up in the seat and readied the camera. Clicking away at the figure, I waited for the person to turn in my direction, I needed a better head shot. Although *I* knew the stalker was Craig, the authorities required more substantial proof. A picture of him tampering with Mrs. Jenkins' car should be sufficient to arrest him for violating the restraining order.

Light from a streetlamp glinted off something in the person's hand. In an instant, a car sped into the lot, its headlamps illuminating the person kneeling beside the tire. The individual stood up, highlighted by the approaching car lights.

My camera snapped off shots. I obtained a clear picture of a man with a paltry, grizzled goatee staring wide-eyed at the car. A second later, the vandal sprinted away. Someone ran out of the apartment building and jumped into the car, which quickly sped out of the lot.

Ignoring the speeding vehicle, my gaze followed the fleeing boyfriend. With my headlamps off, I started the car and followed. Although I had him on camera, I wanted more. I spotted where he'd parked on a side street adjacent to the apartment entrance.

Craig started his Camaro, executed a sharp U-turn, and proceeded down the street away from the apartment building. I wanted to see where he went after his attempted vandalism. When he turned right onto a main street, I switched on my headlights. Nothing in medical school prepared me for this, but I learned fast. Paranoia fueled this secondary education.

Running stop lights and making endless turns, he eventually returned to the pink house.

Once Craig pulled into the garage, I drove away. Over the past weeks, I'd observed his routine, learned his habits.

From the moment I listened to Tamesha's story about life in the pink house, I was determined to make sure it didn't happen again. Noting the time, I calculated an opportunity to return home and shower before work—maybe even walk Lady.

CHAPTER 27

A new workday and another chance to irritate the fractious ego that was Ken. Before I reached the sidewalk leading to the outpatient medical clinics, I detected something amiss. Scanning the area, I searched for familiar faces.

A waving April hurried from her car. She jogged to catch up with me. But she hadn't caused my skin to prickle. Someone unfriendly was watching me. Where are you, Pruitt?

"Thanks for waiting," April said.

"No problem."

We fell in step together as my gaze swept across the employee and visitor parking lots. When we reached the sidewalk, perspiration drizzled down my arms. On a bench not a hundred yards away, I recognized Pruitt.

An unlit cigarette dangled between his cracked lips. Incrementally, as we came nearer, he tapped a wristwatch, gesturing for me to call. I contemplated the next steps in dealing with him when April spoke.

"My family wants to visit for Thanksgiving. But I have to work."

Listening to April with half my brain, I observed Pruitt.

"It's more convenient for me to drive down on Thursday and back for Friday clinic. I…"

He was becoming quite bold. Once I was abreast of where he sat, my vision dimmed. A woman's smiling face appeared.

No, she was shouting. A child handed her a glass. The child had wavy hair, not fine. It looked dark, but lack of lighting could be the cause. But Evens had a short afro with little hair. Thaddeus had fine jet-black hair. I didn't understand.

Don't give in, Julia. You're stronger than this.

As I passed the bench, he glanced up. My finger grazed my wedding ring. Pruitt's scrutiny pressed upon my back, now damp with perspiration. It seemed like he was trying to peer inside my brain. I felt his gaze all the way to the medical center entrance.

"I was hoping to spend Thanksgiving with Lupita and Camile," April said. "Lupita is going to fry a turkey. I've never had it. But my mom would freak out if I didn't spend Thanksgiving with family."

Lost in my own thoughts, I simply nodded.

April's voice softened. "I love my family, but...I don't like them. They always want something from me."

"They're family, not your captors. You're not obligated to give them all your free time—or money."

"Easy for you. They don't call, making *you* feel guilty."

"They manipulate you only if you let them."

She swiped a badge across the door reader leading into B wing. "I try, but I'm not like you. I need family in my life."

I placed a hand on her shoulder as we reached the office door.

"April, you have friends. And often, they're better than family."

Her tiny smile was the last nice thing about that day.

Clinic started busy and remained so all day. Fall ushered in a flood of colds and sniffles, and flu season had barely started. At the end of the day, April stopped me in the hall.

"How about dinner?"

"I have to walk Lady, but if—"

"Julia," Ken said, acknowledging me with a head nod.

I replied similarly.

April said, "Hello, Ken."

Without answering, he strode past us into Bryce's office at the end of the hall near the restroom.

April flushed. "I better finish my charts." She entered her office.

Likewise, I entered my office. A half hour later, someone attempted to enter, but I had locked the door, desiring seclusion to complete my work. For a second, I considered ignoring whomever it was but decided not to be antisocial.

Ken's smug face greeted me.

Next time, don't answer.

I returned to the computer. He walked behind me as I typed. My jaw tensed.

"You haven't signed up for the Christmas party yet."

"I won't be there, but you have a good time."

Swiveling around, I met Ken's glowering, supercilious face.

"What do you mean you won't be there? You have to come." Angry frown lines crisscrossed his sunburnt forehead.

Not this again. I sighed with fatigue. Ken required more effort than Lady.

"I stopped celebrating Christmas when Evens became an adult."

He rushed toward the door and closed it.

Crap. With the door shut, I braced for another one of his melodramatic tirades.

"This Christmas party is about supporting our staff. They look forward to this yearly event. And I expect you to be present."

A semi-religious holiday celebration wasn't mandatory. This was California, the land of liberalism. I took a moment to reflect before capitulating.

"If it's important to you, I'll go." With a shrug, I returned my attention to the computer.

"Good." He exited.

Like any control freak, he had to speak the final word.

Though not a misanthrope, Ken aroused my distrust and suspicion. What disturbed me most was whether his peculiarities reflected the ethos of Noughton at San Marguerite, or simply the bastard running their pediatric department.

Minutes elapsed before I returned to the EHR. After charting, I opened my emails and searched the trash folder to retrieve the notification about the Christmas party. I donated to the fund and returned the RSVP.

Ken would need to be dealt with—which reminded me I needed to call Trevor. The latter wanted an answer about my interest in becoming chief of the department, but I needed assurances about April's transfer to Goleta. Although becoming chief of pediatrics in San Marguerite—let alone chief medical officer—had not been the plan. If it secured April a transfer, I would.

Perhaps I should hint to Ken about the possibility of me becoming an administrator. That would make his tan melt. It might also place Ken on notice about his position being in jeopardy.

Ken rose to third place on my to-do list. However, more pressing matters required attention. Abusers took precedence over narcissists—and blackmailers.

CHAPTER 28

Cool fall weather made long walks tolerable despite the menopausal hot flashes. Lady and I must have walked for at least an hour when she rounded the corner near the house a half minute before I did. She should be leashed, but she obeyed my commands and knew her way around the neighborhood. Once I had the doggy door installed, she'd be more independent.

As I caught up with her, my cellphone rang. "Hello, Camile. How's everyone?"

"Are you running?"

"Yeah—no. I had to catch up with the dog. We went for a walk."

"First, you didn't want a dog. Now, you treat her like a child."

"No, I don't," I said more strongly than intended. "I treat her like any living creature should be treated—with respect and care."

"Julia, you *adore* that dog, and she obviously loves you. Too bad you didn't get a dog sooner."

Evens had begged for a dog, but I had always refused. Not liking the direction of this conversation, I said, "I have to go—"

"Wait. I called for a reason. When was the last time you spoke with Thaddeus?"

I didn't want to admit how long it had been. "Not sure. Why?"

"There was something on the television about a drug bust. I thought I recognized Tonya."

"Damn." I unlocked the front door, and Lady trotted inside. "I'll make some calls."

After I hung up with Camile, I called my lawyer.

"I'll check the Santa Barbara arrest records," the lawyer said. "Do you want me to investigate bail options in case she was detained?"

"Please." Placing the phone on speaker, I lifted the sweaty shirt above my head and tossed it into the hamper.

"Fine. Anything else, Dr. Toussaint?"

I paused. "There's a minor child involved. Tonya Frye had a prior case with child protective services. Contact them about any current open complaints."

The lawyer clarified a few issues before ending the call.

Without taking a shower, I changed into tan cargo pants and a long-sleeve cotton shirt. Covered my hair with a scarf and laced up my high-top sneakers. I applied enough DEET to send a small child into convulsions.

In the living room, I found Lady lying on her back with her limbs spread wide.

"Not an attractive pose for a lady."

Without altering her position, she barked and farted.

"Nice. We'll work on manners next."

I stepped into the backyard. Before sunrise this morning, I dug up the metal box I buried under a small lemon tree. Now, I carried it around the side yard into the garage, where I unlocked it and removed a black vinyl bag.

Before I returned inside, I placed the bag inside the trunk. Lady hadn't changed position.

"Okay. Time to go. We've got work to do."

Scrambling to her feet, Lady followed me around the house as I retrieved several more items. When everything had been gathered, we headed out for our appointment.

***

The San Marguerite nature preserve had rudimentary, poorly tended walking trails overgrown with vegetation. It offered none of the accoutrements of modern parks and consequently had few visitors—a perfect place to meet Pruitt, who suggested the location.

As a precaution, I surveyed the area several times after consenting to a meeting. Sprawling coast live oak trees encircled the parking lot. Adjacent to the preserve, a large walking trail extended for miles, meandering around the southern part of the city. Tall, wild, straw-colored grasses extended like a sea in every direction.

We scheduled the appointment for six o'clock. I arrived at four to make adjustments to the surroundings. I installed two cameras around the parking lot and sensors along the trail to alert me if someone approached. I decided to bring Lady along. She added credence to my appearance as a jogger. I secured the collar around her neck and waited.

Around five o'clock, I spied Pruitt drive into the lot. I lay in the grassy field approximately twenty yards away. With my head down, I observed him from a hand-held screen linked to the cameras I concealed in the trees.

Pruitt circled the lot in his station wagon, parked a moment, then left.

Lying on the hard, rocky ground, my body ached. I checked the time. Lady whined. Without rising, I removed a doggy treat from my pocket and tossed it to her.

She snapped up the treat and laid back down beside me.

At five minutes before six, Pruitt returned. This time he parked near the entrance. He exited the idling car but remained beside the driver's side door.

At six o'clock, I sent a text.

NOT COMING, BAG NEAR LARGE TREE WITH BURN SCAR.

Seconds later, I observed him reading a cellphone screen. He glanced around the area. Removing a cigarette from above his ear lobe, he lit it and took a few puffs while fiddling with the phone.

My burner phone buzzed.

THAT WASN'T THE DEAL.

After a few more drags on the cigarette, he threw it down and strode across the lot. He walked along the border, inspecting the trees. For several minutes, he stared up into the tree branches.

If he searched for the cameras, he would be disappointed. One was hidden in the eye of a woodland creature inside a hollowed-out portion of a tree stump. The other was in the stop sign at the entrance into the preserve.

Pruitt walked over to a large oak partially burned around its base. He removed the black vinyl bag I hid and looked inside.

Things were going according to plan when Lady wandered off.

Shit. I taught her not to approach strangers, but, apparently, she needed a refresher course.

Sniffing around the parking lot, she came within five feet of Pruitt. He whistled, bent down and held out his hand.

If he hurt her... I used the dog whistle. Lady barked but didn't return. Dammit.

Calm down, Julia.

Lady inched toward Pruitt. From a few feet away, he bent down and flicked a lit cigarette at her. With a sharp cry, she dashed toward the trees.

Pissed, I rose and started toward the lot when I heard Lady growl and bark.

Kicking in her direction, Pruitt said, "Go away, bitch. Get outta here." He waved his arms wildly.

Baring her teeth, Lady growled, barked a few more times, then ran away. Several minutes later, she came to my side. After licking my head, she settled beside me.

I slipped her another treat while watching Pruitt. He returned to the car, tossed the bag inside, and sat there.

The sensor I placed along the trail beeped. A couple and their dogs approached.

Grabbing Lady by the collar, I said, "Stay."

Two dogs left the trail and sniffed the grass around us. Fortunately, the couple called them back, and they continued along the trail.

Lifting my body in a plank, I stretched my muscles. What was he waiting for? If he didn't leave soon, I'd have a butt full of chiggers. Several lizards had passed by. There better not be any snakes. A bird had already crapped on my shirt sleeve.

My phone buzzed. Pruitt.

I SAID 30. U SHORT 10.

Deliberately waiting before I replied, I sent a short text. SELL THE DRUGS AND MAKE UP THE DIFFERENCE.

He sent a happy face emoji.

Shaking my head, I whispered, "Jackass."

Sunlight decreased. Pruitt turned on his headlights and exited the preserve.

Several more joggers passed by on the trail. A dog barked at Lady but didn't approach.

I waited a half hour before I rose. Shaking dirt from my body, I trotted up to the jogging trail.

"Ready to go home?" I asked Lady.

We jogged lightly; practicing with April had helped. It took an hour to reach the car, which I left in a different park along the same trail. Once inside, I checked the burner phone for messages from Pruitt. Nothing. Good. I shut down the phone and tossed it in the glove box. It might be useful later.

Lady climbed into the passenger seat.

"We'll go back to the preserve to retrieve the cameras tomorrow. Momma needs a bath."

Bark.

I smiled. "With Jean gone, I guess I'll have to share my thoughts with you."

With her back paws, Lady scratched her ears.

"Exactly. It'll satisfy my itch."

Hopping in back, Lady stretched along the seat and laid her head on her paws.

"Rest, girl. You did well today. Although, you scared me when you got near Pruitt. Momma told you not to approach strangers."

Lady expended a small whine. A few minutes later, I noticed she'd fallen asleep.

Watching traffic, I thought about the next step in my plans. Momentarily, I considered connecting Pruitt with Dr. Griffith. She had lied, and such a sin shouldn't go unpunished. A person should be able to trust their priest, lawyer, and doctor.

On my last day in her office, fear sparked in Dr. Griffith's eyes with that click. She understood I had recognized the sound of a recorder. Why would she be afraid unless she hadn't erased the tapes I gave her?

Her lame attempt to gaslight me and dismiss my suspicions had failed. How many judges, lawyers, and professionals had she illegally taped? More importantly, what had she done with the information?

Let it go, Julia. She can't hurt you.

Right. Move on. Active threats had to be addressed.

What would Pruitt do with the drugs? Given his track record, he knew how and where to sell them, and he clearly needed the money.

Time would reveal if he kept his word and stopped bothering me. If he persisted and contacted me again…

People with skeletons buried in their pasts shouldn't dig around another person's yard.

CHAPTER 29

My schedule looked as usual. While I checked patient messages, my cellphone beeped.

NEED 2 TALK URGENT

I hadn't spoken with Tonya for about a month. Camile had been correct about the drug bust in Santa Barbara. Tonya had been detained but not arrested. I hadn't been able to reach her, but now she wanted to meet. This communication following the payoff to Pruitt confirmed my suspicions.

Ping, ping.

The cellphone display read *"Mom."*

"Hi, Momma."

"That was quick. Were you on a call?"

"No. Is everything okay?" I asked while preparing patient charts.

"Julia, you need to talk to your daddy. He doesn't want to pay to check his bag, so he's bringing one pair of pants, two shirts, and four changes of underwear. I told him that was nasty. He can't wear the same pair of pants for five days."

Daddy must have been listening because I heard him shouting in the background.

"As long as I wear deodorant, I won't stink."

Trying not to laugh, I said, "No one cares if Daddy smells."

Momma spoke more to him than to me. "It's embarrassing. Being old doesn't mean you can't look your best."

Though entertaining, I had work to do. "I'll speak with Daddy later tonight. I have to go."

"Where are you going?"

"I'm at work."

"Oh, right. What day is it? I thought it was Sunday."

"Bye, Momma. Love you." I hung up and returned to patient messages.

Thanksgiving was next week, and I had several unresolved problems—issues I wanted addressed before the holiday.

Usually, Thaddeus spent Thanksgiving with me and Evens. If Tonya was sober, she attended. Thaddeus and Evens grew up together. I fostered their relationship, hoping Evens would grow to love Thaddeus as a brother—and he had.

"Mom," Evens had said, "don't forget the pumpkin pie."

"Yeah, my favorite," Thaddeus had added.

Evens chuckled. "Last year, you ate more pie than turkey."

Thaddeus smacked Evens' shoulder. "Well, you ate enough for both of us."

I stared at a Christmas photo of them together opening presents the Christmas before Evens' last bike ride. Since Evens' murder, Thaddeus and I spent the holiday with Camile and Lupita. Being around other children helped Thaddeus cope—at least, I believed it did. Besides, my house had become a mausoleum for my dead son. Camile's place exuded warmth and gaiety.

Before my parents arrived, I needed to decide whether to have them stay with me or at Camile's. While I worked, they might get bored at my place. Thaddeus would be here, though. His smile could dazzle a crowd—or was that Evens'?

The EHR alerted me to a patient's arrival. Tonya would have to wait. Before I left the office, I texted her.

Where? When?

I grabbed a lab coat and headed for the patient exam room.

Thirty minutes later, despite completing an exam and history, I was no closer to discovering the source of the teen's abdominal pain. While the father berated his daughter for wasting time, I unobtrusively reviewed my schedule on the EHR. Since the next patient was a no-show, I had more time.

While explaining proper dietary habits and exercise, I printed a handout and handed it to the father. "Email me a three-day food diary, and we'll discuss how to proceed." With the appointment concluded, I proceeded toward the door.

The father stood and shook my hand. "Can we get some blood work done or an x-ray?"

I pivoted back inside the room. "What are you worried about?"

"Doesn't she need blood work since she's having pain?"

Another discussion ensued. In the interest of time, they agreed to provide a three-day food diary. If I noticed anything concerning, I would order lab work. Engrossed in her cellphone, the teenager could care less.

In the hallway, I bumped into April.

"Oh, hey. I wanted to invite you to Thanksgiving. My parents are coming down, and we're eating at Camile's."

"Thanks, but I made other plans."

Following her into the office, I shut the door behind me. "With whom?"

She laughed. "My family, of course."

I frowned. "You sure?"

"Julia, they get on my nerves, but I still love them."

"Sorry. I just meant you have so much fun with Lupita and Camile."

A blush spread across her face. "I do." She collapsed in the computer chair.

"Come with us. I'll pick you up, and we'll drive down together."

"I can't. My mom would have a fit."

"April, you're an adult. Spend Thanksgiving wherever you want."

"It's not that easy."

"It should be."

"Oh, my next patient is here," she said, circling around me. "Later."

I shut her office door as she headed down the hall. Ken rounded the corner and barged into her. He grimaced and didn't apologize.

"Excuse me," April said and entered the exam room.

Uninterested in speaking with him, I entered my own office, shut, and locked the door. A second later, a knock sounded quickly followed by the knob turning.

Hell. I opened the door and returned to my desk.

Ken took a seat beside the door.

While waiting for the computer to load, I faced Ken, raising my brows, questioning his presence. He didn't bother with preliminaries.

"You lied."

My back stiffened. "I told you, don't come into my office disrespecting me."

"Huh. You don't deserve respect. I asked you the first day you arrived here if you wanted my job, and you said no."

"At the time, I didn't."

"Stop it. I know you spoke with Dr. Madison about becoming chief. Do you deny it?"

"My conversations are none of your business."

"Anything involving this department is."

"If you took care of *this* department, you wouldn't have to worry about losing your position."

The corner of his lip curled into a snarl. "You're out of your league."

"I was about to say the same thing."

He stood. "If you don't want to work with me, Julia, leave before something bad happens to you."

I grinned. "Well, bless your heart."

"You've been warned."

"Be careful who you trust," I said, swerving back toward my desk. "Carter is a duplicitous ally."

"What do you mean?"

"Duplicitous? Check the dictionary."

His sunburnt face reddened. "I meant about Carter."

"Watch your back. Screwing the staff isn't your only besetting sin."

He left my office, slamming the door.

Before I continued charting, I locked it.

***

Daylight savings time brought sunset earlier in November. I shut the office shades and turned off the overhead light. If I hurried, Lady and I could complete our evening walk before it became too dark. I headed toward the visitors' lot. It didn't take long to identify Tonya's car.

She looked ghastly as if a child had applied her make-up with a trowel. Raccoon eyes encircled her injected conjunctiva touched off with thick fake eyelashes. Tonya rolled down the driver's side window.

"Do you want to go somewhere and talk?"

"This is fine," she said, sniffling.

An alarming odor of mouthwash greeted me. No one used a gallon of mouthwash unless they wanted to cover up another odor.

My shoulders slumped. "You've been drinking again."

"No, I haven't." Her loud reply garnered the attention of several passersby.

195

Repeated questioning produced the same denials of no alcohol or drugs. Skeptical, I let it go. If she wasn't back on street drugs, it had to be alcohol—copious amounts from her appearance.

"Why did you quit your job?"

"I found another one."

"Where?"

"None of your business." She sat up straighter. "I can take care of myself."

Since when? "Why did you want to speak with me?"

Leaning her head out the window, she lowered her voice. "You tell me about the drugs and money. They belonged to Kevin. I should get half."

My survey of the parking lot failed to uncover Pruitt, but I recognized his involvement in Tonya's presence.

"You need to speak with a therapist. Those hallucinations are going to get you into trouble again."

"I'm not hallucinating."

"Right. Delusional is the correct term. It's from the drugs."

"I'm not using," she shouted, starting the engine.

Shrugging, I said, "CPS can find out with a drug test. If this continues, I'll have to call them. I'm required to report abuse."

"Stop threatening me. I'm clean."

Burning tires, Tonya ripped out the parking lot, barely avoiding pedestrians.

In the employee lot, I had come within a yard of my car when Pruitt stepped from behind a tree. He tossed aside a smoldering butt and headed in my direction. A grin teetered on his lips.

Deep breath.

"Dr. Toussaint. I see you spoke with Tonya."

"What have you done? She was clean. You got her hooked again."

"Tonya's a grown woman, who makes her own decisions."

"Like that car? What do you want from her?"

Inserting a cigarette between his teeth, he lit it. "I've gotten what I needed from her. But you still owe me."

I walked toward the car door. "Stay away from me." From the corner of my eye, I noticed people scattered throughout the parking lot.

Pruitt grabbed my arm. "Where'd you get those drugs? And the money."

"Get away from me and leave Tonya alone," I shouted.

From an adjacent row, a fellow physician approached. "Julia, are you all right?"

Removing the cigarette from his mouth, Pruitt withdrew.

"Thank you. I'm fine." I entered the car and reversed out of the parking spot.

Pruitt glared.

At what I thought to be a deliberately slow pace, he crossed in front of the car and headed toward the visitors' lot.

As I waited for the gate arm to rise, my gaze followed Pruitt. As he returned to the visitors' lot, Carter approached him. I stopped at the edge of the medical center campus. From the rearview mirror, I witnessed them conversing.

The light turned green, and I proceeded forward. On the drive home, I considered the possibilities. Would Pruitt confide his suspicions to Carter? What would the latter do with the information?

Carter desired the position of chief of pediatrics. How far would he go to secure Ken's blessings? I couldn't be sure. But if Carter wanted to be added to my to-do list, so be it.

CHAPTER 30

The Santa Barbara airport seemed unusually busy, even for the weekend before Thanksgiving. I shuddered to imagine how busy it would be on Wednesday.

By the time Thaddeus and I exited the highway and turned left onto Fairview Avenue South, traffic congestion had increased. Earlier, I picked Thaddeus up from school and checked him out.

In the spring when Tonya demanded I speak with her at the school prior to taking Thaddeus away for Easter break, I had her sign a release granting me the authority to remove him from school for vacations and holidays. Per her usual modus operandi, Tonya refused to answer my calls about her plans for the holiday week.

While I drove, Thaddeus called Daddy. My parents were standing out front at the departures section of the airport as we pulled up. Thaddeus jumped out of the passenger seat before the car stopped. He helped Daddy secure suitcases in the trunk before following Momma into the back seat.

"Hi."

"Hey, baby girl." Daddy rode shotgun. He kissed my cheek then adjusted his seatbelt.

Momma gave me a kiss. From the rearview mirror, I watched Thaddeus lean across the seat and kiss Momma's cheek.

"Hi, Grandma."

Turning aside, I quickly wiped the tears away. I had forgotten he referred to them as grandparents. After Evens died, I never expected to hear those words again. How did my parents feel about it?

Thaddeus had become part of our family since the day I informally adopted him. We fostered him during Tonya's bouts of addiction. From the moment I saw those enormous brown eyes, I was committed.

Tonya had been more than willing for me to welcome him into our home. She probably would have surrendered him if I had requested. Her interest in Thaddeus had always been fleeting. And Evens adored Thaddeus as much as I did. Had I slighted Thaddeus while mourning Evens?

"Mom," Evens had asked, "why am I an only child?"

"Because your dad and I wanted one special baby, and we got him." I wrapped Evens in my arms, and we curled up on the king bed. "Do you miss having a sibling?"

"Not with Thaddeus around." Evens grinned. "He's my brother from another mother."

We laughed as I tickled him. Evens' smile made my breath catch. It reminded me of Jean. A large grin with those somber eyes. His long black hair. *Wait.* Evens kept his afro short. Thaddeus had long dark hair. I shook my head, trying to realign the facts.

Perhaps in mourning for my natural-born son, I had neglected my adopted one. I hoped not. But Thaddeus wasn't truly my adopted son. He could be, though. It would require more thought and preparation.

Momma held Thaddeus' cheeks between her hands. "You get bigger each day." After giving him a large kiss on both cheeks, she released his face.

In under twenty minutes, we headed north on Fairview Avenue for Highway 101 North.

Daddy said, "The trip wasn't bad until we got to LA."

"The layover was only an hour," Momma said.

"Believe me, Daddy, we would've sat in traffic longer than an hour if we picked y'all up at LAX."

"Humph."

"Stop grumbling," Momma said. "You'll feel better once you eat."

"How long before we get to your new place?" Daddy asked, turning on the radio.

"Depending on the traffic, usually about two hours."

Reclining his seat, Daddy stretched his arms. "You better have something good to eat. I'll be starving by then."

Momma flicked the side of his head. "Don't be rude." She turned toward Thaddeus. "So, how is school?"

Daddy craned his head to look into the back seat. "You playing any sports, Son?"

Conversation continued around Thaddeus's school performance—which, as usual, was excellent. Gaiety filled the car. For the first time in months, I relaxed. This felt good, familiar.

Though I appreciated Camile and Lupita—their home was always welcoming—nothing compared to family. My parents always provided safety and security.

But what about Thaddeus? My hands tightened on the steering wheel. Thaddeus wasn't safe. Tonya's irrational whims dictated his life. *How could I protect him?*

Tomorrow, I would call my lawyers and get answers. The pressure on my chest lightened. After Pruitt showed up discussing Mrs. Copeland, I consulted them. The official cause of death had been accidental overdose. Pruitt lied.

Apparently, the family accepted Mrs. Copeland's death as an accident and moved on. The lawyers inquired about whether I had changed my mind about a wrongful death suit. I hadn't and resented the idea any amount of money could recompense the death of my son. But I had to tell them something to get the information.

Jean and I had done everything possible to protect Evens. We lived in a respectable neighborhood. Evens attended quality schools with goal-oriented friends. Before the accident, he arranged a visit with his father's extended family in Haiti. Evens possessed a youthful desire to change the world. My child did the right things. He shouldn't be dead.

But I should've known better. We've always behaved properly—did what society had expected of us. And in return, we received nothing but platitudes and broken promises. We chose to believe the lies made by politicians, pundits, and the like. Obtain a degree, find a steady job, and you'll be set. Conform to society and you'll obtain equality.

Evens received the DWB lecture, but none of it mattered because a woman with a long record of DUIs ran a light and slammed into his bicycle, propelling his beautiful, perfect body against a telephone pole and crushing his spine. His once lithe form crumpled on the ground as she sped away.

And what about Thaddeus? Entering the world with multiple hardships, he rose above adversity. Despite the poor circumstances of his early life, he maintained a bright, cheery demeanor. How could I protect him from Evens' fate? Could any parent ever completely inoculate their child from harm?

The burnt-orange sun drooped low across the sky. We arrived home right before it set.

After I parked in the garage, Daddy removed suitcases from the trunk as Thaddeus helped Momma inside. Lady jumped on Thaddeus, her tail wriggling endlessly. She sniffed the feet and legs of my parents.

"You didn't tell us you bought a dog," Momma said, rubbing Lady's back.

Locking the door, I said, "I didn't. She's a stray I found at work. Remember. I told you about it."

"You said you found a stray, but I assumed you turned her into the pound."

We entered the living room, and Lady raced to the back door, whining. Thaddeus and Lady went outside as my parents toured the house.

"Not bad," Momma said, opening cabinets and closets.

"It's small," Daddy said. "It's half the size of the place in Goleta."

"Less people live here."

"We miss Evens, too," Momma said, rubbing my back. "Every day."

Daddy removed a soda from the refrigerator. "How are you liking the new office in San…?"

"San Marguerite, honey," Momma added.

"It's okay. I told you about April."

"Umm hmm." Daddy drank. "Are we gonna meet her? Is she coming to Camile's for Thanksgiving?"

"No, she has other plans."

Items piled on the countertop as Momma gathered food from the pantry and refrigerator. "When are you gonna find a new man?"

I rested beside the kitchen island. "Never."

"You need—"

"Sugah, don't start," Daddy said. "Julia's happy enough."

Momma rolled her eyes.

Daddy and I exchanged a look.

Slipping off the stool, I gave him a kiss on the cheek. "Come see your room."

"Do I have to share with your momma?" He chuckled.

"I don't want to sleep with you either. Your daddy only brought one pair of pants. In two days, he'll smell worse than Lady."

My shoulders relaxed as my parents bantered. Finally, this house had become a home. I had a family and would fight for them. Anyone who dared to tear us apart would regret it.

CHAPTER 31

Out the kitchen window, I saw Momma sitting in the backyard. I filled a kettle with water and went outside while waiting for it to boil. Yesterday, Thanksgiving at Camile's house had been loud and celebratory. The party spilled into the yard and well past midnight. When the festivities ended, I retreated to my room to rest. Friday evening, I was scheduled to work in the pediatric clinic.

Lady lay on the stone patio, sleeping. Her chest rose regularly, her snores the single sound besides birds chirping.

"Morning."

Furrows etched Momma's forehead. Wrinkles multiplied around her face.

My throat tightened. "What's wrong?"

"Sit with me."

I pulled a wicker chair close and waited.

Daddy exited the casita, where he and Momma spent the evening and joined us. Generally, I would have slept there, but I believed they would appreciate the privacy. I perceived the slight nod of Daddy's head toward Momma. They were sharing a private communication. This couldn't be good. I squeezed the chair's arm rests.

Momma faced me. "Julia, have you looked over those brochures? We need a decision." She held my gaze with a flat countenance. Nothing in her demeanor expressed disappointment or impatience.

Whether from guilt or selfish avoidance, I had delayed discussing senior living facilities with my parents. But now...

I glanced at Daddy. Likewise, his countenance remained immobile. No wonder they were experts at playing cards.

"Do you want to live in a senior facility?"

Momma answered, "No."

I spoke rapidly. "I can hire someone to come to the house to help you. A nurse. An aide to help with cooking and cleaning."

"We don't need a nurse," Daddy murmured, gazing aimlessly over the yard.

The kettle blared.

Shouting over the hissing steam, Thaddeus asked, "Do you want me to make the tea?"

My heart raced. "Do you want me to come home?"

Before I rose, I saw Momma nod. Tears stung my eyes, and I retreated inside to make tea.

Lady leaped to her paws and accompanied me.

Taking an extraordinary amount of time to prepare the tea, I eventually wandered outside. By this time, Daddy was kicking the ball around with Thaddeus while Lady chased after it. For a moment, I watched them. Slowly, Daddy morphed into an agile young man with a short, cropped afro. A lump stuck in my throat. Evens. As the young man's face swung around, it morphed into Daddy.

Like a mist, tears covered my eyes. I placed a hand on Momma's arm. "I—"

"Help us decide which place would be best."

After sipping tea, I set the mug aside. "I have to...to take care of things here first."

She averted her eyes and nodded.

The silence suffocated me. Mercifully, Camile came outside.

"Morning. Anyone hungry?"

"You must be kidding," I said.

She perched on the arm of my chair. "Anyone want to go to the beach?"

"I work tonight. Momma, do you want to stay here? I can pick you and Daddy up tomorrow."

"No, we'll go drive back with you tonight."

"Actually, I was going to leave this morning. I have errands to run before work."

Without looking at me, Momma called Daddy. They retired to the casita. Thaddeus dribbled the soccer ball with his feet while approaching the patio.

"Can I go, too?"

"You don't want to stay with the kids?" I asked over my shoulder as I entered the kitchen.

"I want to stay with Grandma and Granddad. Are they coming back for Christmas?"

***

The drive to San Luis Obispo took about ninety minutes. Momma sat next to Thaddeus without saying a word during the entire trip. Conversation consisted of Daddy's war stories and Thaddeus asking questions.

At home, I dropped everyone off and went grocery shopping. Because I lived alone, I kept little food in the house. Thaddeus ate more than Daddy—which was saying something. When I returned, Momma was home. Daddy and Thaddeus had taken Lady for a walk. She helped put away the groceries. Neither of us spoke until we finished.

My hand bumped up against hers as we both placed items in the refrigerator.

Lowering my eyes, I said, "I haven't forgotten."

She closed the door. "I know."

"I don't want y'all to leave your home—not if you want to stay there."

Sighing, Momma sunk onto the couch. "We can't stay in the house alone."

"I'll decide soon. I promise."

***

Clinic was busy. I segregated senior living facilities to the recesses of my mind. Coughs, colds, and influenza occupied my attention until the clinic closed at ten o'clock. After ensuring all patients had been treated and discharged, I left.

***

Without the aid of moonlight, the darkened alleyway slowed my approach. Mrs. Jenkins detailed where her boyfriend, Craig, cleaned offices. During my surveillance, I discovered he left work at nine but usually didn't arrive home until close to eleven. Apparently, he had an active social life. Craig was inconsistent, making timing a huge variable.

On a street next to the hospital, I parked and caught the bus to Craig's neighborhood. I managed to arrive at the pink house fifteen minutes before eleven o'clock. I'd been assiduous in formulating my plan, and timing mattered.

Entry proved simple. During my reconnaissance, I noted the rudimentary locks. Neither he nor his neighbors had security cameras. Perhaps they didn't own anything worth protecting. More likely, they couldn't afford it.

Once inside, I hid in a spare bedroom where Mrs. Jenkins' children had slept. From Tamesha's interview with the psychologist, I learned what he did to those children in this room.

During medical school, one of my favorite courses had been a forensic medicine elective. It was fascinating, like a puzzle. Beginning with a corpse, you worked backward to ascertain the method of death.

As a physician, I tried to prevent death—or at most delay it. Pediatrics emphasized prevention. We cured otitis media and streptococcal infections. However, accidents remained the largest cause of death for children in the United States.

Years of practicing medicine left me disconnected. A medical conference led me once again to forensic medicine. While most of the physicians at the conference attended simply to collect continuing medical education credits, I occupied the time considering how to kill people in the conference room without getting caught—a typical locked room mystery.

The mental exercise kept me engaged. When I returned home from the conference, I shared my ideas with Jean. Initially, he thought it was silly, but the more ideas I shared, the more concerned he became.

One night, gripping my arms, he sat me down on the bed. Hours of questions passed as he gave me a psychological evaluation. I swore to him I hadn't acted upon my thoughts. Once he determined I met none of the criteria for anti-social behavior, he made me promise not to carry out my ideas. And I had kept my promise until the day he died.

A half hour elapsed before the garage door rose. I checked the backpack, ensuring everything was in place. Tense, I alternated relaxing my neck and shoulder muscles.

Mrs. Jenkins mentioned Craig exercised in the garage after work. I hoped he followed his routine.

The garage door opened, and voices flittered inside the cracked doorway. A shadowy figure emerged. From the darkness, Mrs. Copeland's face materialized.

Focus, Julia.

Wrong. This wasn't her house. I hid in her house before, and it looked different than this. Spacious and ornate. It took all night before...

Rubbing my eyes brought the figures into view. Craig wasn't alone.

Damn. Before they rounded the corner, I slipped back into the spare bedroom. Steps sounded throughout the home, making it difficult to track their movements.

Laughter came from the kitchen. Bottles popped open, and sexual banter trickled down the hall.

Great. How long would this go on?

Cabinets opened and closed. Conversation faded.

My body tensed, listening carefully. I tiptoed into the hall. Momentarily, I considered leaving and trying another day. A phone rang.

Near the bedroom door, I heard a partial conversation. It wasn't substantial and didn't improve my opinion of Craig. His lady friend complained about him being on the phone. A brief argument preceded by what could only be described as vigorous sexual activity. *Nasty.*

Leaving the bedroom, I hurried into the kitchen. Loosening the cap on two beer bottles, I sprinkled in the white powder before replacing the caps. I had retained a tiny sample before giving the lot to Pruitt. Once finished, I surveyed the room, considering how things would work with a second person.

Vociferous cursing preceded the television blasting on.

"Just a minute, babe," Craig said, exiting the bedroom.

Shit. I couldn't reach the bedrooms. Where to hide? The house had an open floor plan connecting the living room and kitchen. A peninsula separated those two rooms.

On the other side of the kitchen, a hallway led to the guest bedrooms. Even if I sprinted, the children's bedroom was too far. Scrambling, I dashed into the kitchen and dropped to my knees. I hid behind the peninsula countertop. I duck-walked around the opposite side as Craig turned the corner.

In the kitchen, he opened the refrigerator. If his companion left the bedroom…

Lack of planning caused mistakes.

My balled fists left indentations in my palms. I dared not peer around the corner.

Fortunately, Craig retrieved the refreshments and left. As he turned into the short passageway leading to the master bedroom, I crawled into the kitchen.

The master bedroom door remained open. More banal conversation preceded a shorter sexual tryst.

My stopwatch clicked down. The window of opportunity was slowly closing. I despaired of completing my task tonight.

The television blared on again. I inched closer to the master bedroom door. Unable to hear movements over the television, like a ghost, I crept along the floor. Peering around the door, I spotted Craig in bed on the side closest to the door. The other side of the bed was empty. Where's the girlfriend?

Craig lay manspreading, with his hand near his crotch. His chest rose regularly with an occasional snore. He was out. Good.

On the table next to his head were the two beer bottles. I entered the room and glanced down. The bathroom door handle jingled. Dammit.

The girlfriend was about to exit the bathroom.

Like a rock, I dropped to the floor and slid under the bed right as she returned. Bed springs sunk and moaned as she climbed onto the mattress. I glanced at my watch, considering how to extricate myself from the situation.

A minute later, the bed began rocking. An agonized moaning rose above the creaking mattress. Peeking from under the bed, I saw Craig's flailing tattooed arm. He was swatting at the person on top of him.

It took a second for my mind to register what was occurring. The girlfriend was on top of Craig—and she wasn't performing anything of a sexual nature. From the noises, it sounded like she was strangling him.

I dared not peek again. Unsure of who the woman was or what she was doing, I waited, prepared to defend myself. But from whom?

A side lamp crashed to the floor. Something bumped against the headboard. Three agonizing minutes elapsed before the bed stopped moving. The room became dead silent. I held my breath and gripped a can of mace.

The woman climbed off the bed. From my limited viewpoint, I watched her run around the room gathering items. She was dressing.

At the bedroom door, she paused and glanced back. I barely managed to stifle a gasp. Mrs. Jenkins.

Two minutes later, I crawled from under the bed. Craig's face was dusky with blood smeared under his nose. Déjà vu washed over me.

A different face, a woman's. Bloated and covered in vomit, her eyes shot open, and she glared up at me.

"No," I said out loud.

Hush, Julia.

My heart raced. I touched Craig's chest. His head lolled to the side. With my stethoscope, I checked for a heartbeat. Guess I didn't need the GBH from Kevin's stash after all.

Setting the lamp back on the bedside table, I lifted Craig from under his axilla and hoisted him off the bed, dragging him into the garage. In under ten minutes, I managed to position him on the weight bench. Leaving him there, I re-entered the house and retrieved beer bottles from the bedroom.

In the kitchen, I rinsed them out and got others from the refrigerator. After pouring beer into the cleaned bottles, I swirled the liquid around and returned to the garage.

Measuring the distance, I placed the bottles within Craig's reach. I lifted a barbell and set it on the rack above his head. Rigor hadn't occurred yet, so his limp fingers easily wrapped around the bar as if he was performing a curl. Once the scene was complete, I lifted the barbell above his chest and released it.

His chest bones cracked. Ribs snapped. A squelched grunt and spittle shot out his mouth, splattering my clothing. It didn't matter. By tomorrow, these clothes would be free of any DNA. Gradually, the barbell rolled down his chest and onto his neck. I wanted to cause a hangman's fracture, where both pedicles of the C2 vertebra fractured. It didn't always result in death. Occasionally, the person died from asphyxia.

The cold temperature would retard decomposition. GHB reached its maximum concentration at around thirty minutes, with a half-life of about thirty minutes for elimination from the plasma. From my rough calculation, the drug should be untraceable in his urine after about twelve hours.

Craig didn't work on Saturdays. Accordingly, his body shouldn't be discovered until Monday. But the best-laid plans could go awry. As evidenced by Mrs. Jenkins's arrival and the murder of Craig.

If I had known… Forget it. Worry about it later.

The death should be classified as an accident. GHB wouldn't show up on a drug screen by the time of his autopsy, even if his urine was screened for the substance. I hope Mrs. Jenkins created an alibi. Because if the police suspected murder…

Leave it, Julia. Hustle.

Using Craig's finger, I opened the cellphone and brought up his texts. I didn't find any from Mrs. Jenkins. At least she wasn't stupid enough to text her victim the day of the homicide.

I dropped the cellphone near the beer bottles. After securing his fingerprints on the bottles, I left.

At the garage door, I started to turn off the overhead light but, at the last minute, remembered to leave it on. He wouldn't work out in the dark.

Inside, I kept the television on as well as the other lights.

I exited via the master bedroom window, hopped over a chain-link fence, and ran down the alleyway. If anyone happened to notice me, they would see an overweight male wearing a ball cap.

Shadows crept across the sky, chasing me to the bus stop. But the dark felt reassuring. Wasn't there a Bible verse about what you do in the dark being brought to light? I hoped not.

At the main thoroughfare, I waited. Slipping off the latex gloves, I secured them inside the backpack. They would be deposited in a hospital contamination bin on Monday morning.

An hour later, I returned home. I had changed clothes in the car. I quickly entered before Lady woke up my parents and let her outside. Next to the garage, I slipped into the laundry room and tossed my clothes into the washing machine.

After a long, hot shower, I gave Lady a treat.

"Momma did well tonight despite Mrs. Jenkins' surprise."

Lady looked at me with one ear raised and the other dangling beside her head.

Exhausted after the adrenaline high, I collapsed in bed. My eyes closed, but I didn't sleep.

Sharing my thoughts with Jean satisfied any desires I had for crime and murder. But after he died...

Lie to others, but not yourself.

I did have impulses to kill before Jean's death. But I was afraid to share them, even with him. I didn't want to lose his love. Fear reflected in his eyes when I shared some of my ideas.

Successful people compartmentalized emotions which might impede their ambitions. So, that was what I did. And it worked, then he died. The tether binding me to social conventions tore until I remembered my son.

Shivering, cradled against my side, Evens looked up at me with those large eyes. "Momma, what are we gonna do?" He had asked a question I couldn't answer. But I had to formulate a plan. I had to be strong for him.

"Can Thaddeus stay tonight?"

At the door, Thaddeus had watched us. With a gesture, I invited him to sit beside me. I cradled both boys in my arms, vowing to protect them from monsters seen and unseen. It was hard, but I managed until Mrs. Copeland entered our lives.

Now, I had my parents to worry about. As their only child, I needed to support them too. They deserved a decision.

Usually, you're a decisive person.

When I learned Kevin assaulted Thaddeus, I acted. Hearing Tamesha recount her life with Craig, I acted. But helping my parents decide on a senior living facility… I couldn't.

But they depended upon me. Why could I help others but not my own family? I couldn't help Jean or Evens.

My parents deserved an answer, and I would give them one. But when?

CHAPTER 32

For once, I arrived early at the lunch business meeting. Secreted in a corner of the room, I checked local news on my cellphone. Two paragraphs mentioned Craig Norton had been discovered deceased in his garage on Tuesday morning after his fellow workers contacted the police about his absence from work the prior evening. Good. Three days of decomposition would obscure evidence of strangulation.

Grabbing a sandwich and water bottle, I sat next to Kim. People entered and circulated around the room, grabbing food and conversing.

Ten minutes later, Ken stood at the front of the room, and the meeting started. Five minutes elapsed before April entered.

The tip of Ken's nose quivered as his gaze followed her around the room like a shark following a seal. "If everyone could take a seat, we have a lot to cover."

April grabbed a lunch box and plopped down in the nearest chair. We hadn't spoken since the Wednesday before Thanksgiving. On Sunday, I drove my parents to Santa Barbara airport and returned Thaddeus to his boarding school. April had ignored my texts. I considered calling but spent most of yesterday cleaning the house and completing minor errands—like removing DNA from my clothing.

Once the meeting concluded, I returned to clinic and hurried to my first afternoon appointment. Shaking hands with the young man seated on the table, I said, "We need to discuss your lab results."

Over six feet tall with blond hair and angelic curls, Pauly asked, "Is everything okay, Dr. T?"

"Remember when I asked if you'd been sexually active?"

His body tensed. "Yeah."

"Your urine was positive for chlamydia." I allowed the words to penetrate before proceeding. His vacant gaze showed he required more information.

"It's a sexually transmitted disease. When was the last time you had sex?"

He blushed. "I didn't have sex. Couldn't I have gotten it from playing football? Last week, one of the guys was sick."

"Football didn't cause this." Time to break it down. "Did you ever put your penis inside a girl's vagina?"

He gaped. "Yeah, but I took it out right away. I didn't let go inside her."

"It doesn't matter how long your penis is inside—it's sex. Did you ever have anal or oral sex?"

"No, I didn't put my mouth on anything."

"Did anyone ever put their mouth on your penis?"

"Yeah, a few times."

"That's sex."

After explaining sexual activity to Pauly, I gave him a bag of condoms and a dose of oral and intramuscular medication, inviting him to bring his friend in for treatment, too.

In total, afternoon clinic went off without any problems. In a good mood, I closed my last chart and checked my teddy bear camera. No surprise, Carter had been in my office again. Perhaps I could use his curiosity to my advantage. What did he learn—if anything—from Pruitt?

I heard voices next door. April might be finished seeing patients. After locking my door, I made my way to her office and ran into Ken. I'm sure I rolled my eyes.

"Can we talk?" he asked.

"Fine."

"Not here." He walked over to my office door.

I invited him inside. "What was that about with you and April?"

Frowning, he cocked his head to the side. "That?" He shrugged. "Oh, nothing. I wrote her up for not showing up to work."

Colors flickered before my eyes. Hell, not a migraine. My good day evaporated as a heaviness filled my head. "When did she ever fail to show up to work?"

"This weekend."

"What's your problem with her?"

"Ask her yourself."

"I know about the incident in Sacramento, but it occurred years ago."

His mouth fell. "If someone cost you a job, would you get over it?"

There wouldn't have been a problem if you kept your pants zipped, I wanted to say—but didn't.

"So, this is payback."

"This is my department. I told her to leave."

I studied his unflinching face. "You need help. Have you tried Narcissists Anonymous?"

His cackle sent shivers down my spine. My temples throbbed.

Ken's grin was all teeth. "I expected more introspection from you. I told you we're a team—a family."

The Manson family.

"We have to respect each other."

"This has nothing to do with respect. You're a control freak."

217

He turned to leave. "You're being..." His hand hovered over the doorknob. "Confrontational."

"You've got to be kidding."

"I could make a case for it."

"How? With Carter's help?"

"Maybe you should reconsider working with me instead of Madison."

"You're a fool to trust in the perfidy of Carter."

His face reddened. "I..." He bit his lip. "You're a good doctor, Julia, but if you want to fit in, learn how things work. Join me, and I'll dump Carter."

He departed before my double-barrel reply. From the chair, I rolled over to the door and kicked it shut with my foot.

Ken made his desires clear. Get with the program and what? Work in peace. Become chief of pediatrics when he became chief medical officer.

Asshole. I didn't need his help to become chief. Rubbing my temples, I waited for my heart rate to moderate. Dammit. I forgot to call Trevor—again. Grabbing my purse, I returned to April's office.

Seated at her desk, April stared vacantly at the wall. Tears pooled in her eyes.

I shut the office door and gave her a hug, wiping her splotchy cheeks.

"Did you know Ken's dad died?"

"No," I said, pulling a chair over beside her desk. "I covered for him when his dad had a stroke."

"Marsha called me on Saturday to cover his shift. Since I was scheduled to be off until today, I stayed in LA. I refused to come in."

"It's not your responsibility to cover for him. It's Marsha's job. She's the office manager."

"According to the backup schedule—"

"You weren't first backup."

"I was third in line."

"Did he write up the other doctors?"

"Doesn't matter." Tears streamed down her cheeks.

"Forget it." I rubbed her shoulder. "One blemish won't damage your career."

She flushed. "It's not only that."

"How was Thanksgiving?"

April wiped her face and blew her nose. "I should've worked the shift."

My brows knitted into a question, but she stayed silent. "April?"

She removed a manila folder from a side drawer and dumped the contents, two photos, on the desk. One had April's head spliced onto the body of a naked woman masturbating. The other had her face on a woman receiving anal sex.

Bile rose in my throat. Heat suffused my torso, spreading up to my face. "We have to—"

"File charges? Against whom?"

"Did you check the teddy cam I bought?"

Her body trembled. "It's gone. Someone stole it months ago."

"Why didn't you tell me?" I asked, struggling not to shake her.

"There's only one way you can help me."

A minute passed as she shut down the browser and gathered up her items. When we reached the parking lot, April said, "I can't stay."

"Noughton has other campuses."

"I want to work in Goleta."

"There are other employers."

"Who'll hire me with my history? Two different medical centers in five years."

219

"It doesn't matter."

April gave me a side glance.

"Seriously. As long as you're willing to work—and haven't been sued—they don't care."

She smiled timidly. "You're a good friend, Julia. But a horrible liar."

As she strode away, I realized April had poor judgment. In actuality, I was a skilled liar. After she drove away, I scanned the area for Pruitt. Nothing.

Ideas circulated across my mind. Despite the temperature being fifty degrees, I turned on the air conditioner as sweat poured down my face. I didn't know which was wearing on my nerves more: menopause, Pruitt, or Ken.

One I could easily eliminate, the other two required effort. My brain craved rest and nourishment. I promised Momma to call about the senior living facilities, but in actuality, they wanted me to return to North Carolina. I couldn't, though—not yet.

Stuck in traffic, I turned on the radio. My gaze drifted to the rearview mirror. A boxy dark blue station wagon followed two cars behind. Though I couldn't visualize his upper face, the man had a cigarette dangling from his bottom lip. My grip on the steering wheel tightened. Pruitt.

Tapping my fingers along the steering wheel, I considered what to do. The signal light turned green, but the cars heading straight hadn't moved. Cars in the left turn lane had a green arrow and proceeded across the intersection. When the turn signal flashed yellow, I swerved into the left lane and executed the turn before the light became red. With a glance back at the intersection, I noticed the station wagon entered the turn lane.

Continuing down the street, I completed several turns until I found a small side street. Once there, I executed a three-point turn, faced the intersection, and waited. Several minutes passed before I viewed the station wagon. After half a minute, I pulled behind it. The hunted became the hunter.

Sunset tumbled into night, but I kept the vehicle in sight. The distinctive license plate served as a beacon in my headlights. My stomach grumbled. I considered a detour to one of my favorite restaurants when a realization dawned on me. The vehicle was headed for my neighborhood. What did he expect to learn from following me?

Sweat dripped down my spine. Pruitt knew where I lived. From my security cameras, I had viewed his car traveling by my home on several occasions. But why tonight?

My presumption was he wanted more money. I gave him what I took off Kevin Page. Apparently, it had been insufficient—or he had a different motive. Could it have something to do with Carter? Too many possibilities.

As the station wagon turned onto my street, I parked at the corner and observed. Pruitt slowed as he passed my house. Eventually, he proceeded down the street and returned to the main road.

Five minutes. Ten. Eventually, I entered my garage. I didn't turn on the house lights. From the front window, I peeked outside to see if he had returned. After a half hour, I tiptoed into my bedroom.

After changing clothes, Lady and I took a walk.

Pruitt texted.

Need 2 talk

?

More $

So, that was it—or was it a blind. His association with Carter added another dimension. One I didn't understand. What could Pruitt learn from Carter to use to his advantage? Carter might be using Pruitt to gain detrimental information about me for Ken.

I didn't reply to Pruitt's last text. He stated what he wanted. Now, I had to decide on a response.

After our walk, I fed Lady then retired to bed. Before drifting off to sleep, I decided to call the police.

CHAPTER 33

On my way out of the exam room, I used a soapy paper towel to wipe saliva from my stethoscope. The adorable newborn mistook the bell of my stethoscope for a nipple. Hopefully, he would become more perceptive with age. His first-time parents looked terrified we allowed them to take a newborn home without an instruction manual. Thirty minutes of encouragement allayed their fears—I hoped.

In my office, I checked the EHR. My next patient was a no-show. The Christmas party started in two hours, and I had five incomplete charts—not to mention patient messages and labs. Priorities. I called Trevor. He answered on the second ring.

"Hello."

"My favorite pediatrician," he said jovially. "I was going to call you." Papers shuffled in the background. "How are things in San Marguerite?"

"About the same. Did the kids get my presents?"

He chuckled. "I hid them. Otherwise, they'd be opened before Christmas."

After allowing time for pleasantries, I asked, "Have you decided about April's transfer?"

"Who?"

"Dr. April Powell. The pediatrician interested in transferring to Goleta."

Seconds passed.

"Oh, yeah. We need to discuss—"

"What's the problem? I know peds doesn't have a vacancy, but an extra doctor wouldn't hurt. Besides, a few physicians will retire next year."

"That's not the problem."

Another pause.

"Well, tell me."

"Julia, you know I'd do anything for you."

My back stiffened as I prepared for his barrage of bullshit. "Trevor."

"I looked into Dr. Powell's background."

"And?"

"And before joining Noughton, she precipitously left a position in Northern California."

"She wanted to be closer to family." I had no intention of divulging April's history. Although, I suspected he already knew.

"Is that what she told you?"

"Dr. Powell is a board-certified—"

"She reported a fellow colleague to the medical board."

"Oh, you mean the physician proctor screwing a medical student?"

"I heard it was a resident."

"Does it matter?"

"Julia," he said before clearing his throat, "we don't need those types of difficulties in Goleta."

"She reported an inappropriate sexual relationship between a colleague and a person under his supervision."

"Did she have to notify the medical board? Why not the department chief?"

"Perhaps she did." Perspiration trickled down my neck as I clicked on my fans. "This is a conscientious physician who cares about her fellow doctors and patients. Isn't this someone you want on your team?"

"No."

My jaw clenched.

"Look. I do want good, competent physicians in my department. But not someone who runs to the board over a minor infraction."

"A minor—"

"Don't go there. You know what I mean."

Yes, I did. April wouldn't be transferred to Goleta. What next? If I couldn't assist her transfer—

"Julia? You there?"

"Yes," I said, inhaling deeply and wishing unpleasant things upon Trevor.

"We had a deal, and I really want you to take control of the San Marguerite campus. Let's discuss this over dinner. There's a department meeting in ten minutes—"

"Sure, Trevor. We'll talk later." I hung up.

Once I completed charting, I picked up the phone to call my parents when I heard a sneeze. It came from April's office next door. Earlier, she'd been coughing. A concerned friend would go and check on her and I would *after* calling home.

Twenty minutes later, I went to check on April. I tapped lightly on her office door.

"April?"

A fit of coughing answered. Cracking the door open, I peeked inside. With her head buried in a cloud of tissues, April's bleary eyes peered up at me. When I entered the office, I kept a healthy distance between us. I liked April, but I had no intention of catching her cold.

"You look horrible."

She blew me a kiss. "Thanks, friend." Another fit of coughing racked her small frame.

"Count on a true friend for honesty. I'll tell Ken you're ill."

"Oh, no. I'm going to the party." She rose, grabbing her purse and coat.

"Don't take this wrong, but you look like hell."

"Is there a nice way to take it?"

"I could've said you look like shit."

She grinned feebly and sneezed.

"You need to go home. It's Friday night. Two days of rest, and you *might* be able to work on Monday."

Rummaging in her purse, April found a cough drop and popped it into her mouth. "Ken came by today. He said he expected me to be there."

"Not this again." With an audible sigh, I collapsed into a chair beside the desk. "Have you reconsidered filing a harassment complaint?"

"I-I just want a transfer."

"And if you can't? Perhaps you should simply leave Noughton and go somewhere else."

Like a trumpet, she blew her nose. I retreated toward the door.

In a garbled voice, she said, "I'm fine. After a few hours, I'll leave."

"Do you want to carpool?"

"No. I don't want you to leave early because of me."

"Oh, I promise, I'll be leaving before you do."

On the way to my office, I heard hurried footsteps. Curious, I ran to the end of the hallway and saw Carter departing—eavesdropping snake. I wished I knew what he learned from Pruitt.

***

The Christmas party was held at one of the local vineyards. California had more vineyards than a drought-stricken state ought. Being December, the sun had already set. In the dark, drizzling evening, I parked in the rear—for an easy exit—and donned my rain slicker.

After avoiding the sinkhole-size puddles, I entered the restaurant and found the festivities had begun. Maneuvering around the celebrants, I joined Kim and Juanita at a large, round table in the rear beside a floor-to-ceiling window.

"How's it going?"

"You made it," Juanita said between sips of wine.

"I hope you aren't driving," I said in all seriousness.

She shook her head. "My husband's here."

My gaze followed the direction of her finger. A long line of people waited for a photo with Santa Claus.

"Pictures with Santa. They take this party seriously."

Leaning back in her chair, a visibly pregnant Kim said, "This is Ken's pet project. He loves this more than the picnic at his house."

"Kim, where's your husband?" I asked.

"Getting food. The line's pretty long."

Our conversation drifted toward work. I scanned the room for April.

She sat at a table with Carter and several staff members. Dark circles gathered under her eyes, accentuating her illness. Those usually full cheeks were sunken. How long would she last?

Juanita's husband and twins returned to the table. Eventually, Kim's husband arrived with plates of food. I declined to eat—not because I wasn't hungry—but I had graduated from buffet food years ago. If I couldn't order a plate, I ate at home.

An hour later, Ken rose and replaced Santa Claus at the front of the room. The low lights were turned up, spotlighting his exuberant face. His scrawny mustache hadn't grown much. I fantasized about ripping that piece of fuzz off his smug face.

There's my Christmas wish.

Speaking into a small microphone, he welcomed everyone to the gala, gave a brief history of the department's Christmas party tradition, and thanked the event's organizers. Once the applause diminished, he said, "Now, we'll hold the annual raffle."

My attention drifted from him to April, or at least it would have if she were still seated. While Ken rattled off numbers and the attendees gasped and giggled over who won, I left the dining room in search of April. After the food line, I checked the bathroom. Empty. Where could she be?

Beside the entrance, I found a shivering April sneezing into a wad of tissues.

I rushed over. "It's cold *and* rainy. Why are you outside?"

"The air is stuffy. I started coughing and couldn't breathe."

"You sound worse."

"I know. It's just…" Her eyes became watery. "I don't want trouble with Ken."

"What more can he expect? You showed up. Besides, if you don't go home, you'll end up in the hospital."

"I need a breathing treatment."

Leading her toward the parking lot, I said, "I'll drive."

"No, I can drive myself."

"Fine, but I'll follow—make sure you don't need anything."

We got in our cars and snaked along the windy, slick roads. Twenty minutes later, we arrived at April's house, located in a planned community in south San Marguerite. She parked in the garage, and I parked on the street.

Her house was tidy and quaint. Cleaned to obsession. I could relate. In the kitchen, she got a glass of water before offering me refreshments.

"Do you have any soup?"

"You hungry?"

"The soup isn't for me. It'll open your sinuses."

For several minutes, she checked cabinets. "Afraid not."

"I should've known. You don't cook, so why buy groceries."

Grabbing my purse, I headed out the door. "I'll run down the street and get some pho."

"Julia, you don't have to."

"I'll be right back." I left before she could reply.

***

By the time I returned, April had changed into pajamas. Directing her to go to bed, I searched the kitchen for a bowl and spoon.

In all the times I had visited, I hadn't seen April's bedroom. It revealed another aspect of her personality—feminine and tender.

Frilly pink and lavender pillows covered a four-post bed surrounded by cream-colored wallpaper. A silver tray held glass perfume bottles on the delicate dressing table. The dainty jewelry container played classical music when opened.

Curled up in the middle of the bed, April had covers layered up to her neck. I handed her a bowl of pho, then retired to a far corner of her room onto a velvet settee.

"What did you think about the party?" April asked, clearing her throat.

Slurping pho, I said, "Forget the party. Eat."

Once April finished, I removed the dishes and cleaned up the kitchen. When I returned to the bedroom, a drowsy April had slipped under the covers.

Perched on the side of the bed, I asked, "Anything else I can get you?"

Her head shook. "I took some medicine. Now, I need to rest." Her eyes started to close. I got up to leave, but she grabbed my hand.

"Please, would you stay with me a while?"

"Sure."

She inhaled deeply and sighed into the pillows.

Minutes passed. April's eyelids drooped. "I called my sister. Told her I was sick."

Though I waited for an answer, I already knew her money-grabbing sister wouldn't drive up Highway 101 from LA to care for April—unless she got something for it. Kicking off my shoes, I reclined against the headboard and lay beside April, softly rubbing her hand.

"Julia, do you ever feel lonely?"

My chest tightened.

"This world isn't designed for single people. Family, marriage, children. You need help, or you won't survive."

Rain pinged off the roof. The only sound as we both separately pursued our thoughts. With Jean and Evens gone, I felt alone even in a crowded room. Jean had been at my side for over twenty years. Memories remained, but his absence was palpable.

And Evens… His smile anchored me to Jean. Without it, I felt adrift. But I wasn't.

Thaddeus, my parents, Camile, Lupita, Anjelah. There were people in my life who loved me and cared about my welfare. Who did April have—besides me?

"Did I tell you my younger sister is getting married?"

"When?"

"She's not sure. My mom is planning a huge wedding."

I wondered who was paying for it.

April motioned with her hand, and I passed over a box of tissues.

"Mom asked to borrow money for it, but I refused."

"Good for you," I said, rubbing her arm.

"She hasn't spoken to me since." A coughing spasm interrupted, and I rushed to the kitchen for a fresh glass of water.

"Does your family's approval matter to you?" I asked after April sipped some water.

"It's cultural. As the oldest, my mom looks to me for support."

"*She* chose to have more kids than she could afford. You are her daughter, not a paycheck."

Tears clouded her eyes.

"They are not your responsibility. I can be your family. Camile, Lupita, Thaddeus. You deserve to be loved."

I slipped down on the bed and hugged her. Though our situations differed, I understood the importance of family. Jean adored me despite my flaws. Camile loved me even when I emotionally crumbled. My parents tolerated my indecision.

April glanced up at me. "Thank you, Julia. You're a good friend."

Before her eyes closed, I whispered, "I love you, April."

Other than a fluttering of her eyelids, she didn't respond. I kissed her forehead and flicked off the lights. In the living room, I curled up on the couch.

***

Hours later, I returned home. Paws scampered across the tiles in my direction. Lady gave me a look which said, "Where the hell have you been?" She ran around in circles and then shot like a rocket at the glass doors leading to the backyard.

Opening the doors, I released her outside. I seriously needed a doggy door.

In my bedroom, I undressed and showered. Before bed, I set the alarm. I'd check on April tomorrow morning.

In the mirror, I considered my reflection. Years of love and pain created those wrinkles along my brow. When Jean and I moved to California for his fellowship, it was supposed to be temporary. But after he graduated, we stayed and created our own family. Although I'd been raised by two staunch atheists, Jean was Catholic, and we observed his religious traditions. Daddy's parents were atheists; Momma's were Baptists.

Momma told me that in my grandmother's home, a picture of Jesus hung between Martin Luther King Jr. and John F. Kennedy. As a teenager, Momma came home one day and replaced the European Jesus with a Black Jesus sporting an afro. Although her parents tolerated the modified Jesus, they objected when Momma replaced JFK with Malcolm X. Soon afterward, they threw her out. Unrepentant, Momma managed to support herself and never returned home.

Once Jean died, Evens continued to attend church—even while in college. He said he wanted to be near his dad. I hadn't detected Jean's presence there, but I was raised a heathen.

Right after Evens' death, I attended church and lit candles for him as he had done for Jean. However, I detected no special connections there. I attended several times per week. Nothing comforted my heart. I received no assurances my son dwelled safely in heaven with his dad. After three months, I stopped going.

Lying in bed, I considered a life back East, caring for my parents. California was all I had known for the past twenty years. My friends lived in California. While I had friends in North Carolina, we mainly messaged each other and sent cards for holidays and birthdays.

Lady whined and scratched at the screen door. I let her back inside, refilled her water bowl, and returned to bed. She followed, stretching out beside the door.

Maybe moving back home would give me a fresh start. Perhaps San Marguerite wasn't far enough away from Goleta to escape my demons?

As I drifted off to sleep, an image of Evens appeared. I saw him as he looked the night before his fatal bike ride. Each night,

I kissed his forehead and told him I loved him. At least he knew he was loved.

April craved affection. Instead, she had an enormous burden. Family could wound worse than strangers.

The vision of Evens blurred, replaced by the face of Pruitt, then the female police officer. Both of them were pointing at me and repeating, "It's your fault," and "Where were you?"

I slept poorly.

CHAPTER 34

The weekend transpired faster than expected. Fortunately, April was on the mend. I encouraged her to take Monday off. However, she showed up anyway. Late, but breathing easier.

Once I closed the last patient chart, I scoured the internet and scheduled a contractor to install a doggy door for Lady. Despite initial misgivings, I had become quite attached to the dog—my dog. It shouldn't be so hard to claim her, but everyone I made a home with died.

Stop it. You're being morbid. That's Dr. Griffith speaking.

That psychiatrist did more damage than... The greater distance I placed between myself and her treatments, the more I remembered. Fatigue and dizziness simply topped the list of the side effects I endured. Suppressed homicidal tendencies weren't the problem. Things spiraled out of control after—

"Dr. Toussaint, can you help?" a medical assistant asked, rushing inside my room.

All three of my desk fans whirled. Drenched, I felt like I slogged through a humid Alabama summer day. "What's wrong?"

"Dr. Jacobs is running behind, and her patients are about to riot."

Frustrated with always being asked to help—while experiencing another mercurial hot flash—I asked, "Did you try another provider?" How about Kim, Juanita, Carter—not to mention our sociopathic leader?

"Everyone refused."

I retrieved my lab coat. "Fine. Where?"

Cursing internally, I proceeded down the hallway to the patient room. I knocked before opening the door. "Hello, I'm Dr. Toussaint. Your doctor—"

"I don't want to see you!" a thin woman hollered, neck veins popping out along her throat. "*Where's my doctor?* I have been waiting almost two hours!" A torrent of obscenities, along with spittle, flew out the woman's mouth.

"Ma'am, Dr. Jacobs is with another patient. If you want to wait for her, fine." I left. In my office, I used the EHR to remove her from my patient list and placed it back on Dr. Jacobs's.

In the next patient room, I entered and said, "Hello, my name is Dr. Toussaint. Your doctor is running behind, but I would be happy to see your child."

"Oh, yes. Please," the parents stated graciously.

They listed their concerns about the child's speech. The examination was brief. I ordered a speech therapy referral and provided a school note. At a quarter before six, I stopped by April's office.

"Hey, lady. You ready to leave?"

She looked anemic. "I have two more notes."

"Girl, you look worse." Closing the door behind me, I leaned against her desk. "Have you eaten?"

Her head shook. "Too busy."

"Come on. Let's grab dinner—my treat." Free food couldn't persuade her to leave.

"I need to finish these notes."

"You have sick days. Call off tomorrow."

"I'll still have to finish the charts when I return—and the backlog of patient calls, messages, labs…"

"This is ridiculous." I paced around the room. "You need to rest."

Unable to convince April to leave, I returned to my office determined to wait for her. My cellphone buzzed at the same time the burner phone beeped. I set my purse in the bottom desk drawer and removed both phones. The burner phone displayed Pruitt's number—again.

WE NEED 2 TALK

Disregarding his message, I answered my personal cellphone.

"Hey, Camile. What's up?"

"Lupita wants a head count. Is Thaddeus staying with us?"

Damn. I needed to call Tonya. She had withdrawn permission again for me to remove Thaddeus from school. If I couldn't reach her, he would have to stay on campus all winter break.

"Julia?"

"Sorry. Tell Lupita he'll stay with me, but we'll visit. Tell her to make enough food."

Laughing, Camile said, "She makes enough food to feed an army."

"And yet there are no leftovers."

"True. Okay, I've gotta go. Oh, by the way, Trevor asked about you."

"Really?"

"He asked if you decided about the CMO position in San Marguerite?"

"I see."

"Gotta go."

"Bye," I hung up and phoned Tonya. The call went to voicemail as I tapped my fingers along the desktop.

The clinic sounded too quiet. In the hallway, I noticed April's open office door. Inside was empty. Where was she?

On the way to the bathroom, peripherally, I spied Carter departing. For a second, I considered following him. Instead, I would confront him after I decided about becoming chief medical officer.

There would be difficulties. Ken wouldn't cede his position willingly. Despite *my* dislike of him, he had supporters. Trevor might want to extend his influence in San Marguerite, but at the moment, he had little. As I stood in the hallway of two minds, April exited the bathroom.

"Were you waiting for me or the restroom?"

Accompanying her back inside the office, I said, "You shouldn't leave your door open. Carter was snooping around."

"In here?"

Light shimmered on the desk phone receiver. I pointed. "What's that?"

April leaned in; her hand reached forward to pick up the phone.

"Wait?" With a tissue, I wiped the phone, removing a sticky, clear substance.

"What is it?"

Holding the tissue under my nose, I delicately sniffed. "Don't know, but it smells like piss."

"Do you think Carter would urinate on a phone?" April's chin quivered.

I slid the desk away from the wall. A used condom clung to the wall. "Filthy bastard."

Sobs choked April's speech. "What are you doing?"

After assisting her to a side chair, I checked the bookcase. From the spine of a huge medical book, I peeled off a miniature camera.

"Where did that come from?"

"A spy store in Santa Barbara."

"But I told you—"

"If you won't file a complaint, I'll deal with this."

"Julia, you'll make things worse."

Doubt it. Quickly, I deposited the condom between a piece of paper and wiped the phone clean.

April clicked off the overhead light, and we departed.

Time passed. Before we separated, she asked, "Have you spoken with your contacts in Goleta? I want to know if a transfer is possible."

"There's nothing available." I refused to share Trevor's comments. April was upset enough.

She studied me for a moment before driving away.

Damn Trevor and hospital politics. As I exited the parking lot, the burner phone pinged an alert. Pruitt again.

U BETTER ANSWER ME I CAN HURT U

He was aggravating my already brittle nerves. Apparently, my anonymous tip to the Santa Barbara Police Department hadn't produced the desired result. I would have to escalate to step three. This could get dangerous.

Careful, Julia.

CHAPTER 35

The lawyer promised to call me the moment she received an answer from the court, so I left San Luis Obispo early Friday morning for Santa Paula. I requested the day off to attend Thaddeus' school Christmas party.

Lady rode up front for the first hour. She became less enthralled as the journey continued and curled up on the back seat by the time we arrived at the boarding school. I scrolled down the window so she could sniff the air. That was Christmas for her.

The school parking lot had already filled up. In the rear, I allowed Lady to stretch and relieve herself.

"Come, let's find Thaddeus—and you better behave. Dog-friendly doesn't mean they'll tolerate shenanigans."

To my surprise—and delight—I discovered quite a few dogs on the premises.

For two hours, we watched the school holiday production. During the choir hymnals, I read emails. Thaddeus hadn't participated in the activities but sat in the front row of the auditorium with other theatrically-challenged students.

At the end of the ceremony, the dean made departing comments. He barely stepped away from the podium when people stood and milled around the room. People streamed by, exiting from the rear. Minutes passed before we spotted Thaddeus.

He smiled so large I thought his face would split. Once Thaddeus disentangled himself from the crowd, he rushed over. Lady cannoned into him and licked his face.

"Down, Lady." I regained the slack on the leash. "Sit, sit."

She obeyed, her tail drumming along the floor.

"You came," he said, giving me a long hug. "I thought you wouldn't."

I kissed his cheek, noticing the first signs of acne on his brown, chubby face. "You say that every time. Have I ever let you down?"

The smile vanished. "I-I'm afraid one day you will."

Emotions clogged my throat. I thought about Evens. The one time he truly needed me, I failed. A drunk slammed his body against a pole and served only three months of a fifteen-month sentence. Without justice, I would have no peace.

"I will always be here. Wherever you are, I am."

He cried. I brought his head to my chest, kissed his head, and held him tight. Lady jumped on his back and licked his neck. Between his sniffles, I handed him a tissue.

The dean approached, extending a welcoming hand. "Hello, Dr. Toussaint. How are you?"

I returned his greeting, and a conversation of platitudes ensued. He praised Thaddeus' academic performance, mentioning the upcoming school term.

"Will Thaddeus be spending the holiday at home or on campus?"

Wide-eyed, Thaddeus' face fell.

"His mother is coming up tonight." I deliberately avoided a direct answer because I didn't know.

Having completed his duty, the dean zeroed in on another family. Once he left, Thaddeus, Lady, and I departed. As we crossed the parking lot, Thaddeus froze.

"What's wrong?"

He didn't answer with words. I followed his eyes.

Tonya strutted across the blacktop on three-inch heels. Her arms flung wide open. The aggressive make-up and skin-tight body suit brought her disapproving glares.

"Come give Momma a kiss." She planted a loud, dramatic kiss on his neck.

Thaddeus' arms hung limply at his sides.

"I missed you so much." She stepped backward and stumbled. "Aren't you going to say anything? Didn't you miss me?"

Her boisterous protestations of love brought undesired attention. Thaddeus grimaced and withdrew.

"Stay here," I said, addressing Thaddeus. I unlocked the car door, and Lady climbed on the passenger. "Tonya. Let's talk." With my hand, I guided her away.

Families crowded the lot, piling children into cars and carefully navigating around spectators toward the exit.

Pulling away from me, Tonya asked, "What's going on?"

"It's winter break." I waved my hands around the parking lot. "These are parents taking their children home for the holidays."

A frown creased her pancaked brow. "You mean I have to take him home?"

My teeth gritted. I itched to smack the hell out of Tonya. "I'll take him, but you have to sign the permission slip."

Her face brightened. "Great. You take him. Where do I sign?"

"Why did you withdraw permission in the first place?"

Averting her gaze, Tonya scampered toward the school. "Hurry up. I'm going to a party tonight."

We rushed to the admissions office without speaking. It was packed with people. It took thirty minutes to obtain Tonya's written permission. Thaddeus had waited near the school's entrance, a question behind his weepy eyes.

"Go get your stuff," I said. "I'll be at the car."

His grin stretched from ear to ear. Before he left, Tonya grabbed his arm.

"Now, Thaddie. Be a good boy. Understand?" She kissed his cheek. "Mommy will call you later."

Without responding, Thaddeus ran upstairs to the student suites. Tonya strutted outside, tottering on thin FM heels. At a slower pace, I followed.

"Where is this party?"

Her eyes narrowed. "Why?"

"Because I'm worried about you."

"Since when?" Tonya departed.

Forever.

***

Five minutes elapsed before Thaddeus hopped in the passenger seat, and we left campus. As I pulled onto the highway, my cellphone rang.

"Hello?"

"Dr. Toussaint, I spoke with the child advocate," my lawyer said. "We weren't able to see the judge today, but probably early next week."

"It won't be necessary. She gave permission for me to remove him from campus for the holiday break."

"Did you want to pursue the long-term solution we discussed? It will take some time."

Did I want to fight Tonya for custody of Thaddeus? It would be an ugly, contentious process. I didn't want Thaddeus to see me take his mother to court.

"Let me think it over."

We were driving north of Santa Barbara before Thaddeus spoke.

"Why did you bring my presents to the school if you were taking me home?"

"How—"

"While you were talking to Mom, I looked in the trunk."

After turning off the radio, I gave Thaddeus a side glance. *Tell the truth, Julia. He can handle it.*

"I wasn't sure your mom would give me permission."

He stared out the side window. His shoulders shook.

Damn, Tonya. She didn't appreciate Thaddeus. I bit the inside of my lip. Don't cry.

"Hey, she gave me permission, so let's not worry about what might've happened. We're together. And next week, we get to have Christmas dinner at Camile's."

He wiped his damp cheeks. "Is Aunt Lupita cooking?"

"Of course."

Lady barked.

We both laughed.

Thaddeus found a radio station playing Christmas carols, and we sang hymns all the way to San Luis Obispo. At that moment, I decided to fight Tonya with everything I had.

CHAPTER 36

Over the past week, I'd made three trips to the grocery store. I forgot how much teenagers ate. With my parents arriving this weekend, I decided to stock up on provisions.

Initially, they had planned to spend Christmas in Charlotte. When I told Thaddeus, he asked why since they had always spent the holiday in California before Evens died. I immediately called my parents. They were thrilled about the invitation.

Because of the congested highway, I arrived home late Friday evening. I wanted to call April before my parents arrived. Though she sounded weak over the phone, April insisted she was better. She simply didn't want me to come over and feed her more soup. But a hearty holiday meal with friends would cheer her up.

Thrum, thrum.

While navigating traffic, I hit the cellphone speaker button. "Yes?"

"Julia?"

"Hey, Anjelah. What's up?"

"I wanted to remind you about the SOS ceremony."

"Did you think I would forget?"

She chuckled. "No. How're things?"

We discussed our respective holiday plans.

"I was going to invite you over for dinner," Anjelah said, "but since your parents are coming…"

"They fly into Santa Barbara tomorrow."

"How about Christmas dinner?"

"With Camile and Lupita."

"Are you trying to avoid me?"

"Absolutely not. It's been busy. How's Mrs. Jenkins?"

"There's something different about her. She's a new person."

I bet. Murder did change your perspective. "It's been over a month since I heard from her."

"Yeah. She moved out of temporary housing. But she returned the RSVP."

"Well, I'll see her then."

"You won't recognize her. She's confident and happy."

Killing your abuser delivered positive results. "Talk later," I said, hanging up while pulling into the garage.

Thaddeus and Lady helped unload groceries—the latter carried a large bone I obtained from the grocery butcher.

Did killing alter a murderer's appearance? Should I tell her what I saw?

"Lady's hungry," Thaddeus said. "Can I unwrap the bone?"

Later. I decided to wait until we spoke. Right then, I had a family to feed.

CHAPTER 37

Saturday passed pleasantly. Daddy and I walked Lady around the neighborhood while Momma and Thaddeus prepared breakfast. Later, we shopped for presents and drove over to Morro Bay. I forgot how entertaining my parents were.

Damn. I must visit more often. It wasn't as if I didn't have vacation time. I simply didn't want to leave California.

Why not? What's left for you here?

Pulling into the driveway, I yawned as exhaustion washed over me.

"Tired, baby girl?" Daddy asked. "I told you I'd drive."

Momma said, "In the dark, you're blind as a bat."

"Bats see well in the dark," Daddy shot back.

"Using sonar, not GPS."

Thaddeus unleashed Lady, and we entered the house.

"Can we finish the tree?" Thaddeus asked no one in particular.

"Of course," Momma said.

They removed their coats and headed for the naked Christmas tree and boxes covering half the living room floor. Lady performed her "I need to go outside" dance. Daddy sat at the kitchen island, drinking a soda.

"I'm making hot chocolate," I announced.

"Yum," Thaddeus said, holding tinsel as Momma draped pieces along the tree.

Daddy's piercing gaze made my ears itch. Between us hung an unspoken question. I refused to acknowledge it, wanting to bask in the moment of holiday bliss.

"Everything okay?" I asked, between heating milk and melting chocolate.

"We made a decision," Daddy said, glancing at Momma. She handed Thaddeus the remaining tinsel and headed for the kitchen.

My heart skipped. No one spoke until Momma joined us.

"Julia, our doctor said it was time."

Emotion gathered in my throat, preventing speech.

Lady barked and pawed at the screen. I forgot her doggy door collar. Glad for the distraction, I rushed to let her inside. She bolted past me and into the kitchen.

Sliding off the bar stool, Momma said, "Lady, you hungry? Huh, girl? I got something for you."

She removed a plastic container from the refrigerator. I recognized remnants from last night's dinner of fried chicken, mashed potatoes, and vegetables. Strip by strip, Momma tore the meat into smaller pieces, tearing them off the bone. She placed the container of food in the microwave.

Daddy waved me over to the seat Momma had vacated. "The doctor said we need to prepare our estate."

Momma laughed. "Estate?"

Scratching his bald head, Daddy said, "I don't know what to call it."

The microwave beeped, and Momma tested the food. She stirred the contents together before setting the container on the ground. A beat hardly elapsed before Lady rocketed up to the bowl and gobbled it up.

"Come," Momma said, "it's better to talk in the living room."

My parents sat together on the couch. I sat alone and waited.

"We decided to move into a senior facility," Momma said. "The one we emailed you about."

"We're old," Daddy said, hanging his head. "The house is getting to be too much."

His strong, wrinkled hands reached for Momma. He squeezed her fingers and smiled. Their love engulfed the room. Their faces blended and morphed into Jean and I, vacationing in Jamaica, holding hands on a veranda. Together, forever— like it was supposed to be.

"I'll never leave you," Jean had said, kissing my neck tenderly.

But he had. The vision dissipated.

Daddy touched his head to Momma's. I had imagined growing older with Jean like they had. A tear escaped before I had time to prepare myself. My chest heaved. Momma misunderstood my sentiment.

"Don't cry, Julia." She leaned forward. "We decided it wasn't fair to ask you to decide for us. This is best."

"Is that what y'all want?" I forced myself to swallow the sadness clawing at my throat.

Neither spoke. Instead, they exchanged glances.

"I can make arrangements for someone to help out if you want to stay in the house."

"It's not only about taking care of the home," Daddy said, glancing distantly.

Momma's bottom lip trembled. "We need someone to help us. In a senior living facility, we know someone will always be there."

Guilt tightened around my chest. "Do you want me to move back to North Carolina?" I avoided the word home. Why?

Although I faced Momma, from the corner of my eye, I saw Daddy's shoulders relax. I knew the truth but avoided it for over a year. Dammit, they needed me. My family...

"Julia," Momma said, sighing, "you're not obligated—"

"What about California? I can get a house big enough for the three of us."

Lady barked.

My gaze shifted to her. "Four of us."

The terrier whined and lay on the floor of the living room close to the kitchen. Her head rested on her paws.

"Five of us." Thaddeus stood beside my chair.

"All of us," I said, hugging him around the waist.

He sat on the chair's arm.

"I can't live in California with all these weirdos," Daddy said, grimacing.

"Like no weirdos live in Charlotte."

He chuckled. "Well, I'm used to those freaks."

"Charlotte is home for us," Momma said.

"We're not from there."

"But it's closer to family than California," she said.

"Baby girl, we want you to come home."

Home. Wasn't this my home?

Momma rose and hugged me. She hadn't hugged me like this since Evens' funeral. For a minute, we simply held each other. A weight lifted off my heart, but now my shoulders weighed down with responsibility. Was this how April felt?

Opening my eyes, I saw Daddy crying. I started crying, then Momma and Thaddeus. Lady whined and joined in our group hug.

Pushing away from me, Momma said, "I'm sorry we made you an only child. It's hard, but whatever you decide, we love you so much."

Sniffling back tears, I croaked out, "I know."

"So, who's up for Scrabble?" Daddy said, walking over to the bookshelves and retrieving the board game.

I shared a glance with Momma, who shook her head. Daddy didn't do well with emotions, *and* he really liked Scrabble. We cleaned our faces and joined Daddy at the kitchen table. Thaddeus returned to decorating the Christmas tree.

The first game ended with Momma winning. Daddy shared a couple curse words and threw his tiles into the bag. He wasn't a good loser and insisted on playing another game. As we gathered the tiles, my cellphone chirped.

Excusing myself from the table, I said, "Hello?" before checking the caller ID.

"Julia?"

My body stiffened at the crack in Juanita's voice. "What's wrong?" It couldn't be good news for her to call me on a weekend evening. My initial concern was Kim's pregnancy; she was due in less than eight weeks. "Is Kim—"

"It's April. She's dead."

My grip on the phone increased. "What happened?"

Probably in response to my expression, Momma rose.

"Julia Marie, is everything okay?"

While on the phone with Juanita, I shook my head. Momma sat back down.

"She committed suicide."

As if a million tiny acupuncture needles stung me, my skin prickled. Sweat trickled down the center of my back.

After a momentary pause, Juanita provided the few details she knew. Saturday morning, because April hadn't shown up to work and wouldn't answer her cellphone, police were dispatched to the home for a welfare check. They discovered her in bed. Authorities suspected an overdose but would conduct an autopsy.

Thanking Juanita, I hung up. In a daze, I leaned up against the kitchen countertop. My parents gaped at me. Their faces expanded and shrunk, distorted and misshapen. Another migraine.

Deep breath. Remember what happened the last time you lost control.

"Baby girl, what is it?"

Don't upset your parents. They're watching you. They'll tell Camile.

"My friend died. She killed herself."

Vocalizing the words made it permanent. Once stated, it became truth. April was gone from my life. Like Jean and Evens, she wouldn't return. Pain sweltered at the base of my neck, slowly seeping up to my brain. A familiar, uncomfortable pressure. I knew what would come next. It felt like my head would explode.

"Give me a moment."

In the bedroom, I collapsed on the bed. Not until a wetness touched my hand had I realized Lady followed me.

Why did April commit suicide? I knew the flu weakened her spirits, but to kill herself. I couldn't grasp... Why did the people I love die? Was I the problem?

After cancer claimed Jean's life, I coped. Pushed forward for the sake of our son. When Evens died, I fell apart.

Throbbing in my head prevented further thought. I lay on the bed, staring up into the darkness. Darkness. It had seeped into my heart such that I thought only violence would cure my pain. How to keep out the darkness?

And sorrow. It dragged me down into despair. But I wasn't going back to a psychiatrist. No way. This time, I would find a better solution. A healthy way to address my impulses. Dr. Griffith might have been an anomaly, but I wouldn't trust anyone with my deepest secrets again.

Over the past year, April and I had become close. I thought I understood her. It must have been something dramatic to make her choose suicide. When we last spoke, she hadn't returned to her cheery self but was on the mend. Had her voice sounded different, worried?

I reflected on our last conversation. What had I missed? I failed another person. Why didn't I protect her? Daddy said regrets were like assholes. They stank and were always behind you. I loved April. Tears drenched the bed beside my head.

Pictures of lost loved ones floated before my mind. *Jean's calm face with a touch of wrinkling at the corners of his eyes. Evens' deep, soulful eyes. April's infectious laugh ringing in my ears.*

Choking, I hurried into the bathroom and vomited in the toilet. Hugging the porcelain bowl, I sobbed.

Time passed, and I fell asleep.

CHAPTER 38

Sunday morning, I drove to April's house. Birds flew overhead in the clear skies with mocking joviality, unconcerned with the grave injustice committed inside. A neighbor glanced at me from their driveway. I gave a slight nod before entering.

April gave me a house key after our trip to Carmel. It came in handy during her bout with influenza. Inside, the house felt hollow, but I recognized the scent of April's favorite perfume. Each step toward her bedroom pricked my heart with renewed pain. Could my sanity withstand another loss?

Yesterday, my parents, Thaddeus, and I played board games and visited the city. Now, I searched for answers in the home of my dead friend. Why did April kill herself?

The house felt less welcoming, the world less colorful. I saw none of the prior beauty of April's bedroom. Pink frilly pillows looked gray in the absence of their vibrant owner.

On a padded stool, I sat in front of April's dressing table, preparing to call her family. Would they grieve her death? Those vultures were probably searching for life insurance policies. Did she have one? Who benefited from the estate?

Leave it, Julia—and this place.

In honor of my friend's memory, I would extend compassion to her family. Five rings, no answer or voicemail. Figured. They were probably on their way to stake a claim on the house.

Bam, bam.

The devil doesn't knock, so I started for the front door when I noticed April's cellphone on the bedside table. In the time we spent together, I had memorized her PIN—recording it automatically without effort. Another peculiarity I acquired when researching how to commit murder. Touching the phone conjured up a picture of April during our cycling trip in Carmel. She—

Boom, boom, boom.

Dropping the cellphone in my purse, I hurried to the front door. Without checking the peephole, I flung the door open.

"Yes."

Rashema, April's sister, glowered. "What are you doing here?"

"I have a key." Without inviting her inside, I turned and headed for the kitchen.

Two women accompanied her. They all entered.

"You have no right," Rashema said, joining me in the kitchen.

Piece by piece, I cleaned out the refrigerator. "Someone has to look after April's place. And, as I said, she left me a key." Over my shoulder, I said, "Apparently, she hadn't trusted you with one."

A hand slapped onto my shoulder as Rashema swung me around.

"She was *my* sister. I'll look after her things."

"You mean you'll take her stuff." I glanced around her. "Where's the truck? Are those your movers?"

"For your information, she's our mother," Rashema said, gesticulating like a strutting cock.

In the living room, I found the two women admiring photos on bookshelves beside sliding glass doors.

"Hello, Mrs. Powell. My name is Julia Toussaint." I shook hands with both women. "April was a dear friend. We worked together at Noughton."

The older woman's gaze widened—not easy given the heavy fake lashes. She grinned. "So, you're a doctor too?"

"Yeah, mom," Rashema said, storming up behind me. "The one April was always talking about."

"The lesbian?" Mrs. Powell said with a gloomy expression.

"No," Rashema said, circling around me to stand beside her mom. "The one who's always interfering." She sneered.

Clearly, she hadn't appreciated my advice to April regarding finances. I ignored Rashema and studied the younger woman, who remained silent and slightly behind the mom. "And you are?"

She shot a quick glance at the older woman.

"This is my youngest daughter, Tia," the mom said, striding away.

"Nice to meet you."

The girl—not more than a teen—trailed after the mom like a frightened mouse. She resembled April in appearance *and* attitude.

"You can leave now," Rashema said, stepping into my space. "We'll take care of things."

"Have you planned a service yet?" I asked, holding my ground though losing patience.

"Not yet."

"Looting April's house takes priority."

"Look—"

"Doctor... What's your name again?" the mom asked, exiting April's bedroom.

"Toussaint."

"Whatever." She set a large purse on the couch. "We're family. We can take care of April's stuff. So, you can—"

"Leave," Rashema hissed.

"Do you have power of attorney over April's estate?"

The mom glared quizzically. "A what? We don't need—"

"I'm afraid you do." I walked away from Rashema and hopped on a kitchen stool. "Simply being related to April doesn't mean you can seize her property. And seeing how she hadn't given you a key to her home, I question whether she left you executrix of her estate."

"Let me tell you something," Mrs. Powell said, pointing a stubby finger at my face. "I raised April by myself. Her—"

"You don't deserve a reward for being a mother? Who was supposed to take care of her? You brought her into this world. Was it to simply service your needs?"

"Don't, Mom," the teenager wailed as Mrs. Powell flew in my direction.

Rashema caught her mom before we connected. I wish she hadn't. Slapping that cheap wig off Mrs. Powell's head would've made this day a tad brighter.

"Fuck her," Rashema said. "I'm calling the police."

"Please do. And I'll explain how I entered with a key." I held it up proudly. "While you'll bark about needing to gather April's personal items for a funeral you haven't planned."

Holding up her cellphone in mockery, Rashema pushed the number nine.

"Of course, the police will run a background check on each of us before they allow us to leave. Make sure no one has any warrants or arrest records." As predicted, the cellphone returned to Rashema's purse.

"Let's go," Mrs. Powell said, pulling Rashema down the hall toward the front door. "This ain't over. You can't steal my baby's things."

"I was going to say the same to you."

"We'll get an attorney," Rashema said, anger rolling off her in waves.

"Please do. Maybe they can educate you on property laws." I followed them to the door. "And ask about April's will. It might prove enlightening."

Rashema swung around to reply, but I shut the door in her face. After cleaning out the refrigerator and emptying the trash, I secured the front door with the deadbolt and exited the garage using the door opener from April's SUV.

Before leaving, I removed the picture of us in Carmel from April's shelf. A lovely soul had departed. Perhaps she was in a better place with Jean and Evens.

Since the authorities apparently believed April's death was a suicide, I saw nothing wrong with keeping her cellphone. A quick glance at her messages confirmed what I had feared. Another pornographic picture mockup of her performing a sexual act.

Those bastards would pay.

Once the Powells left, I walked next door to speak with the neighbor. She could be useful in keeping an eye on April's house. Some family members *were* worse than enemies.

CHAPTER 39

Because I hadn't finished mourning, yesterday was my first day back at work. All morning, Clarence Carter's *Patches* played in my head. The haunting, cryptic tune made me wonder how I failed April. Why wasn't I there for her? I knew she was struggling but never thought she was suicidal. What she did all those years ago to protect a young woman ultimately led to her murder.

Not murder, Julia. Suicide.

No, murder. They killed her. Ken alienated and harassed her after the medical system misled her into believing they cared. Lies about abuse reports being anonymous and protected. Encouraging medical providers to uphold standards they lacked.

If you see something wrong, report it. But when you do, they withdraw support and treat you like the villain. April reported a colleague for abuse, and the hospital system ostracized her as a snitch. Hypocritical bastards.

I intended to confront Ken and beat the shit out of him. Fortunately, I didn't find him. Marsha had no idea where he was. Maybe it was best. Going to jail wouldn't address what happened to April—but it would alleviate some of the pain crushing my soul.

Before I entered the patient exam room, I took a second to collect myself. Breathing in and out for several cycles, I straightened my lab coat and opened the door.

"Good morning, I'm Dr. Toussaint." The EHR booted up, and I noticed Ken was this patient's regular doctor. Why was she on my schedule?

"I understand Aaya suffered a concussion last weekend."

Aaya said, "Yes" at the same time the mom said, "No."

With a stern look at her daughter, the mom said, "Aaya bumped into another player. She didn't have a concussion."

As I washed my hands, I asked, "Did she pass out?"

"We need a note to return to soccer," the mom said, avoiding my question.

"But—"

"Aaya passed out because she was tired," the mom insisted. "The day before, she played three tournament games. She just closed her eyes for a moment."

I regarded the mom, trying to ascertain if she genuinely believed that. Unsure, I interviewed Aaya. "Tell me what happened."

"I don't remember." She stared up at the ceiling. "First, I was standing in front of the goal. Another player ran toward me. The next thing I knew, people were looking down at me."

"I understand you were taken to the ER by ambulance."

"She went home the same night," the mom said. "Aaya's being scouted by colleges. She can't miss the game this weekend."

All too well, I recognized their dilemma. Often, the surest way for kids to attend college was on an athletic scholarship. And sports provided a gateway to escape poverty. Pressure was immense. Those high stakes led families to take risks with their children's lives.

Over the next twenty minutes, I conducted an exam and concussion screening. Aaya scored poorly on memory and balance. She admitted having headaches, feeling in a fog, and fatigued.

"Your daughter suffered a concussion," I said after completing the exam. "At this time, she cannot be cleared for sports." I printed documents detailing the return to school and play criteria.

The mom slapped the papers aside. "This is ridiculous! Aaya didn't have a concussion."

My head throbbed. While I understood the mom's position, it still frustrated me. She didn't appreciate having a child. What I wouldn't give to have Evens alive, to see his eyes, feel his hug. People failed to appreciate their blessings.

"Yes, she did. A concussion is a form of traumatic brain injury. She needs to rest and allow time for her brain to heal. If she returns to sports too soon, she could suffer a second injury, compounding the damage. I will not clear her to return to sports."

Peripherally, I noticed the teen's shoulders relax. The mom continued to argue. We reached an impasse.

Snatching up her purse, she leaped from the chair. "Fine, I'll talk to Dr. Brady. Come on, Aaya." She wrenched the door open forcefully, slamming it against the wall. It ricocheted and knocked her in the ass.

Aaya gave me a tiny grin. "Sorry." She hurried after her mom.

In my office, I tossed the papers into the recycling bin. A glance at the wall separating my office from April's made me tremble. Thoughts of hunting down Ken increased. A quote from Agatha Christie came to mind where Hercule Poirot said, "Do not open your heart to evil. If you do, there's no turning back." Well, I crossed that bridge years ago.

Staring out the office window, I watched the breeze toss leaves along tree limbs. Why did I stay in California? I'd lost so much.

Now, biking along Carmel's coastline would remind me of Evens and April. Numerous places in California reminded me of a dead loved one. Why was I determined to stay in a place which held so much sorrow?

Knock, knock.

Juanita entered, shut the door, and collapsed in a chair. "Phew. Flu is bad this year."

I nodded.

"You okay?"

How did you respond to that when someone you loved committed suicide? I rubbed my temples. Why didn't I see the signs? My eyes watered.

Juanita gave me a side hug. At first, I accepted it stiffly. Did I deserve love? Why did people close to me die? It took seconds before I could return the gesture.

"Thank you. It's...it's hard."

"I know." She sat back down. "Did you hear the medical center announced she died from a heart attack? Liars. They'll say anything to keep from admitting they work us to death or accept responsibility for the stress we deal with."

"Work stress didn't kill April."

We shared a weighted look.

"Julia, I know you're hurting, but this isn't a particular person's fault."

My head tilted slightly to the right. "Isn't it?"

"The system is broken. We need better mental health services."

"An asshole harassed April and pushed her over the edge."

"I'm sorry, but I don't agree." She stood. "I know how much you cared about April. Maybe you should take more time off to rest."

"Where's Ken? I saw one of his patients this morning."

She gaped. "Seriously, you don't know?"

My wrinkled brows deepened. "No, I don't."

"He's giving a deposition. One of his patients died."

"What hap—"

A medical assistant tapped and opened the door. "Dr. Williams, the nurse in C wing is looking for you."

Once Juanita left, I reclined in the chair, staring at the computer screen. I couldn't chart. Disparate thoughts swam around my head. I closed my eyes, but stomach acid scratched at the back of my throat. Massaging my temples wouldn't prevent a migraine. Where was my medication? In the past two days, I'd swallowed enough ibuprofen to cause a gastrointestinal bleed.

Opening my eyes, I gazed upon a heart-shaped framed photo of April and me dining at one of our favorite restaurants. I stared at her laughing smile, wanting to cry.

Leave.

Patients would have to wait. I needed to escape this condition of lassitude weighing upon me. Slipping out of the lab coat, I grabbed my purse and exited the clinic.

On my second trip around the medical complex, I received a call from Thaddeus' boarding school. Shit. My heart raced. I couldn't handle more bad news.

"Hello?"

"Dr. Toussaint?" a woman's voice asked.

"Yes. What's wrong? Is Thaddeus ill? Is he hurt?"

"It's not about Thaddeus. He's fine."

"Then what's wrong."

"I'm sorry to call, Dr. Toussaint, but the school didn't know who to notify. We haven't spoken to Thaddeus about it yet. We thought you might want to call him first."

"Speak to him about what?"

"It's his mother. Mrs. Frye is in the hospital. She overdosed."

My body relaxed.

CHAPTER 40

Early in the morning, the medical center felt its age. Without people occupying the hallways, its cracks winked at you. Loose-fitting joints became visible. Plumbing groaned, straining to meet the needs of a medical staff stretched beyond what the architects and builders expected. However, I found the halcyon hours of the morning alone in the decrepit monster peaceful.

Last night, I went to bed late. Most of the evening, I spent in the Santa Barbara ER. According to the intensivist, Tonya would live. She had more lives than a cat. I wasn't sure that was a good thing—at least not for Thaddeus.

Tired, I wore sneakers to cushion my feet, unsure if jogging caused my foot pain or tripping over Lady's dog toy this morning. Either way, the sneakers made walking comfortable and quieted my steps as I entered the clinic.

Voices reached my ears before I turned the corner onto the hallway where the physician offices were located. Light from Kim's office illuminated the surrounding area.

"Come on," Carter said. "What's the big deal?"

Inching up behind him, I watched Kim shuffling papers.

She said, "It doesn't matter. He's already in trouble. Besides, everyone knows you encouraged the family to sue."

Looking past Carter, Kim spotted me. "Hello, Julia."

"Morning. What brings you in so early?" I addressed her over Carter's shoulder.

Stepping aside, he said, "She's preparing cases for M&M."

The monthly morbidity and mortality conferences covered unusually complicated patient medical cases. Each Noughton campus held a monthly session. Quarterly, a system-wide conference occurred across all the Central California medical complexes, attended by physicians and psychologists. It could be a privilege to demonstrate your ingenuity in identifying and managing a complicated medical condition or an embarrassment at your failure. Occasionally, a high-profile medical liability case was presented. Carter's interest—I presumed—concerned the latter.

With grim lips, Kim tossed a pen on the desk. "I'm not going to submit Ken's case because you want him humiliated before the entire medical center."

Carter leaned against the door jamb. "Ken should be exposed for his incompetence. This isn't about me. It's for everyone—for his patients."

I watched their exchange, listening for anything useful.

"Stop lying. You're angling for his job."

"Are you gonna do it or not?"

"No."

"Fine." Carter's freckled face curled into a frown. He stomped out of her office.

"Come on," I said, pointing toward my door.

With a lopsided grin, he followed.

Turning on the office lights, I motioned for him to be seated. I closed the door before sitting in the lounger in a far corner of the room. The tan leather lounger had belonged to Jean. As I relaxed on the cushions, confidence surged along my spine. Carter wanted something I could provide.

"What's going on?"

In two minutes, he explained Ken's malpractice lawsuit.

One of Ken's patients, a little girl, complained of intermittent abdominal pain for over a year. Despite rapid weight loss and intermittent bloody stools, Ken had treated her for chronic constipation and what he perceived to be anal fissures. Six months ago, she presented to sick clinic with escalating severe abdominal pain. Ken ordered lab work and a CT, which had been scheduled for two weeks later.

Unfortunately, the little girl didn't live to keep the appointment. She decompensated and her parents rushed her to the ER, where she was diagnosed with an acute abdomen. In the OR, surgeons found a large colonic perforation with multiple intestinal erosions. Two days later, the parents buried their youngest daughter. Inflammatory bowel disease—likely ulcerative colitis—was diagnosed on autopsy.

"I encouraged the family to sue and gave them the name of an attorney."

My brows raised in question.

"Ken deserved it. You know this isn't his first malpractice case."

"Do tell."

"After his residency—somewhere in northern California—Ken missed jaundice in a three-month-old."

Carter shook his head.

"Idiot. He probably thought the baby was mixed or something. Anyway, the baby developed kernicterus, resulting in permanent brain damage. The medical center settled a few dollars on the family. The amount was below state-reporting requirements."

According to California law, if the apportioned settlement amount attributed to the physician was less than $30,000, it would not be reported on the medical board's website. Curled into my lounger, I considered the information.

"So, Ken is an incompetent pediatrician."

"Yes, which is why I'm trying to get rid of him."

"Dude, seriously. You've been acting obsequiously, hoping to be appointed chief medical officer." My brain worked furiously over the information. Could I use this? Realizing Carter was watching me, I set my private thoughts aside.

"And Kim refuses to present the case for M&M."

"She's the pediatric department quality improvement officer. The request must come from her." He stared out the window. "If Ken received enough humiliation, Howard would have to replace him."

"Possibly."

Dr. Howard Cummings was the medical director for Noughton's San Marguerite Medical Center. I'd met him but hadn't been impressed. Small wonder this medical center failed to reach the standards of the other campuses.

"How long have you been kissing Howard's ass?"

Carter bristled and readjusted his position in the chair. "I haven't—"

"Tell the truth—at least with yourself."

He leaned forward in the chair. "Can you help me?"

Climbing out of the lounger, I traipsed over to my desk and sat down. "I can arrange for Ken's case to be presented at the quarterly regional M&M, but not here. I have no influence at San Marguerite."

His eyes grew wide. "Really? Thank you, Julia."

"Not so fast."

Carter slowly sat back down.

"What did you discuss with Pruitt?"

"Who?"

Crossing my legs, I leaned against the backrest. "Oh, now you're playing stupid?"

A smirk stretched across his mouth. "Well, what about it?"

"What did he want?"

Again, the smirk. It required self-control not to smack the freckles off his face.

"He asked about work—what you were like, who you talked to."

I studied Carter, confident he wasn't telling me the truth. But even lies helped if you understood the liar.

"Why were you snooping in April's office?" I withheld the fact I had filmed him rifling inside my desk.

Carter shrugged. "If someone leaves their door open, they invite people inside."

"Did you leave the pornography in her office?"

"Now, you want me to incriminate myself." Carter rose.

"Did Ken put you up to it?

From the doorway, Carter spoke over his shoulder. "Let me know if you decide to have Ken's case presented at the quarterly M&M. I don't want to miss it."

I gripped the sides of the chair as my left finger grazed my wedding ring.

Calm down, Julia.

His chuckle hung in the air as he departed. I closed the office door. Time to think. Before I could see my first patient, my cellphone vibrated. The screen read Trevor.

"Yes?"

"Sorry it took so long to get back to you. Ready to come back to Goleta, or do you prefer to manage the San Marguerite campus?"

Gaiety intermixed with his words. His joy in close proximity to April's suicide made me nauseated.

"I'm not interested in returning to Goleta."

In the background, his chair scraped across the floor. "You want to be chief of pediatrics at San Marguerite or chief medical officer?"

"What's the status of the current pediatric chief?"

"Ken Brady? You heard already?"

"No, tell me."

"The directors are discussing his continued employment with Noughton."

"Hmm." The situation had progressed quickly. Hiding surprise from my voice, I said, "I wanted to get the facts straight. Is he being removed?"

Over fifteen minutes, Trevor and I discussed the state of the department. I made my position clear.

After we disconnected, I remained in my chair gazing, absently out the window, considering the many variables. Hospital administration had postponed their meeting to discuss Ken's tenure until after the malpractice suit had been settled.

I needed to speak with Ken. His response would determine what happened next.

CHAPTER 41

Three weeks had passed since April died. Each night, her heart-shaped face greeted me as her laugh reverberated around my mind. Lack of sleep left me tired and irritable. I'd been unable to speak alone with Ken. Though I could've pressed the issue, I judged it prudent to allow things to settle.

Clinic was winding down. Removing my lab coat, I slipped out of my wing and entered Ken's. He occupied a large office near the staff bathrooms—the tradeoff for more space and windows.

Administrative activities and court depositions had apparently consumed his time. Either way, he hadn't been in his office whenever I stopped by.

Listening at the door, I overheard a one-sided conversation. Unless Ken talked to himself, I presumed he was on the phone. Pushing the door aside, I entered at the same time he hung up.

Ken glanced up but quickly returned to the papers littered across his desk.

With my foot, I closed the door behind me. I didn't bother taking a seat, nor was I invited to. "We need to talk."

He sighed heavily and turned haggard eyes upon me. "I don't have time, Julia. Send me an email or take it up with Marsha."

My hands rested on my hips. "This is about April."

Slit, cat-like eyes shot up at me. His sky-blue eyes became thunderous. "There's nothing to talk about."

"Why was she scheduled to work two weekends in a row?"

He leaned back in his chair. "Because I run this department."

Humph. Not for long.

"Did you assign her to cover Thanksgiving *and* Christmas?"

His scraggly mustache twitched. "Why not? April is—was—the newest member to the department. She had to pay her dues."

"Bullshit. April transferred from another campus. She had seniority over at least two other pediatricians in our department."

"I make the rules!" he shouted, his neck veins taut.

"You harassed her with pornography and worked—"

"She cost me a job." He sat up straight, his voice fast. "I have a family to support. Do you have any idea what it felt like to be fired? To have no job to feed your family."

My nostrils flared. "Then keep your pants zipped."

As he pivoted back toward the computer, the back of his neck shined brick red.

"I'm busy. And if you're smart, you'll stay out of my business." He gave me a side glance. "Carter's been telling me about your relationship with a Tonya Frye."

I stood stoically.

"Oh, and if you're thinking about stepping into my job, forget it. I heard this Frye woman has a son you care about. If I lose my position, I might have to let the kid's court-appointed attorney know what I've learned."

Before departing, I asked, "Would you really hurt a child to remain chief of pediatrics?"

Under his mustache, the corner of his lip curled. "Without a second thought." He glanced at his cellphone. "Why do you care about some cunt? April was weak. She's better off dead."

My body absorbed the ugliness of his words like shock waves. With great effort, I avoided smacking his dumb ass right then. *Count to ten. Swallow your anger.*

"You don't accept any responsibility for her death?" I heard a strange timber rise in my voice.

Ken snatched a stethoscope off the desk and strode right up to my face. Heat from his heavy breath blew across my face. My fists clenched. The slightest impetus would release a torrent of vengeance upon him, and I would most definitely be sent to prison.

"You can waste time on that dead bitch, but I have patients to see." In an aside, he said, "And get out of my office."

As he proceeded forward, I bumped him with my arm, propelling him against the door frame. For a second, he glared into my face. I knew he wanted to lash out—verbally and physically—but my action hadn't actually been aggressive. It could be dismissed as an unintended accident. He circled around me and stormed down the hall.

I glanced down at his cellphone in my hand. In a minute, I finished and positioned the phone on the floor under his desk. It should look like he dropped it when we collided.

Glancing around the office, I noticed a picture of his family—well, of his children and parents—on his desk, but no photos of his wife, Nancy. Ken cared for his children but no one else's.

***

Before I returned to my office, I noticed people rushing into C wing. I followed.

Huddled inside the treatment room, I viewed Carter and a nurse standing over the gurney.

"How can I help?" I asked no one in particular and received no reply.

The nurse inserted an IV into the child's arm. At the foot of the gurney, Carter examined a bent and bloodied limb. On closer inspection, I noticed an approximately two-centimeter portion of glistening white bone protruding from the skin.

"Did you call ortho?" Carter asked a medical assistant.

On the other side of the room, a medical assistant spoke into a phone. "Yes. They said—"

A stream of doctors in white coats and scrubs entered the room. They barked out orders, which the nurse and medical assistants fulfilled. Useless, I stood aside. Carter questioned the parents, obtaining a history while the orthopedists stabilized the fracture. A medical assistant retrieved Carter's lab coat from the ground and draped it across the countertop.

"Do you have any morphine?" an orthopedist asked.

Walking over to the medicine cabinet, the nurse said, "How much?"

Making my way over to the counter, I watched the proceedings. Carter's lab coat slipped to the floor again, and I picked it up.

In a flurry of activity, the orthopedists stabilized the now-sedated child. Encircling the gurney, they wheeled him away. Carter accompanied the parents, directing them to the hospital waiting room next door. The medical assistants and nurses cleaned up. I helped.

"Anyone need anything?" I asked.

Ken strode into the room. "I need a breathing machine. The one in our wing is broken."

He glanced over at me. A tiny snarl ticked up the edge of his mustache. My head tilted slightly to the side as I returned his gaze with equal intensity.

Accompanied by a medical assistant carrying a nebulizer machine, he left the room.

I returned to B wing and retrieved my purse. On the drive home, I abstractedly tapped my purse. Confident the vial of morphine would prove useful.

CHAPTER 42

Menopause was a mean, vicious taskmaster. Exiting a patient exam room, I hurried to the restroom. Between hot flashes and an irritable bladder—I could care less about my desiccated vagina, which I didn't use anyway—having to urinate every two to three hours was madness.

On my way to the facilities, I heard voices emanating from Bryce's office. She had the large corner office next to the staff bathroom. My pace slowed as I picked up tidbits of conversation.

A male voice said, "How can you be like this? After everything we've meant to each other. I need you."

"You want me—there's a difference."

"Let's talk."

"It's over, Ken. Accept it."

Without seeing his face, I heard the threat in his voice.

"Even if I lose my position as chief, I can still make your life miserable."

Seconds passed.

"Fine. Where do you want to meet?"

"The usual place."

The tracker I placed on his phone *would* prove handy. I hurried to my office, needing to prepare for tonight.

***

Later, I sat in my car waiting. Lady would forgive me for being late. She had water, food, and a doggy door. On the radio, the oldies' station played *Sitting on the Dock of the Bay* by Otis Redding. My thoughts flowed to Jean. He had admired San Francisco from our first visit. He would always insist on riding the trolley. I hummed to the lyrics.

As the song ended, Ken exited the medical office—finally. He pulled out of the parking lot, and a minute later, I followed. The tracker app showed a toy car moving on a map. With one eye on traffic and the other monitoring the app, I turned onto Main Street, headed north of San Marguerite.

Ken whipped off the road onto a side street at an unsafe speed. At a moderate pace—and distance—I followed. Powered down with its SIM card removed, I placed my cellphone within easy reach. I might need its mapping device to return home because I was unfamiliar with this area.

Traffic lessened. Fearing Ken might grow suspicious, I allowed another car between us. Three miles down the road, he took a tiny side street. At the corner, I hesitated a quarter of a minute before proceeding. The street ended at a park. Night had fallen, but streetlamps illuminated the parking lot and walking trails.

Ken parked in a far corner of the lot.

Outside the park entrance, I left the car among a patch of trees, but not before wrapping a scarf over my head and changing into sweats. Hiking through the brush with a backpack, I scoped out a surveillance location.

Sauntering aimlessly around his car, Ken eventually reclined against a tree kicking at dirt. In the lot, I noticed two other cars without occupants.

Fifteen minutes elapsed before another car entered the park, stopping adjacent to Ken's. As the Jeep passed, streetlamps highlighted Bryce's profile.

Once Bryce stepped out of the car, Ken rushed over. He grasped her shoulders and kissed her lips. From behind a large oak tree, I watched through binoculars, wishing I could hear them. Removing a burner phone from my bag, I snapped pictures. Heavy petting and vertical lovemaking ensued. I filmed enough to document their tryst. Careful of my footing, I tiptoed closer, trying to overhear their conversation.

Straightening her clothing, Bryce spoke hurriedly. "We can't keep doing this."

"Why not?" he asked, running his finger along her jaw.

"I told you. It's over."

"Don't worry about the deposition. One malpractice case isn't going to sink my career."

"But it's not only one case, Ken. It happened—"

"I'm not giving up my position."

"Will you have a choice?" She retreated, adjusting her hair into a clip. "Listen, I'm back with my husband. We decided to work on our marriage. His wife now has full custody of the kid, so we can work on our relationship."

"I don't care. Stay married. It doesn't mean we can't get together." His hands flowed down her hips, pulling her up against his groin.

Smacking his hands away, she pivoted toward the car. "It does for me."

Ken grabbed Bryce's arm and swung her around. "Let me tell you how this works. This ends when I say so. Otherwise, you can kiss your cushy job goodbye."

"What do you mean?"

"I'll hold you to the same standard as everyone else. If I evaluated you like them, you'd be fired in a month. No more time off so you and limp dick can ski in Tahoe or cruise the Caribbean."

He leaned into her face. "When was the last time you showed up to work on time? You're the only doctor in the department who doesn't work a full weekend each month."

Bryce's chest rose and fell like an ocean wave.

Conspiratorially, Ken whispered, "Who ordered April to work your holiday shift? Not to mention the backup schedule."

A squirrel scampered by as I strained to hear.

"If you end this, expect to work *hard*. No more adjusted patient statistics. Admin will learn how lazy you've been."

Jutting out her chin, Bryce asked, "What about Nancy? How would she feel about our affair?"

Joggers streamed by on a nearby trail, obscuring his reply. Bryce slapped him in the face, rushed into her car, and sped away, kicking up rocks. A moment later, Ken departed.

I tramped back to my car and headed home, careful to check my rearview mirror for any boxy 1970s station wagons. Confident with my plan, once home, I undressed and showered.

An effective plan depended upon detailed preparations. Mentally, I made a list of supplies. That night, I slept—not comfortably, but for the first time since April died.

CHAPTER 43

Because I needed to leave early, my clinic schedule was abbreviated. The lengthy commute to Santa Barbara required a hasty departure. In the bathroom, I changed clothes and fashioned my thick mane into twists before hurrying out of the clinic. Before leaving home, I placed the package inside the trunk so I wouldn't forget it.

As I jogged to my car, Pruitt approached. Reflexively, my eyes scanned the area for a boxy 1970s station wagon. It rested in a far corner of the lot. Pruitt called out from a few yards away.

"Dr. Toussaint, I'd like a word."

On a tight timeline, I had no interest in sparring with him.

"A moment of your time. I promise." His dingy teeth and receding hairline resembled a predator.

I made a deliberate show of looking at my wristwatch.

He frowned. "Oh, I'm sorry. Am I keeping you from something? Tell me. Anyone else about to die? Were Kevin and Mrs. Copeland your only murders?"

His smirk irritated me, but he wouldn't be cocky for long. Cognizant of the traffic I said, "I don't know what you're talking about. Now, leave me alone."

"Mrs. Copeland. I understand. She killed your son. Simple revenge." He stepped closer. "But Kevin Page, a patient's mother's boyfriend. Pretty extreme."

I regarded the detective's suit coat. "I don't have to explain California law about illegally audiotaping someone without their permission. Unless you applied for and received a warrant, which you did not because there's no probable cause *and* you're no longer a detective."

His thin hairline receded further as his gaze widened.

"The papers reported your departmental suspension and the district attorney's investigation into the Santa Barbara police department due to your... Shall we say nefarious activities. If I recall, the article mentioned bribes, blackmail, and extortion."

Circling around him, I reached for the car door handle.

"I'm not sure why you're pursuing me—former detective now disgraced PI—but I suggest you stop. This behavior borders on criminal obsession."

Because he lurched forward abruptly, my hand bumped up against the acoustic audio jammer in my purse as I reached for the mace.

"I'm not obsessed, Doctor, just determined," he huffed.

"To do what?"

"Get what I'm owed."

"Didn't you profit from Kevin Page's illicit activities?"

His face went slack a moment before he snarled. "I didn't kill him."

"What about the car you gave Tonya? And supplying drugs to a woman with an extensive history of addiction. Who's been paying for her motel?"

His mouth opened, but I cut him off.

"Mrs. Copeland was an alcoholic who avoided jail time because of her family's influence and her husband's money. I had nothing to do with her death. And Kevin Page succumbed to a life of debauchery."

Pruitt's nostrils flared as he glared from under thick, overhanging brows. "Watch your back. You're messing with the wrong person."

Men were so unoriginal. I glanced at my watch. "As for you, surveillance cameras recorded you driving by my home—repeatedly."

I scanned the parking lot. Several people were entering and exiting.

"Your presence will substantiate my allegation of stalking. Now, move. I have somewhere to be."

Inside the car, I rolled down the window. "Oh, by the way, I have a camera mounted on the car's rear window. If you tail me, it'll record your plate."

Suddenly, Pruitt reached into the car and grabbed the steering wheel.

"I'm working for Mr. Copeland," he snarled. "What can you do against his wealth and connections?"

Now, I knew Pruitt was a liar. With my elbow, I jabbed him in the arm. When he released the wheel, I quickly rolled up the window and exited the lot. As I glanced momentarily in the rearview mirror, his icy stare almost made me turn on the heater—almost.

Once on the freeway, I floored it for Santa Barbara. The heavy traffic was devoid of boxy, dark-blue station wagons. I didn't expect to hear from Pruitt again, but I would remain cautious.

***

Highway 101 South led me into Ventura. From there, smaller streets steered me away from the ocean toward Thaddeus' private school. Fifteen minutes passed before I approached the tall wrought-iron gates.

After the guard verified my name on the roster, I proceeded forward and parked in the visitor lot left of the main building. I removed the gift from the trunk and entered the lobby.

Ten minutes elapsed before Thaddeus joined me in the gathering room. Tall and gangly, he must have grown over an inch since Christmas break. April's suicide hampered the festivities, but I believed he still appreciated the holiday. If I didn't take him home, he actually preferred to remain on campus for winter break. In fact, I couldn't recall the last time he spent a holiday with Tonya since he enrolled in this school.

We exchanged hugs. For a moment, I admired his appearance. "You're taller than I am."

"I didn't think you would come."

I frowned. "Stop it. Have I ever let you down?"

We sat. No one spoke for a half minute.

His gaze rested on the table. "Sorry. You've been…"

"What?" I asked, squeezing his hand.

Absently, he glanced around the room. "Mom was arrested—again."

Lifting my chair, I scooted closer to him, lowering my voice. "I know. I bailed her out."

"Why?" he asked, glaring at me. "You should've left her there."

Tears poured down his cheeks. I fished a tissue from my purse and slid it over to him.

After Tonya recuperated from her overdose, she fled the hospital. I reached out to her, but she blocked my number. In the hospital, I couldn't get her to admit Pruitt was using her to get to me.

Several minutes elapsed before Thaddeus composed himself. Draping my arm over his shoulders, I brought him close. "If she goes to jail, you'll return to foster care."

"Better than—" His mouth snapped shut.

282

I held him for another moment, then kissed his forehead.

Wiping his eyes, Thaddeus vacantly stared forward. A minute later, he asked, "Would you adopt me?"

I swallowed hard. "Is that what you want?" A knot grew in my chest, and my throat constricted.

He nodded. After a moment, he said, "I want you to be my mom. I wish Evens could've been my brother."

Tears blurred my vision. "He was." I didn't want to become emotional, not in front of Thaddeus—or in public. Biting my lip, I squeezed his hand. "I miss him, too."

Removing my package from under the table, I smiled as his gaze brightened. "This is for an excellent report card. All As and one B."

"I'm not good with literature, but I love math."

"I'm sure there's a medication to cure that."

Laughing, he tore apart the wrapping paper. "A new laptop! Thank you." He practically leaped onto my lap, hugging my neck.

"You deserve it."

For the next half hour, we discussed school and his friends.

"Next term, I take physics," he said, grinning.

I chuckled. "And you're happy about it?"

He laughed.

From my purse, I handed him a package from my favorite Santa Barbara chocolatier.

"Mmm. My favorites."

Before I departed, he hugged me tightly. I rubbed his back, and he eventually released me.

"Careful with the laptop, and don't loan it to anyone."

"I won't."

The school would set up controls on the device to keep him off restricted websites, which I appreciated. Too bad they couldn't restrict news sites. I didn't want him looking up Tonya's criminal record.

"Thaddeus don't worry about your mom. She's not your responsibility."

He nodded. "Will…will you think about what we talked about—about adoption?"

"Of course." My eyes watered. "I love you. Be good. And don't worry."

"I won't. Love you too."

As he ran back up the stairs to his room, he said, "Thank you."

In the car, I wound down narrow roads until I reached Highway 101 North. Night settled over the sky, making the trip cumbersome. Though I could spend the evening at Camile's place in Montecito, it would require getting up early to beat the morning traffic to San Marguerite.

Two hours later, I arrived home. Lady had expressed her anger at missing another evening walk by vomiting a frog onto my slippers.

"Bad dog. No treat for you."

She farted.

"I should've named you Tramp instead of Lady."

With two barks, she trotted over to her water bowl and ignored me for the rest of the evening.

After shedding my clothing onto the bathroom floor, I popped into the shower. Steam melted the day away.

A pint of chocolate ice cream would complete the evening. Chocolate and I have had an intense relationship for ages. Chocolate drowned my sorrows and alleviated my stress, and I didn't question what it did to my body. This indulgent cooperation served me well during medical school, residency, and marriage. It hadn't worked so well since I relocated to San Marguerite.

Could I justify my actions? I didn't try. I wasn't a sociopath *or* a psychopath. I understood the difference between right and wrong and didn't believe my desires were more important than another person's.

Right after Evens' funeral, people called to ask how I was doing. With considerable effort, I maintained a charade, keeping myself intact. Psychotherapy didn't help, nor did the tranquilizers the psychiatrist prescribed. I wanted the woman who murdered my son dead.

Once the court case concluded, Mrs. Copeland's family abandoned her to their immense estate at the end of a cul-de-sac in the hills above Santa Barbara. She had no close friends, and the neighbors shunned her. Sneaking into her house and pouring GHB into her drink was simple, given she was drunk most evenings.

GHB hadn't been detected in her system at autopsy. A known illicit drug user and alcoholic, her death was ruled an accidental overdose, and the case closed. I couldn't tell anyone, but her death healed my pain.

What made Pruitt suspicious? Supposition. He had lied about the police department opening an investigation into her death. Pruitt lost his job due to his illicit activities. If I detected him sniffing around again...

Kevin Page had been a parasite. I was sure many people celebrated his death—except Tonya and Pruitt. The latter claimed Kevin was his informant, but he'd been much more. Pruitt profited from Kevin's illegal activities. What criminal activities was the private detective up to now?

Clearly, he was using Tonya. But I couldn't make her understand. He offered her what I wouldn't—drugs and money. If I couldn't persuade Tonya of his dishonest motives, she would have to be dealt with, too.

The pint of ice cream was almost finished, and I hadn't reached a decision. Thaddeus' request changed things. I licked the spoon and tossed the empty container into the trash. I got a water bottle from the refrigerator, brushed my teeth, and went to bed.

Lady lay on the floor beside the bed. Apparently, she forgave me.

I loved Thaddeus too much to hurt his mom. During Tonya's incarcerations, I fostered Thaddeus. Years ago, I had considered persuading her to surrender parental rights but refrained, believing every child deserved a relationship with their biological parent. Was I wrong? Had I acted in Thaddeus' best interest?

"Come to bed, Julia," Jean had said, rolling over in the bed with open, welcoming arms.

Happily, I had joined him, cocooning myself in his comforting embrace. He kissed my lips, and we made love.

Before falling asleep, I had asked, "So, you're okay with adopting Thaddeus?"

"I'm not the problem. We should've made it official the last time we fostered him."

"I-I don't like the idea of taking a child from his mother. It seems so colonial."

Jean chuckled. "It's your analytical mind." He touched my chest. "What does your heart say? Sometimes, figures and calculations aren't the best options to find a solution. Feelings matter."

He had given me a peck on the cheek and fallen asleep. I had remained awake, trying to reconcile my desires against the needs of a child.

Tonya would self-destruct without my intervention. Thaddeus might want me as his mother, but as a child, he failed to appreciate the complexities involved.

Drifting off to sleep, a vision of Evens and Thaddeus playing soccer in our Goleta backyard came to mind.

"Mom," Evens had asked, "can Thaddeus sleep over?"

"I'll have to call his mom," I had said.

"She'll agree," Thaddeus had said, diverting his eyes. "She never—"

"Come on," I said hurriedly. "Let's make caramel popcorn balls and sundaes."

"I'll get the ice cream."

"Where's the caramel?" Thaddeus asked.

"Mom makes it fresh from sugar," Evens said.

"Wow." Thaddeus joined me at the stove. "Can I watch?"

I brought him close to my side. "Better. You can help."

"Awesome."

A pediatrician, Dr. Donald Winnicott, once wrote, "A baby cannot hate the mother without the mother first hating the baby."

Tomorrow promised to be busy. But for the first time in months, I slept well.

CHAPTER 44

From the employee parking lot, I dialed Ken's number. He answered on the final ring.

"Who's this?"

"It's me."

"Fuck off."

"Don't hang up if you want to stay chief."

"I thought *you* wanted my job."

"No, but Carter does. He's scheming behind your back."

"I'm not worried about an M&M."

"You want to talk or not?"

Minutes later, I hung up, started my car, and exited the lot.

Traffic was heavy, but I managed to arrive in downtown San Marguerite in time to find a parking spot. Tonight, at the SOS ceremony, Mrs. Jenkins would receive her diploma.

At a large table in the rear of the banquet hall, I joined Anjelah and other women from SOS. We conversed about current events while waiting for the ceremony to begin. Rubbing my aching feet, I slipped out of the high-heeled shoes I wore for the event.

Anjelah leaned toward me. "Did you read the *Santa Barbara Standard*?"

"No." I scooted closer, tilting my head toward hers.

"They reported the judge—what's her name—the one at Evens' trial."

"Judge Donaldson." Her name had been imprinted on my brain—as had all those involved in the trial.

"Yeah, her. I read she's stepping down. There's an allegation she accepted bribes."

"What?" I feigned surprise because I'd read the item in the paper, confirming what I had felt that day in the courtroom.

Anjelah nodded.

Overhead lights lowered, and a woman took the stage. The room erupted in applause. As the ceremony proceeded, I searched the room for Mrs. Jenkins. It took a few minutes to locate her at a table up front with her children. Dressed in an ankle-length dress and boots, she'd styled her curly hair like a beauty queen bouffant. Make-up made her quite attractive. Murder *had* improved her appearance. The Jenkins family happily laughed and ate.

The ceremony started with a children's performance. The room darkened, and the play began.

Tapping Anjelah on the shoulder, I said, "I have to use the restroom. I'm going to sit by the door in case I have to keep getting up. I don't want to distract anyone."

She nodded, and I exited the auditorium.

***

Twenty minutes later, I walked across a dark, abandoned lot in southeast downtown. Like silent giants, empty warehouses towered over the area. Their shattered windows peered down upon me. Did they judge me?

Never mind. I stopped caring long ago what people thought. In sweats with a scarf over my head, I jogged up to a car idling in the cracked gravel lot. My surveillance confirmed the driver arrived alone.

The car's headlamps were off, but my eyes had adjusted to the dark once I left the rail station. From the driver's seat, Ken's profile was clearly visible.

Confident he was the sole occupant, I tapped on the passenger-side car window. Hearing a click, I opened the door and quickly slipped inside. Interior car lights came on long enough for me to see Ken's grinning face. His straight white teeth resembled those traps which snapped off an animal's leg.

Without preamble, he said, "It took you long enough. Why did we have to meet downtown?"

"It's close to my gym. Besides, this place is convenient *and* private." My gaze took in the car's interior. I noticed a soda can in the cup holder.

"Did Carter follow you?"

"No, but he's been following you."

Removing my backpack, I reclined against the door and handed him a burner phone. "Take a look."

While Ken scrolled through pictures, I palmed several tablets in my fist and dropped them into the soda can. My shoulders relaxed. Step one: completed. Now suggest he drink.

"Would you like some water?" I offered him a water bottle.

"No, I have a cola." His eyes stayed focused on the phone. He picked up the can without looking at it and guzzled.

I checked my stopwatch. Two hours before the graduation, attendees received their diplomas. The preliminaries should still be going on.

Deep breaths, Julia. You have time.

"Carter's following you."

Ken shook his head. "How did you get this?"

"His office. He boasted about having dirt on you, so I wanted to confirm it."

"Bastard. He's been playing both of us."

"He's sly."

Striking the steering wheel with his hand, Ken cursed. "I'll kill him. He told me you were arranging to have my malpractice case presented at the quarterly M&M to discredit me and become chief of pediatrics."

"I overheard him discussing it with Kim. She refused, so he tried blackmailing me into helping."

"Humph. He told me some bullshit about you and some Tonya chick. Claimed you had something to do with this woman's boyfriend's death. What an idiot. I believed that asshole."

Ken cut his eyes at me.

I shook my head. "Carter's manipulative."

"All this time, he was playing me. Me!" Leaning his head back, Ken yawned. "Lying, claiming you were scheming to get my job, when the entire time he was the snake."

"He played both sides." I handed Ken a water bottle, but he pushed it aside.

With the back of his hand, he covered a yawn. "And you didn't want the position?"

"No. I'm going home." Why did I say that? Maybe because it didn't matter. I checked the clock.

Ken blinked long and heavy. "I-I'm tired."

"I noticed."

He attempted to drink more soda, but it dribbled from his lips. "What's…what's happening?" His lids flickered. "Something's wrong."

Reaching across him, I took the cellphone from his shirt pocket.

"I need help."

"Yes, you do. I got it."

Manipulating his body over the console between the seats, I managed to change positions with Ken. Once I got him settled on the passenger side, I buckled his seatbelt and slid behind the steering wheel.

Ken's head lolled to the side. "Ju-Julia. I can't keep my eyes open. Call 911."

"Don't worry. I'll take you to the hospital."

"Thanks." His head fell forward onto his chest.

I exited the lot and proceeded across town. Twice, a police car passed us. I positioned Ken down in the seat where his head wasn't easily visible. Police cars recorded license plates, which coincided with my plan. I must ensure no one saw me with Ken, though. Fifteen minutes later, we arrived at the park where Ken and Bryce met.

Heavy chains roped off the entrance. Reconnaissance told me it closed at seven o'clock. Driving through the underbrush, I bypassed the blocked entrance. Trees scraped the side of Ken's car, but body damage would be the least of his worries. Nancy would probably want to replace the car after finding his dead body inside.

Once on the asphalt, I parked in a far corner of the lot. The exact position where pictures captured Ken and Bryce's rendezvous.

My watch beeped, signaling sixty minutes remaining. Working with purpose, I replaced Ken in the driver's seat. His head slumped against the steering wheel, startling him awake. Blood trickled down his nose.

His dull blue eyes regarded me. "Why… Where are we?"

"Now look what you did." I resisted the temptation to look at the blood on my latex glove.

"Where's the hospital? Julia, what are you doing?"

"Out of respect for your family, I'd rather not create a bloody scene."

"I don't understand."

"You never did. Ken, you're about to die."

"What? No!" He smacked at my hands and reached for his cellphone.

"Behave. I don't want to shoot you. Can't have the police suspecting homicide. Given your present employment situation, suicide is more plausible. And gunshot wounds to the head are complicated. I have to calculate angles and hand position. And it's not the most likely manner of death for narcissists."

"You're not killing me." Ken tussled sluggishly to exit the car.

With little effort, I restrained him and reapplied the seat-belt. "Stupid man. You're no longer in control—never were."

Disregarding his mumbling, I removed a syringe and a tiny glass vial. Popping the needle holder off, I filled the syringe with insulin. I rolled up the sleeve of his button-down shirt and searched for a vein.

"Stop it," he said, slurring his words and snatching his arm away.

I bitch-slapped him in the face. "Enough. Do you want your kids to see their daddy's brains splattered against the car windows?"

He gaped. While he contemplated the possibility, I shot insulin into his vein.

Ken cried. "Please."

"Where's all that machismo bullshit from the office? Pathetic baby."

"I don't want to die," he said, slurring his words.

"Neither did April. But you didn't care. Did you?"

"It's not—"

"You didn't put the pornography in her office, but you enticed Carter to."

His head shook slowly from side to side. "No. I... The dildo but no pictures."

"Doesn't matter. You lit the fuse."

Time ticked away. Ken's breath became ragged. When his head lolled forward onto his chest, I measured his pulse. The irregular rise and fall of his chest slowed. Periodically, I scanned the area for joggers or other interlopers.

Before departing, I checked for any incriminating items. I pressed Ken's fingers to the syringe and top, even wiping the plastic needle tip cover along his tongue for saliva.

Everything had to coincide with suicide. I placed his cellphone in the cup holder next to the water bottle. Using his finger, I opened the cellphone and scrolled his texts and messages.

I dropped the burner phone with the pictures of him and Bryce on his lap. It also contained the audio recording from the night of the medical conference. Carter had been in the building that evening, so it would be plausible he had recorded their conversation.

Tempus fugit.

I poured the remaining liquid from his soda can on the ground, filling it with cola I brought with me. Wait. A person about to commit suicide would not worry about seatbelts.

Minutes later, I checked for respirations and heart rate with my stethoscope. Detecting no pulse, I started to leave.

Damn. I almost forgot the tracker on his phone. In under a minute, I exited the car and jogged down the street to the light rail station. Thirty minutes later, I slipped inside the community college where the graduation ceremony continued.

In the bathroom, I changed out of my sweats and into a dress and heels. The watch alarm beeped. Traversing the hallways, I returned to the auditorium.

Lights flooded the room as I entered. I joined everyone in applauding the participants. The ceremony emcee rose to the podium.

"Now for the main event. Graduates of our adult GED program…" She continued for several minutes, detailing the requirements for the program.

I returned to my seat.

Anjelah leaned in my direction. "You should see a doctor about your bladder."

"It's not bad enough to endure the medication side effects. Besides, sometimes a leaky bladder comes in handy."

She laughed. "True. I would've liked an excuse to miss the children's play. It was particularly bad this year."

One by one, the graduates were announced and walked across the stage to accept their diplomas. When Mrs. Jenkins took the stage, I and the women of SOS stood and applauded—her children did likewise.

When the ceremonies ended, people ambled about the room, conversing and socializing. Trudging against the crowd, I approached Mrs. Jenkins. Beside the table, her children surrounded her while she spoke with another graduate.

I addressed her kids. "Tamesha, where did you hang your framed picture?"

"It's on the wall in my bedroom. The frame is orange, like my favorite fruit."

Once she finished speaking with another attendee, Mrs. Jenkins smiled at me. "Dr. Toussaint. It's so good to see you."

"I wouldn't miss it. Congratulations."

She hugged her son standing next to her and said, "It took years, but now I have a GED *and* an associate degree. I even applied for a supervisor position at my office." Her eyes widened, and her smile grew.

"I'm sure you'll get it." Opening my purse, I removed a small package and handed it to her.

"Oh, I couldn't. You've done so much already."

"You've focused on the children, but this is for you."

She teared up. Handing the package to her son, she gave me a huge hug, slightly knocking me backward. "If you hadn't helped me…"

Dabbing her eyes with a tissue, she said, "I didn't know life could be this good."

My gaze fell over her kids. "It's been hard, but you did it. You simply needed to know *you* could provide a better life for your family."

She nodded.

Flicking her hand toward the table, she told the kids to gather their things. As they dispersed, we stood together, watching them for a minute.

"How's Tamesha doing with the therapist?"

"Better. We're all going to counseling. It's really helping."

"Good. Especially after what happened to Craig."

She gaped. "What do you mean?"

"You heard about his death."

"I... Well... Yes. Yes." Sweat beaded along her upper lip. "But I heard it was an accident."

"The newspapers wrote he was killed while exercising at a gym."

"I thought it was in his garage."

Gotcha. Clearly, she *had* read about Craig's death. My left eyebrow rose.

"Horrible." She shivered. "He was always showing how strong he was, working out day and night. This time, the dumbass got drunk, and a weight slipped on his neck. Serves him right."

Humph. "Do you miss him?"

She snorted. "He terrorized my kids, smacked me around in front of them." Taking a deep breath, she said, "He got what he deserved."

After giving me a short hug, she called her children together. "Come on, guys. Excuse me, but I have to speak with Anjelah. Thank her and the other ladies at SOS. You know, they asked me to speak at one of the support groups."

"Why wouldn't they? You're a role model—to your kids and other women." *As long as they don't find out you killed your boyfriend.*

For a moment, I watched Anjelah conversing with Mrs. Jenkins. Suddenly, I saw a familiar face in the corner of the room. The last person I expected to find at a graduation ceremony for survivors of domestic abuse.

Surrounded by a half dozen people, Mr. Copeland spoke animatedly. Unsure how long I had been staring at him, I flinched when he noticed my observation. With a somber face, he left his entourage. Slowly, we approached each other in the rear of the room.

"Dr. Toussaint."

He didn't offer to shake hands, and I didn't either.

"Perhaps we should speak."

He inclined his head toward an abandoned area near the stage. I followed at a polite distance.

"I didn't expect to see you here."

"I've supported SOS for over a decade," I said, observing his rigid demeanor.

He cleared his throat. "Yes. I believe I've heard your name mentioned before."

Seconds ticked by as we scrutinized each other like a chess game with human pieces.

"Am I to presume this was a chance meeting?"

"Why are you here?"

"My family has supported other charities in San Marguerite. At the suggestion of a colleague, this year I made a sizable contribution to SOS."

My brows raised. "Well, thank you. Surprising, but appreciated."

A smug grin crossed his lips. "Why surprising?"

"Neither you nor your family were charitable when it came to—"

"I…" He paused, seeming to reconsider his words. "Your son's death was tragic. Evens was a promising young man."

Dual emotions percolated in my chest. While I didn't like my son's name coming from his mouth, at least he remembered the person his wife killed.

"You didn't have to protect her. She should have paid for—"

"Her sins? Didn't she?"

My chest heaved.

Don't, Julia.

A minute passed.

"Are you planning to blackmail me?"

"What?" I asked, frowning.

He turned his back to the auditorium, facing the wall and angling his head toward me. "A Detective Pruitt sent me a letter. He said…" Concisely, Mr. Copeland outlined the gist of Pruitt's missive.

"I didn't send him, *and* he's no longer a cop."

"Then how did he know?"

"Conjecture. He's been hounding me, poking and probing for details."

"So, you didn't tell him?"

"Why would I? It was an accident." I placed emphasis on the last word.

Mr. Copeland's shoulders relaxed. "When I received his letter, I sent Cynthia overseas—in case things became contentious."

"You have nothing to fear from me. Cynthia was a child. She acted out of emotion. Besides, it would be difficult for me to explain being in your house."

Tears welled up in his eyes. "My wife hurt so many people, including our children."

I retreated, needing air and space from the entire Copeland family. Before he left, Mr. Copeland thanked me for my discretion.

***

In the parking lot, I gulped air like I'd been underwater for ages.

"Dr. Toussaint."

My chest tightened. Had someone seen me sneaking into the building during the ceremony? I vacillated between turning around and running for my car. People streamed out of the building.

Witnesses could be useful. With a deep breath, I swung around. A large man wearing a three-piece suit advanced upon me. I braced myself. When he came into view my shoulders relaxed.

"Julia, wait up," Mr. Henderson said. "I'd like to speak with you."

What did the Santa Barbara district attorney want to discuss? I hadn't seen the district attorney since the trial of Evens' murderer. I remembered him as a kind, intelligent man. My finger rubbed against my wedding ring.

Breathing heavily, Mr. Henderson shook my hand. "Hello. It's been, what, about three years?"

"Close."

"I hoped you'd come. Your work with SOS has continued, I see."

Nodding, I detected sweat dripping from my armpits. Uncertain of his motives, I gritted my teeth and allowed him to lead me away from the exiting crowd. Somehow, I'd forgotten he stood a half-foot taller than me.

"It's about a former Santa Barbara police officer. A Detective Pruitt."

My gaze widened, and he released my arm.

"I see you're aware of him."

I inhaled deeply. "Unfortunately."

"Do you mind telling me how?"

"Tonya Frye. She's the mother of a prior patient. A little boy I fostered. I believe Mr. Pruitt is the reason Mrs. Frye is using drugs again. He bought her a car. She wouldn't explain why, but soon afterward, she quit her job. Someone has been providing her with money and drugs. I bailed her out of jail when she was charged with possession and solicitation. Then, last year, she relapsed and overdosed."

Stroking his chin, Mr. Henderson listened as I explained how Pruitt surveilled my office and home.

He cleared his throat. "I wanted to speak with you personally since we have a history together."

I nodded.

"You may have read about our investigation into the Santa Barbara PD."

"Yes."

"There's evidence of police officers working with local drug dealers. Pruitt's name came up during the investigation, and he was dismissed from the force. The case will head to court later this year. His attorney suggested you were also involved with one of the dealers."

My jaw dropped. "What?"

"Kevin Page. Do you know him?"

"No—yes."

You got this, Julia.

"I didn't know him personally but knew who he was. He dated Mrs. Frye and served time in prison for assaulting Thaddeus—the little boy I mentioned."

"Mrs. Frye's son?"

"Yes. I'm concerned about his welfare. I had my lawyer contact his advocate. Mrs. Frye's been in and out of jail since he was born, and I've tried to help the child. I arranged the scholarship which pays for his boarding school."

He nodded. "I thought I remembered him. He was at Mrs. Copeland's trial."

"Thaddeus has been a part of our family for most of his life."

He exhaled. "I thought it was something like that. Pruitt's lawyer is trying to drag you into this. I wanted to give you a chance to explain. There's nothing worse than a crooked cop. Makes all the hardworking ones look bad."

I didn't reply. None was required.

"Well, it's getting late. I don't want to keep you. I'll make sure Pruitt doesn't harass you anymore. If you see him again, call my office. I know about Mrs. Frye and her prior convictions. Some people can't be helped, but I admire your tenacity, especially your work with SOS and the families at the shelter."

"Thank you. It's good to see you, too. I heard you're considering a run for state office?"

He chuckled. "True. And when I do, I hope I can count on your support."

"Absolutely. Like you said, we have a history."

***

Back home, I removed sweats and other items from the car trunk and dropped them in the washing machine. Then showered.

Afterward, I treated myself to a large piece of chocolate cake—Evens' favorite. I made it for special occasions.

Lady wandered into the kitchen.

"Another monster destroyed."

She cocked one ear upward and twisted her neck.

Once the tea kettle whistled, I sliced another piece of cake.

"Momma helped rid the world of another piece of vermin, which deserves a celebration."

Bark.

"No cake for you. It's chocolate. I'll get you a treat." I removed a large bone from the refrigerator, oiling and seasoning it before popping it in the oven. "Wait. It has to warm up and cook the meat."

While sipping tea, I reclined on the couch. Lady remained in the kitchen watching, the oven.

In Goleta, during a medical conference or a particularly lengthy meeting, I'd get an idea about how to commit a perfect murder. Having read mysteries and thrillers for years, occasionally concepts circulated around my mind—but I hadn't considered acting upon them.

Often, I wondered if killers looked different after their crimes. Could people detect a hint of their nefarious intentions? Did I look different now?

All those years ago, when I visited Thaddeus in the pediatric intensive care unit, I yearned to kill Kevin. I couldn't rest until—

But the judge sentenced him to prison before I could act. Within days of his parole, Tonya hooked up with him again. She had no qualms about inviting the man who assaulted her son back into her life—into their home. Consequently, I arranged for Thaddeus to attend a private school. He deserved better. *Why didn't I adopt him then?*

Inside the courtroom on the day Mrs. Copeland was sentenced, I believed people knew I meant to kill her. Lines etched along my forehead from my intense gaze. Did my actions convey my intentions? But I'd been under heavy medication prescribed by the psychiatrist. Perhaps the drugs masked my desires.

Judge Donaldson sentenced Mrs. Copeland to fifteen months in jail. Time enough for me to formulate a plan. After three months, the authorities freed her to home confinement. She would've been safer in jail.

But Ken.

The day I found Lady, when I dropped her off at the emergency vet, I thought they would euthanize her. Matted down to skin and bones, she was suffering. It would be an act of humanity to alleviate her misery. But they saw something in her—a spark of hope. Likewise, I recognized something in Ken. A flaw or kink. He derived pleasure from power, controlling people and hurting them.

Bark.

"Okay, I'm coming."

Fatigue hit me like a San Francisco fog. Drowsy, I prepared Lady's treat then retired to bed. The evening had required a lot of energy. The clock read 11:55 p.m. My eyelids grew heavier. I had work tomorrow.

Remember to maintain your composure. Pretend surprise when Ken's death is announced.

I wanted to call my parents, to tell them I loved them, but sleep came.

CHAPTER 45

Perfect weather for a funeral, windy and cold. Winter with a peek of spring. Because of seasonal allergies, I was sedated on diphenhydramine. Since my last morning patient canceled, I took a quick snooze in the office lounger.

Knock, knock.

Relishing this rare moment of peace, I didn't answer the door, hoping whomever it was would leave—quietly.

"Julia."

Reluctantly, I peered from under one eyelid. "What?"

Kim entered. "Aren't you coming to the funeral?"

Chuckling, I rolled over on my side and waited for her to leave.

"Come on. You're a former department chief. This is to show respect for a colleague."

"When did the death of a bastard become a team-building exercise?"

Kim wouldn't relent. Sleeping in the car would work as well as the office, so I agreed. Being in a haze would make the funeral tolerable and give time for my drowsiness to wear off before seeing afternoon patients. Juanita drove.

On the way, they discussed work, movies, and books. I tried not to drool while sleeping across the rear seats.

The church service had been a private family affair, but the medical director encouraged staff to attend the public graveside memorial. Too many people milled around for me to spit on Ken's grave, but I sincerely planned a return visit to do just that. During a poem recital, I scanned the grounds, comforted the only corpse I'd added to this cemetery was Ken's.

The man reciting the poem started crying. He must have been a relative. Ken didn't do friends. Sociopaths were often charming, though—when it served their purposes.

Nancy stood between her children. The single redeeming characteristic of Ken had been his devotion to those kids. Not sufficient reason to spare his life, though. Too bad he didn't care as much about other people's children.

Off to the side, a woman approached wearing a black blazer over a cream shirt and black pants. A hat tilted low over her face. She trembled, sobbing quietly. I strained to identify her through my tinted lens. With an elbow, I nudged Juanita's arm. Her bent brows questioned me as I directed her attention toward the woman.

"Who is she?"

"Bryce. She's crying because now she'll have to work. No more blow jobs for weekends off."

She laughed, and I chuckled.

Kim smacked Juanita's shoulder.

"Ouch," she said.

"It's a funeral. You're not supposed to laugh," Kim said.

Juanita said, "They're lucky we aren't breakdancing."

I lowered my face, hiding a grin. Juanita pinched my side, and I swatted her hand away.

Kim said, "If you two don't stop, we're going to leave."

Her body shaking with laughter, Juanita said, "Please. I'd electric slide if we could leave now."

"You guys are being disrespectful," Kim said. "This is for Nancy, not Ken."

Wiping tears of laughter from my eyes, I said, "You're right. I'm sorry."

Looking at Juanita expectantly, Kim raised her brows.

"What? It'll be a cold day in hell when I apologize for laughing at Ken's funeral."

For several minutes, we listened to the ceremony. During a pause in the proceedings, Bryce's wailing broke the silence.

"I can't believe she's so broke up about his death," I said to Juanita.

"Reality's a bitch," Juanita said in a voice too loud to be ignored.

My body shook with mirth. Kim walked away. Speaking over her shoulder, Kim said, "I'm going to pay my respects."

"Don't take too long," Juanita said. "Afternoon clinic starts in twenty minutes."

Several people glared at her.

She returned an icy glance. "What're you looking at?"

The onlookers returned to listening to the speaker, who was dismissing the attendees. Services ended.

Pulling out her cellphone, Juanita said, "I'll be in the car."

Nodding acknowledgment, I watched people disperse.

Noughton was a major medical center with at least five major hospitals in Central California. Their San Marguerite campus alone employed over a thousand people. Given those facts, the funeral attendance was sparse. Not surprising given Ken's personality.

Nancy lived with Ken, so she knew he was an ass. Now she understood his colleagues did too.

Unsure of the proper protocol when you killed someone's spouse, I judged it improper to offer condolences. Therefore, I didn't approach Nancy. In *my* mind, I did her a favor. Between the hospital life insurance policy and Ken's pension, she'd be financially secure. Emotionally, she owed me. I removed a cancerous growth from her life. Her children would remember their dad fondly, without knowing the manipulative bastard he had been.

I recognized some of the people strolling by and acknowledged several. After Kim spoke with Nancy, we returned to the medical center.

Life continued. I learned that painful lesson after Jean died and Evens was murdered.

***

At the end of the day, while exiting the clinic, I heard someone yell, "Hold the door."

Carter carried a box overflowing with books and papers.

For a moment, I considered shutting the door in his face. I might be a killer, but I wasn't a bitch.

"Thanks." He preceded me outside.

Although I slowed my pace, so I didn't have to walk beside him, he adjusted his stride and stayed by my side. Clearly, he wanted to talk.

With a side glance, I noticed a lack of that impish gaiety in his eyes—even his freckles lost their shine.

"You win."

I ignored his comment.

"I'm leaving. Won't become chief now."

Nor at any Noughton facility.

"What you did with the cellphone was genius. When did you give it to Ken?"

Whether Carter learned about the phone from the police or Nancy, I didn't know or care. It sufficed that people considered he was a factor in Ken's death.

"Right now, I'm toxic in Central California." He shrugged. "Time to relocate."

Good idea.

"When *did* you give Ken the cellphone?"

Crossing the parking lot, I broke away from him and headed toward my car.

Across the lot, he said, "I underestimated you. I bet a lot of people do."

Settled into the car, I reversed out of the parking spot while Carter placed items in his trunk. What a waste.

CHAPTER 46

My hand reached from under the covers to find my cellphone. The Sly & the Family Stone *Family Affair* ringtone signaled the call came from Momma. On the fourth ring, I threw off the sheets, rolled over to the edge of the bed, and caught the call on the final ring.

Groggily, I asked, "Momma, what's wrong?"

"Nothing, baby. Can't I simply call—or are you busy with company?" She sounded too chipper.

Yawning, I sat up. "Momma, it's five in the morning, and I'm alone."

"Oh, too bad. So, what's up?"

Rubbing my eyes, I checked the time again. "You keep forgetting I'm three hours behind you."

Her voice increased. "What time is it again?"

Stifling another yawn, I said, "Five."

"Oh." Seconds passed. "Well, since you're up, what are you doing today?"

"Work. I have a job."

Momma sounded lonely. After forty years of marriage, my parents sometimes bored each other. While we talked, I placed the phone on speaker and prepared for work. Over the next hour, we discussed everything and nothing. Eventually, I managed to get her off the phone, promising to call more often—not that it mattered.

Once I arrived at the office, I completed messages until patients arrived.

Camile called during lunch, insisting I come down for the weekend. I agreed because it would be convenient. Her house was closer to Thaddeus's school, making it convenient to visit him.

Clinic ended on time—at least for me. I reviewed my last lab and sent an email to a family regarding the results. As I hit return on the keyboard, Juanita entered, kicking the door closed with her foot.

"Come in. Have a seat," I said with a smirk on my face.

Extending her legs forward, she reclined into the chair. "Did you recommend me for chief of pediatrics?"

"Directly to the point. I like it." Without answering, I powered down the computer.

"Did you?"

"Do you want the position?"

Somberly, she stared at me. "I thought about it, once. But with Ken and Carter conniving for leadership positions—"

"You don't have to worry about them anymore."

"Noughton placed Carter on probation, but do you believe they'll fire him?"

"Not sure. They may have grounds based on him snooping into our offices—but not likely. Noughton won't risk a lawsuit."

"Well, if nothing else, from now on, he'll mind his own business."

I decided not to share Carter's plans to leave. "Let's hope so."

"After you mentioned the teddy cam, I bought two. One for the office and home. I'm a believer in surveillance systems now."

I laughed.

"So, did you recommend me?"

Pushing aside the keyboard, I rose. "I believe you'll make a good chief. You don't participate in office foolishness and truly care about patients."

Juanita smiled. The first genuine smile I'd seen from her.

"At work, all I care about is patients."

"Exactly."

At the doorway, she pivoted back inside. "Why are you leaving?"

"My family needs me."

"Too bad." She left.

Out the window, I stared at the parking lot, recalling my first day at the medical center. A phantom had visited me. The ghost of the police officer who notified me about Evens' death. Now, the sidewalk opposite my office was empty. My shoulders relaxed.

In a few months, no one would care about Ken's death except his family—and probably not for long. I removed a hand-held mirror from my purse and scrutinized my face. Did I resemble a murderer?

If I intended to adopt Thaddeus, I needed to make changes. Reform. I didn't possess a god complex or have antisocial tendencies, and I understood the difference between right and wrong. But could I stop dreaming about how to kill people?

After bailing Tonya out of jail for the umpteenth time, I had to take an assertive move. No more help. Whether or not Pruitt forced her to confront me didn't matter. In my heart, Tonya wore out her welcome.

Checking the clock, I realized it was time to leave to reach Camile's house by dinner. My mouth salivated in anticipation of Lupita's cooking.

Before leaving, I touched the heart-shaped photo of April with its chipped frame. Picking it up, I rested it on my heart. I allowed myself to shed tears for the beautiful friend I lost.

CHAPTER 47

Santa Barbara was one of the most beautiful places I'd ever visited, but even the Garden of Eden contained evil. Five miles from the sunny beaches revealed a darker side, inappropriate for tourist postcards. Though the calm Pacific Ocean flowed a few miles away, the people who frequented this part of the city didn't enjoy the beachfront's bucolic loveliness.

Ring, ring.

At the next stoplight, I answered my cellphone.

"Dr. Toussaint?"

"Yes?"

"Are you sure you don't want me to accompany you? The hotel where I found Mrs. Frye isn't in the best area."

"Thank you, but I can handle myself. Besides, Tonya might recognize you. If she realizes I hired a private detective to follow her around town, she'll run."

The detective spent several minutes trying to convince me, but I insisted on speaking with Tonya alone. Ten minutes later, I pulled up to a building that made the Bates Motel look like something out of *Homes and Gardens*.

Cautious, I parked in front of the motel under a streetlight. It provided a modicum of security. Even the tawny-colored alley cat crouched beside the lobby entrance glared menacingly. It hissed as I navigated the broken asphalt across the parking lot.

I glanced in my purse, making sure I had brought every-thing. After two deep breaths, my pulse calmed.

Two-inch-thick plexiglass separated the motel clerk from guests—or more like inmates.

"Hello," I said, directing my voice toward the circular speaker. "I'm looking for a friend. Her name—"

"You a cop?" The spindly man rubbed his protuberant abdomen and yawned.

"No, I'm not."

Without another word, he retired to a side desk and turned the television volume up.

For a moment, I stared and considered bribing him. His glum expression didn't promise success. Biting the inside of my lip, I returned to my car.

The idea of staking out the motel didn't appeal to me; how-ever, my options were limited. Tomorrow, I'd call the lawyer. These games with Tonya had to end. Thaddeus deserved a con-sistent home.

***

After visiting my favorite chocolate shop downtown, I cruised by the motel. If I didn't find Tonya this time—

On cue, the car Pruitt bought Tonya pulled into the motel parking lot. I reversed and parked on a street opposite the motel.

"Tonya," I called, jogging across the street.

Even from a distance, I saw she needed help.

Wearing a long black coat extending to mid-calf, Tonya wore a long scarf draped around her neck with her hair pulled taut in a ponytail. The severe hairstyle accentuated her aged face. More than ten years my junior, she looked at least twenty years older.

Pale hands held the coat close to her shivering body. Although it was February, this was Central California.

313

Hollow eyes confirmed no soul inhabited her body. Six months of rehab helped Tonya overcome a methamphetamine addiction. How long would it take this time?

Alcohol wafted across the space between us. Stumbling, Tonya tripped over her own feet. I reached forward to stabilize her, but she snatched her arm away.

"I don't need your help." She swayed to-and-fro.

As if she just recognized me, she said, "Dr. T, I need to speak with you." Conspiratorially, she waved me over.

"Of course. Let's sit in your car."

"Come on." She plopped inside.

I hurried into the passenger seat and gave her a quick hug. Releasing her, I attempted to adjust the scarf around her neck.

She smacked my hand aside. "I'm fine. It's cold." Shaking, she wrapped her arms around her body.

My shoulders slumped, weighed down from years of dealing with Tonya's relapses. I rolled down the window, not only because I detected a hot flash beginning, but because the car smelled of alcohol and marijuana.

"Is this yours?" I bent down and picked a cellphone off the floor.

Tonya accepted it and flipped it open. "No, I—"

"My mistake." I grabbed it. "You're using again, aren't you?"

"No!"

A passing couple gawked. Tonya lowered her head and became silent. Neither of us spoke until the couple entered the motel lobby.

Settled against the seat, my gloved hand admired the car. "Nice. But you aren't working, so who's paying for this?"

"None of your business." She spit the words out. "I have friends."

"No, you don't." I placed my hand on hers. "Don't trust Pruitt. He's using you, Tonya. Let me help."

"He's my friend. He gives me money just for talking."

"And what does he want you to talk about?"

She nibbled on her fingernails and averted her eyes.

"Why won't you let me take care of Thaddeus?"

Her eyes glazed over. "Who?"

My jaw clenched.

Don't hit her. Stick with the plan.

"Your son."

"Oh…" Tonya's dull-brown cow eyes stared into the night. "No. You can't have him." She poked her chest with a dirty finger. "My son. He belongs to me."

"He deserves better."

Tonya glanced down the street. I followed the trajectory of her eyes. "It's always been about him."

People sauntered around the street, a few gathered in a corner of the lot adjacent to the motel. Cars hurried away to safer places. Nothing in particular stood out. I didn't notice any station wagons. Pruitt knew I could recognize his car. He was a dishonest private detective, but not necessarily a stupid one. If he staked out the motel, he'd make sure I couldn't identify his car.

Tonya avoided looking me in the face but spoke in my ear. "You did it for him. Not to protect me, but for Thaddeus."

My nostrils flared at the odor of alcohol. Fatigue washed over me. Between Tonya's funk, my sweaty clothes, and the late hour, I had nothing left. The day had been long, and my patience had expired.

"I love Thaddeus, and I'd do anything for him."

"And me? What you gonna do for me?"

"We're done. No more bail or rehab."

"You should've let me go to prison," she said, slurring her words.

"I wish I had."

"Then you could've adopted Thaddeus."

I didn't reply.

"Help me, and I'll sign the papers."

"I don't need your consent. Your conduct is my best resource."

"Stop threatening me," she said as spittle dripped down her chin.

With the back of my hand, I wiped droplets from my face. "I can't believe you're this selfish. Thaddeus is simply your pawn. Why are you fighting the adoption?"

Trembling, Tonya's bony fingers flew in my face. "You never cared about me. Never! Kevin took care of me. If I lose Thaddeus, I'll have no one."

"You've already lost him."

She stumbled from the car and ran into a room on the first floor of the motel, shouting that Thaddeus was her son.

People stared.

I made no attempt to stop her. While onlookers focused on Tonya's theatrics, I slipped the burner phone, which I used to communicate with Pruitt, between the car seats, snugly, where it wasn't easily visible. Now, it had Tonya's prints on it. Confident of its position, I returned to my own car.

As I took the exit to Highway 101, I considered Thaddeus. He'd been the only one of Tonya's babies to survive. Four live births and each premature infant died shortly after delivery—except for Thaddeus.

He survived and thrived, an example of true resilience. I became his pediatrician shortly after he left the neonatal intensive care unit. Such an adorable infant. It would've been hard not to fall in love with him.

Tonya had always been a mess, but I worked with her. Struggled to get services to assist her *and* Thaddeus. She'd been correct about one thing; it was never about her. Thaddeus deserved a chance—every child did. I had determined to give him the chance his drug-addicted mother would not.

Addicts cried about wanting a second, third, fourth, fifth chance—never considering their children hadn't even received a first one. Thaddeus would have opportunities.

Years ago, I unofficially adopted him, enrolling him in activities and providing access to resources his negligent mother couldn't. Absorbed with her useless boyfriends, Tonya had teetered on the edge of drug addiction and incarceration since I'd known her. Each time I rescued her, believing Thaddeus deserved a mother, even a piece of shit like Tonya. But she'd become my Achilles heel.

I made a mistake. I should've adopted Thaddeus years ago and allowed Tonya to drown in self-abuse. Now, in order to help Thaddeus, I would have to trust the legal system. The same institution that failed Evens. It terrified me that Thaddeus' happiness depended upon strangers. Shivering, I turned up the car's heater. It would be a long drive.

CHAPTER 48

While stranded in bumper-to-bumper traffic, I spoke over the speakerphone.

"Promise. We'll be there in June."

"Why?"

"Momma, school ends in June."

I hung up and exited the freeway, heading for Camile's house. The family lawyer wasn't sure I could take Thaddeus with me until Tonya's rights were permanently removed. But once the legal adoption was approved, I'd return to North Carolina.

If Thaddeus was to become my son, I would have to commit to changing my life. Become a law-abiding, upright citizen all the time, not only when convenient.

At the stoplight, I noticed a blue station wagon trailing behind. Pruitt.

Pressure caught in my throat. I drove to a nearby grocery store. Hypervigilance was a side effect of murder because, legally, homicide had no expiration date.

In a parking lot, visible to the passersby, I waited in my car. When the station wagon entered the lot, I waved at Pruitt. He glowered. Displaying my cellphone, I placed a call.

He zipped out the lot.

After speaking with Mr. Henderson, I drove to Camile's place. Maybe leaving California was what I'd needed all along.

Bury my ghosts and leave them thousands of miles behind. No more Pruitt or Tonya. Simply cherished memories of Jean and Evens to carry back to North Carolina. And April. Our few memories had been tender and poignant. Camile and Lupita would visit.

It was past time for me to return home.

***

On the porch deck, curled up on a recliner, Camile sipped tea. "Are you sure about North Carolina?"

The children played soccer in the yard as tawny sunlight slipped away in the darkening sky.

"My parents need me," I said, sipping on the margarita.

"I suppose you're right."

Stretching her curvy legs, Camile refilled our glasses from a pitcher on a side table. "Well, they better appreciate you. North Carolina has no idea what's coming their way."

We clinked our glasses.

"No idea."

CHAPTER 49

Before I set the parking brake, Lady bounded out of the car with Thaddeus seconds behind. Understandable. The three-day road trip from California made me not want to drive for a long time. We crawled into Charlotte around three in the afternoon, but with traffic, it took another half hour to reach my parents' home.

The garage door scrolled up, and Momma and Daddy welcomed us.

"Hey, baby." Momma hugged Thaddeus as Lady sniffed the yard and relieved herself. Like a sloth, I joined my parents and Thaddeus.

"Baby girl," Daddy said, "you look exhausted."

"I am so tired. A bath, drink, two days sleep, and maybe I'll feel human again." After hugging my parents, I collapsed on the living room couch.

Momma and Thaddeus talked in the kitchen while preparing dinner.

"And, Grandma, I got second place at the science fair," Thaddeus said, removing plates from the upper cabinets.

"Well, let's celebrate," Momma said. "I'll make my special Mississippi mud pie."

"Mmm."

Evens' favorite pie. Fatigue and sadness brought me to the edge of tears. Closing my eyes, I heard Evens' voice.

"Grandma, my favorite," he had said.

"Anything for my grandbaby."

Stop it, Julia. Thaddeus is not Evens.

I strained to hear his voice again, but Evens didn't speak. His words forever silenced. My body relaxed as sleep came.

"Julia."

Sleep felt sweet. I didn't want to wake.

"Julia."

A dream. Someone called my name. Was it Jean?

"Julia," the voice said loudly.

I awoke to Daddy shaking my shoulder. "Wake up."

"Sorry." Using my shirt sleeve, I wiped my face.

"Come on. Time for bed."

Daddy led me to the bedroom. The room where I grew up. Teddy bears lined up along a narrow wall shelf a foot below the ceiling, encircling the entire room. Before I collapsed on the bed, Daddy held my arm.

"I'm glad you came home."

"Me, too," I said, smiling in a drunken, sleepy way.

His voice lowered. "Camile told me what happened."

I frowned, unsure what he meant.

"About the man's death."

"Whose?"

"Julia." Daddy perched on the edge of the bed. "Jean told me about... He told me to watch you."

Fatigue and sleep prevented me from focusing. "What—"

"It has to stop. No more," his voice lowered, "deaths."

"Daddy, I—"

"It's not your fault. Jean said you didn't mean to, but you had these impulses about killing people."

Thick with sleep, thoughts and conversations tumbled around my mind. What had Jean told Daddy?

"He made me promise to watch you. Make sure you didn't hurt anybody." Daddy sat beside me on the bed.

"But now you're home, I can keep an eye on you." At the bedroom door, he turned around. "I understand about Tonya's boyfriend, but no more."

The door shut, and I flopped on the bed.

Jean read a lot of philosophy and talked often about Nietzsche and Sartre. One evening, we discussed crime and consequences—a philosophical exercise initially. But I explained how—when bored—I formulated murders, down to the minute details, accounting for contingencies. However, in medical school, I swore an oath to save lives—and I had. As long as it remained fictional, Jean hadn't worried. As I shared more, his concern grew.

"Julia," he had said, "these aren't innocent thoughts, are they?"

For a moment, I studied his countenance. Was he upset? "I...I haven't murdered anyone."

He hugged me. "Of course, you haven't." His eyes bored deep into my core. "But you want to, don't you?"

Seconds passed before I slightly inclined my head.

Jean inhaled deeply. "Promise me you won't—ever."

Again, I didn't speak but simply nodded.

"I'm serious, Julia. Don't destroy the life we've built. What would happen to Evens?"

I hadn't tempted fate. Risks carried consequences. My interest in committing the perfect murder remained hypothetical, but Jean still worried. After I described a particularly gruesome manner to dispatch a corpse, he gave me a psychological evaluation. Though I assured him I had no intention of acting upon these ideas, he hadn't believed me.

As his illness worsened, he asked me to confide in Camile. I refused. Apparently, he had shared his concerns with Daddy.

When I saw Thaddeus bruised and beaten in the pediatric ICU, I fantasized about killing Kevin. I shared this with Jean. He had said my feelings were understandable. As Kevin was in prison, I had limited opportunities to act upon those thoughts.

Once Kevin had been granted parole, I tracked him around Oxnard as he conducted his illicit drug trade. Jean had realized I was spending time away from home and confronted me. But he was battling cancer and had other priorities.

Plans to murder Kevin fomented for weeks. When he had cruised down a side street devoid of streetlights, I saw an opportunity. After ensuring the area was clear, I caught up with Kevin and found him already dead.

Tonya hunched over him sobbing, clutching a metal bat matted with blood and hair.

Should've called the police.

Thaddeus had to be protected. I thought he needed his mom.

My murderous plan morphed into a coverup to protect Tonya. I hustled her out of the alley and Oxnard. A stint in rehab kept her away from police scrutiny. While I hoped sobriety would erase her memory of the event, I'd been naïve. It had not, and Pruitt attempted to capitalize on her weaknesses.

From the moment Tonya visited me in San Marguerite, I realized she was trying to set me up. Initially, I didn't understand why. I'd done so much for her, but she realized it had all been for Thaddeus. *Jealous heifer.*

Time passed. Six feet of earth protected Thaddeus from Kevin. Tonya continued to cycle in and out of jail and rehab. Her demons preceded Kevin and persisted in his absence.

Life was good until Jean died. It took years, but I had achieved a new peace. Then, a drunk murdered my child.

Mrs. Copeland served three months of a fifteen-month sentence. Fine with me. On a cold October night, I slipped past the security system and entered her house. Surveillance taught me her schedule.

Abandoned by her family, Mrs. Copeland drank her supper around seven in the evening, usually dozing off before eleven. In the library, I tiptoed over to her body flung across a divan. Things took an unexpected turn when I found a sobbing teenager sitting beside the dead woman, holding a packet of white powder in her hand.

Quickly assessing the situation, I contacted Mr. Copeland, and he rushed over. Arriving in minutes, he scooped up his daughter while I prepared the scene. Before leaving, he offered me money, realizing his error from my stern glower. Until the SOS GED graduation ceremony, we hadn't spoken about what occurred at his house.

Twice, I had desired to kill, and both times, someone beat me to it. In each situation, I covered up the homicide to protect a child. But Ken...

I could use April's suicide as an excuse or Ken's incompetence as a physician, but I wanted to kill him not long after we met. I sensed his deficiency right away. But I had tried murder twice before and it didn't work. Hearing Ken insult April after her suicide compelled me to proceed. And I had no regrets.

Fortunately, I wouldn't need to eliminate Tonya. She'd drink herself to death—and soon, from the last time I saw her in Santa Barbara. Too bad I couldn't use the morphine I swiped from the pediatric clinic. It wouldn't have made sense to use it on Ken. Insulin was easier to acquire. It supported the idea of an impulse decision based on his current situation.

It was also difficult to detect on autopsy *if* you wanted to mask a suicide. A nugget for future endeavors. But who knew? The morphine might come in handy.

Thaddeus didn't have time to wait for Tonya to die a slow death from drugs. She'd taken enough of his life.

Time to make changes, Julia.

I simply wanted to know if I could commit a murder. Escaping detection was only part of it. Would I be riddled with guilt? Clearly not. I eliminated a parasite. Like a surgeon excising a diseased limb, I removed Ken. And the world said, 'Thank you.'"

If you want a new life...

That psychiatrist was a fool. I had impulses, but I also possessed restraint. Jean believed I killed Kevin—interesting and disappointing. Instead of speaking to me, he shared his suspicions with my dad.

Humph. Should I correct Daddy? Tell him I didn't kill Kevin, but I had killed Ken.

I laughed.

Oh well. Parents realized their children weren't perfect.

Lying on my back, I stared up at the ceiling. *Lord, help anyone who bothers Thaddeus. Old habits die hard.*

But the South was supposed to be quiet, filled with wholesome religious people. Surely, there couldn't be anyone in Charlotte worth killing.

Thank you for reading *Hollow Voices*.

As a self-published author, I depend upon reader reviews to increase my visibility and credibility. Please post an online review. Want more mystery and suspense? Visit my website at www.MichelleCorbier.com.

Sign up for MrsDoctor Writes newsletter and receive bonus content, information on new releases, and resources regarding the writing community.
https://lp.constantcontactpages.com/su/paEPQ3x/MrsDoctorWrites

Want pre-release full-length novels and gifts for honest online reviews? Click below and join my reading team.
https://forms.gle/US75ZcACrN6HysDW7

Check out Write Club Mysteries. The first book, *Murder Is Revealing*, is available in all formats at multiple retailers. Want a free eBook? Click on the link below.
https://BookHip.com/KMSDCHS

Paranormal and fantasy fans check out the Mwindaji series. The first book is *Dark Blood Awakens,* widely available in eBook, paperback, and audiobook formats. In addition, a free prequel novella is available. Click on the link below.
https://BookHip.com/VKJLKDT